Snapshots from a
Black Hole
& Other Oddities

Snapshots from a
Black Hole
& Other Oddities

Stories by K.C. Ball

Edited by Cat Rambo

Hydra  House

First paperbound edition.

978-0-9848301-0-7 (print)
978-0-9848301-1-4 (ebook)

Editor: Cat Rambo
http://www.kittywumpus.net/blog/

Cover art: Christopher Sumption
Copyright © 2011 Christopher Sumption
http://www.chrissumption.com/

Book design: Tod McCoy
http://www.todmccoy.com/

Hydra House
1122 E Pike St. #1451
Seattle, WA 98122
http://www.hydrahousebooks.com/

Printed in the United States of America.

0 9 8 7 6 5 4 3 2 1

Publication information:

"Snapshots I Brought Back from the Black Hole," *Lightspeed Magazine*, June 2011.

"Dial Tone," *Kasma Science Fiction Magazine*, December 2010.

"At Both Ends," *Flash Fiction Online*, June 2009.

"According to His Substance," *Benefictions Chapbook*, en theos press, July 2011.

"Tin Man," *Big Pulp Magazine*, March 2009.

"Flotsam," *Analog Science Fiction & Fact Magazine*, September 2010.

"Nosing with the Four-Stroke Kid," *Murky Depths*, May 2009.

"Gossamer Yellow," *Dark Valentine Magazine*, May 2011.

"Bringing in the Dead," *2013: The Aftermath Anthology*, Pill Hill Press, October 2010.

"Serves Him Right," *Every Day Fiction*, March 2011.

"A Bannockburn Night," Static Movement (www.staticmovemnet.com), November 2008.

"A Son of the Night," *A Thousand Faces Quarterly*, November 2009.

"To Each His Niche and Task," *Morpheus Tales*, June 2009.

"Coward's Steel," *Writers of the Future 26* anthology, October 2010.

"In His Prime," *Every Day Fiction*, October 2008.

"The Mixture," *Every Day Fiction*, July 2008.

"We Who Are Ernest Now Salute You," *AlienSkin Magazine*, October 2009.

"And Bay the Moon," *The Absent Willow Review*, March 2009.

Contents

Preface

I confess.

I'm a story junkie. I was first hooked when I was six. An elderly librarian named Emma Huber got me started with *The Hardy Boys* and *The Black Stallion*. She introduced me to the hard stuff—Stevenson, Defoe, and Dickens—by the time I turned nine, and had me mainstreaming Hemingway, Faulkner, and Steinbeck at eleven.

I became addicted to science fiction all by myself. It's a long list. Bob Heinlein, Murray Leinster, Larry Niven, Ron Goulart, and so many more. I didn't care so much about the names as I cared about the stories.

Of course, there came a time when reading wouldn't satisfy my Jones. At first I fed my habit by writing non-fiction. Got paid for it, too. Newspaper Reporter. Public Information Officer. Media Relations Coordinator.

But, over the years, that grew pale and thin, as well.

So I began to turn out a bit of fiction now and then. Short stories. You know, as a hobby. And I told myself I could quit any time I wanted.

Uh huh.

Four years ago, January 2008, I gave myself over to the love of story. I began to write fiction full-time, with the notion of going professional. I made my first pro-rate sale in May 2009 when "Coward's Steel" (which is somewhere in this book) won the L. Ron Hubbard Writers of the Future Award. Since then, I've sold enough fiction to become a member of the Science Fiction & Fantasy Writers of America.

There are twenty-four stories in this book. For seven of them, this is their first publication. There is a bit of this and that, some flash fiction (which I love), and some longer stuff. Hard science fiction, fantasy, and horror. Time travel, dinosaurs, aliens, and monsters lurking in the dark.

It's all what's known these days as speculative fiction—SF.

Other writers tell me that my stories are "old school". That doesn't bother me. Old school is what I grew up reading. It has fed my habit, my need for story.

I hope my stories satisfy your habit, too.

K.C. Ball

A Thank You Note

I want to say thank you to Tod McCoy of Hydra House, my publisher, first for buying this book and second for being so damned patient. I also want to thank my editor, Cat Rambo, for all her hard work and good advice, and Chris Sumption, for his fantastic cover art.

And I want to tip my hat to the members of Horrific Miscue, the Seattle critique group, and to the SF veterans who have been so kind to me over the past four years—Jim Gunn, Kij Johnson, Mary Rosenblum, Maureen McHugh, Mike Brotherton, and Chris McKitterick. Thank you, each and every one.

Most of all, I must say thank you to my life partner and soul mate, Rachael Buchanan. Four years ago, she gave me wonderful advice. She said, "Sit down in that chair, stop whining about what you haven't done, and write."

This book is dedicated to her. Thank you, Babe! These are your stories, as much as they are mine.

Introduction

One of the advantages of being an editor is that sometimes you look deeper than most readers. You examine conjunctions, correspondences, how stories fit together, and the patterns that emerge when reading one creates an overlay of relationships and interpretations that strengthen each one you come to.

K.C. Ball's collection lends itself well to such a reading. As I've journeyed through her landscapes of haunted yellow scarves, fledgling superheroes, and sailors of both sea and space, I've noticed a few things I'd like to share, in the hope that they'll enhance your reading too.

Worlds and time are fluid in K.C.'s stories. Travelers move through time and space, through memory and possibility, always continuing onward, seeking home, redemption, loves lost or yet to come. And while the dimensions around them shift, those characters remain solid, true to themselves, reaching out to one another in a way that inspires us in a modern world that shifts around us as quickly as the worlds in which K.C. writes change from story to story.

Because that's another thing about her stories. She writes with equal ease in the hard science atmosphere on the edge of a black hole or a fantastic Seattle where a midnight runner may encounter something entirely unexpected. Horror, sf, and fantasy all appear within these pages, showcasing why she's established herself as a writer to be reckoned with in a very short period of time.

So here's K.C.'s collection, the first of what I'm sure are many to come. I hope you enjoy it as much as I have.

Cat Rambo

Snapshots I Brought Back from the Black Hole

A Panoramic View: See that dead spot, centered in the two whirling, luminescent rings suspended in the void of space?

Call the luminescent rings accretion disks, gas and dust forever sucked away to who knows where. The dead spot, a black hole dubbed BH/Hawking.

It's the aggressive half of a binary star system known as V-4641 Sagittarii, all the way to hell and gone, one thousand six hundred light years from Earth.

The crew of *Albert Einstein* has traveled all that way, hoping to unravel a mystery. No one know what happens when an object crosses the balk point around a black hole known as an event horizon and falls into the singularity.

No one.

Physicists do their calculations, make educated guesses, but not a soul has spiraled down with the luminescent dust and gas and returned to tell the tale.

Not knowing never stops people from poking. You humans push at boundaries. Surf space-time bubbles sixteen hundred light years across the galaxy. Open doors you shouldn't touch, shine lights into dark and scary places just to see what's there.

And there's the rub at BH/Hawking. Any physicist will tell you. Nothing can escape a black hole. Not even light.

An Establishing Shot: Here's *Quantum Wanderer*, Chloé Dubois' exploration ship. This one's recorded through a single-use sensor drone, fifty kilometers up-slope from BH/Hawking's event horizon. If you care for the big words, that's one-point-five Schwarzschild radii. Do the math. You'll see.

Thirty years ago, this voyage would have been impossible. BH/Hawking's not very large, but its intense gravity would have torn *Einstein* and *Wanderer* apart. Now, thanks to the new tidal-gradient compensators, the mission's only dangerous as hell.

Instruments aboard *Wanderer* ceaselessly collect data while its massive nuclear-pulse engines struggle to maintain a stable orbit against forces that want to suck the ship into oblivion.

The engines produce a fearsome racket but inside *Wanderer* it's church quiet. Each of the ship's one-point-six-five-million pieces has been tuned to exact specifications. A perfect jigsaw puzzle that nullifies the noise.

Sensor arrays, drives and fuel-containment systems, tidal compensators, communications gear, and radiation shielding fill almost every square centimeter. The bit of room left for Chloé and her life-support suit accepts just that and not one single scruple more. She doesn't so much ride in the ship as wear it.

Of course, Chloé doesn't have to be on board. A level-four A.I. orchestrates the show just fine without her. But humans hate to be replaced by a machine, even when you know we can do the job better at far less risk.

So Chloé lays her life upon the line, two subjective hours out of every twenty-four, to orbit BH/Hawking, hoping to wrestle free its secrets. Two shifts left. Still so much to learn.

Of course, she hasn't come alone. See that gleaming speck? That's *Einstein*, riding the tidal gradient in chrono-synchronous orbit to *Wanderer*, two Schwarzschild radii away.

And twelve kilometers above Chloé, tethered to *Einstein* by a tractor field, Andy Mercer hunkers in a shielded observation pod too small to have a name.

Andy makes immersives—you know, grabbies. He watches Chloé's every move, hears each grunt and exhalation, captures what she tastes and smells and touches, everything except her thoughts, through long-range sensors. He's risking his life too, recording every little detail of this grand adventure for all of you back home.

You're curious, aren't you? You want to see what's in the darkness, as much as any of the twenty members of *Einstein's* crew. And you want to know why the world directorate laid out one hundred, ninety seven billion for the trip.

It's your money. You paid for a ticket, you deserve to see the show. Let's be honest though. The science stuff is boring. You really want to be around in case it all goes wrong.

In the deepest, darkest, meanest corners of your hearts, all humans want that. You watch disaster from a distance and if someone dies, so much the better. You can whisper to yourself, "Thank God that wasn't me."

The Obligatory Portrait of the Boss: This is my favorite. Captain Sergei Kolenkhov, caught in a quiet moment in the zero-gee command bubble at *Einstein's* nose. Sergei sits with eyes closed, listening to crew chatter via the command-band sweep.

A plasma-foil screen molded to the forward bulkhead allows me to show Sergei anything he cares to see. BH/Hawking in real time. The ship's exterior from fixed and mobile sensors. Interior shots of the operations and service pods or the giant spinning cylinder that contains the living quarters.

Sergei makes the narrow command chair look spacious. Slim and wiry, a ferret of a man, with sleek dark hair shot through with threads of gray. Andy Mercer interviewed Sergei in that very chair, the day before *Einstein* broke Earth orbit. Of course I listened, and thanks to chip-assisted memory I recall every word.

"Serge, most folks would figure they'd been punished, to be crammed into a rotating cannot much bigger than a high-school gymnasium with nineteen other people for three years."

Andy looks as if he's waiting patiently for Sergei's reply, but that look's pure flim-flam. Andy never waits for anything but an opening to deliver his next line.

It doesn't matter. Sergei can bullshit with the best, but this time every word he says is true. "It's Sergei, Andy, and I'm not most people. I love this ship, I love my crew. We're doing important work."

"There must be times when someone upsets you, when you'd rather be doing something else?"

Sergei's pulse spikes, his respiration climbs.

He's about to tell a lie but what the hell. Everybody does it, don't they? "I can't imagine what, Andy. There's nothing about my job that I don't like. There's no place I'd rather be right now than sitting in this chair."

Sergei's ear bud chirps, breaking his reverie.

"It's engineering, Seryozhenka," I whisper. The name's a diminutive, a term of endearment. Sergei's grandfather used to call him by that name.

"Put it on, Mishka."

That's his diminutive for me. The project shrinks would have had a field day if they had uncovered our little name game before we departed Earth. Sergei's grandfather was Mikhail, Mishka to his only grandson. I'm A.I., a level six, assigned to *Einstein* as communications officer, but I'm so much more. There are just five sixes. I'm senior, the biggest brother, the only one named after a dead man.

I route the call.

"You have a minute, Sergei?"

Engineer Edyta Shamanski's round peasant's face fills the plasma foil screen. That unassuming face hides an intellect almost as sharp as mine. This woman knows which way is up, knows how to move that way. She's a certified genius, helped to design *Einstein*, but like all humans she has quirks. Edyta worries.

Sergei knows her tone. He sits up straighter, murmurs sub-vocally to me. "Mishka, drop to private band."

"Da." My baritone sounds just like his grandfather, gone a decade now. He waits for the click I use to signal I've made the link. I listen in, of course.

"What is it, 'Dyta?" Sergei asks.

"Power spikes in the tractor field."

"We need to reel the pod in?"

"I'd like to. I'm running diagnostics, but right now it's just a gut feeling. I can't see what the problem is from here. I want to check the on-board couplings."

"She thinks it's very serious," I whisper to Sergei. "Her heart rate's up ten points. Look at how she holds her shoulders, how she twists her mouth."

Sergei taps his thumb knuckle on the armrest of his chair. "Let him hang while you finish running numbers."

"All right." She's not happy with his decision.

"Tell him what you're doing, though. Yes?"

"Yes." There's no enthusiasm in Edyta's voice.

"What's wrong?"

"He'll argue with me, waste my time."

"All right, I'll talk to him."

"He'll argue with you, too."

"Even so."

Edyta is silent for a time. Sergei waits her out.

"I don't mean to kick sand your way," she says, at last. "I hate talking to that man. *Vo pridurok to.*"

"I said I'll talk to him."

Edyta pauses for a time before answering. Sergei gives her time again.

She sounds tired when she speaks. "Thank you, Captain. I'll keep you posted."

Edyta breaks contact.

Without being asked, I shift Sergei back to command band-sweep. "She has reason to worry, Seryozhenka. I don't care for how the tractor diagnostics look, either."

"She helped design the system, she'll deal with it. I'll deal with Andy."

"Edyta's right. Andy can be an idiot."

"Even so. We're stuck with him."

Sergei's right, of course. Every member of the crew tested over and over to weed out the claustrophobics, neurotics, and socially inept. Every one of them had to have a specific set of skills, a proper education, but there are folks aboard fifth or eighth or twenty-third on a credentials list because the ones above them couldn't find the cheese in that maze of tests.

But Andy's not a member of the crew. He's celebrity. An award-winning director, a big-shot American used to getting his own way. He's physically a big man, too. He takes up more space, uses more resources, than anyone else on *Einstein*.

And his only job is to produce a piece of propaganda.

The real problem, though, is Chloé. Her two-hour approaches to the black hole are the reason we're all here and the clock's ticking. Einstein can't stay at BH/Hawking forever. Supplies are limited. Even more important, if we stay too long, everything we know of home will have ticked away. We have two more subjective days, no more. On the seventh day, even God rested.

As if that weren't enough, Andy's married to Chloé. If Sergei reels in the pod ahead of schedule, Andy will be pissed. It's his nature. He's not a bad sort but, like all of you, he likes to get his way.

He'll bitch to Chloé and she'll take his side. Maybe she'll go down there again, hang at the edge of hell's abyss, or maybe not. Chloé can be a stubborn bitch.

Sergei can't take the risk of losing those last two days of data gathering. And he can't put off talking to Andy any longer. Sergei's grandfather used to say, "You cook the porridge and you eat it."

"Well?" I ask.

"Put him on."

I meter signal in both directions. It's one of the reasons I'm *Einstein's* communications officer. No human is quick enough to manipulate the time dilation. This close, it's not much, but enough. Faster going down than coming up. I'm a master juggler.

"What's up, Serge?"

Andy's boyish, big-jawed face almost pops from the screen. He sounds likes he's across the cabin, not sixteen klicks down the BH/Hawking well. The sound's almost in sync with movement of his mouth and there's only a hint of red shift.

Sergei shifts in his chair, trying to hide his irritation at being pushed into this situation. "There's a problem with the tractor field. We're running numbers now."

"Chloé's still here. I'm not coming up 'til she does."

I monitor the system closely. Even so, Andy has the sort of voice that can make communications systems squeal. His rise in volume almost gets away from me.

"It's procedure, Andy. If the final analysis looks bad, I'm going to bring you up."

"Bullshit. I'm getting crystal data through the gear, but any more delay on up-link time, even micro-seconds, and it could turn to mush. I have to stay."

He's lying, of course. Even across the distance I can pick up his vital signs. He's arguing because he wants to have it all his way. I know his recording systems. He can fix imperfections when he does the final edit back on Earth, push the data through graphics interpretation coldware, clean the edges, let his own A.I. work on it.

Andy's a genius, too, in his own way. He could fake the whole thing. No one back home would ever know unless he felt guilty and told them. Fat chance of that. He's got his pride.

He's still ranting. "Why even bother to bring me along if I'm not down here watching over everything, making judgments? I could have stayed home, sent out drones to AIGI everything."

What a swell idea. I can almost hear Sergei think the same thing. The band is silent for a moment.

"Serge, talk some sense to that damned engineer of yours. Tell her to stop playing Chicken Little. She's ruining my work."

"She's being prudent."

Andy pauses before he plays his trump card. "Prudent, huh? Hell with this. Let's see what Chloé has to say."

The audio goes dead, the screen blanks.

"*Mat' tvoyu rastak*," Sergei mutters.

"Easy, Seryozhenka," I say. "A fool's tongue runs before his feet." Another of his grandfather's favorite sayings.

He tips his head, his way of shrugging. "You're right."

"Shall I reconnect?"

"Yes."

Sergei closes his eyes, pinches the bridge of his nose. He whispers, so I'm the only one who has to pay attention. The crew at the consoles can pretend they didn't hear.

"Grandfather," he says. "Why did I take this job?"

Ein Strasenverkäufer Photographie: This one's from Earth, from before we left. Chloé and Sergei sit beneath the multi-colored spread of a table umbrella, at a street-front café along a narrow cobbled street in Cologne. Not too far from European Astronaut Centre at Linder Hoehe.

The tables around them are full. The street's crowded too, even though it's still before noon. Pedestrian traffic only, of course. The city banned vehicles from this section at the turn of the twenty-first century, all those years ago.

Sergei wears the new implants that allow me to hear and see and smell everything he experiences. I feel like I'm there.

For those of you who wonder how I feel, how an artificial intelligence might believe it's real, let me ask you this. How do you feel? Do you even have an inkling of the mechanics that make you real? Until you do, pipe down and listen.

Around about, Japanese, Swahili, English, Russian, Spanish, Portuguese, German, and a dozen other tongues somehow blend into a polyglot buzz that's pleasing to the ear. The rich, comforting aromas of coffee, cinnamon, and burnt sugar lay upon the air.

The late August sky is crystal blue. Temperatures hover at twenty cee. Forecasts calls for warmer weather in the afternoon with a flash of rain just before sunset. The Germans like their weather the old-fashioned way, without meteorological controls, so they take their chances.

"You must be firm, Sergei, for me," Chloé says. "Tell them he'll disturb the work. Tell them he'll make me nervous. Merde, tell them he takes up too much space."

She scoops up her espresso cup and drains it, returns it to the linen-covered table with a snap.

"The man's an over-sized American clown," she says. "And I refuse to be a stooge in one of his grabbies."

Sergei lets her rant. Like a summer storm in Cologne, her anger swells, rages for a short time, and then fades. He'd let her talk forever if she wanted to do so.

Truth be told, he loves her, even though he's never told another soul. Not even her, although they've shared each other's victories and losses. He's been her wingman since academy. They have flown in combat together, jumped from the black heights, and know each other's secret fears.

That's why he agreed to accept command of Einstein. Not for the adventure of a lifetime. Not through an exaggerated sense of duty. He's on board to stay close to Chloé.

And it pains him but he knows her well enough to realize that, once she meets Andy Mercer, it won't be long before the two of them will be in bed together. Chloé's always has been drawn to *gromy i molnii*, the thunder and lightning relationship. She's steady on her own, like ice when she flies, but with a man she wants drama.

It's why Sergei has never professed his love for her.

He can give her lightning but he never could maintain the noise. There is nothing else to do. Sergei's grandfather used to say that falling in love is like a mouse falling into a box. There is no way out.

"The decision has been made, Chloé."

Sergei doesn't say that he helped make it. She knows. The vertical crease between her brows, the mark his grandfather used to call an "I'll have my way" line, becomes a crevice. "Come on, my friend, do it for me."

My friend. Sergei works not to grind his teeth, to control his breathing and his heart rate.

"It's been decided," he says again.

To hell with Andy. Sergei wants to take *Chloé's* hand, to tap upon her wrist to the rhythm of her pulse, wants even more for that imagined loving touch to be returned.

Her left brow arches.

He hurries to still the storm. "You know the size of the investment in the mission. The directorate believes that news accounts won't be enough. People want to share the adventure. Mercer can provide that."

"I don't care what people want. I'm the one going down to the damned event horizon."

Sergei sighs. "All right, I'll try."

A Publicity Shot: Here's another one from Earth. Chloé, standing at a window at Fifty-Eight Tour Eiffel, the restaurant in the Eiffel Tower, fifty-eight meters above Paris.

Sergei watches from the restaurant's entrance, waiting until the photographer gets the shot she wants. Over *Chloé's* shoulder, through the window, I can see the Palais de Chaillot and its grounds across the Seine. Everything in sight has been scrupulously maintained. The whole damned city's a museum, not a living, breathing entity like Cologne.

Still, Chloé *is* French, so the party to introduce the *Einstein* crew to the press will begin in ten minutes, here in Paris. The crew has assembled to preen and answer questions. The technicians have even set up a special sound system for me.

But Chloé will be center of attention. Little wonder. Her evening dress is blue silk, elegant and simple. She's blond and tanned, not much taller than Sergei, with the muscled, rangy body of a competitive runner. She *is* a runner, won three gold medals ten years ago in Oslo. She's also earned doctorates in physics and engineering, holds a world record for high-altitude skydiving.

Chloé's never known what it means to fail.

Sergei leads the way across the room. "Chloé?"

She turns from the window, smiling, already moving forward to hug him, only to have to tilt her head to look up into Andy Mercer's sea-blue eyes.

Mercer's enormous, well over two meters tall, weighs in at something over two hundred kilos. He's shaggy-haired. Bearded too, looks like a bear in a tuxedo. He looms over everyone. And there's a scent of danger all about him, mixed with the faint aromas of cedar and of lime.

Sergei has to feel like *karlik* next to the bigger man. A midget. He glances up at Mercer. "Andy, I'm pleased to introduce Chloé Dubois. Chloé, this is Andy Mercer."

"Bonjour, Mme Dubois. C'est un plaisir de vous rencontrer." Mercer's French sucks. Chloé should laugh at him.

"No, Mr. Mercer, the pleasure is mine," she says.

Her English is excellent, better than the big man's French. That's to be expected. English is the default language of the mission and Chloé has told Sergei repeatedly over their years together that the only way to speak French properly is to be born to it.

Mercer relaxes, grins at her, and takes her offered hand.

"Call me Andy. I've got to say I'm a big fan of yours. I've worn out two v-chips watching your world record. Magnificent."

Bullshit. V-chips can't wear out, but Andy loves hyperbole. He's referring to Chloé's high-altitude jump. Sergei has a copy of the chip, too, recorded by a free-falling sensor drone, all the way from twenty-five-thousand meters. Sergei jumped from the drone that day a thousand meters lower.

Chloé smiles. "Thank you."

She's intrigued. Mercer bows his head, lifts her hand, and touches his lips to her knuckles. She should laugh at that too. No one kisses women's hands anymore, not unless they figure to get punched with that same hand.

Chloé doesn't laugh, she blushes. Sergei's own cheeks pink as well. I can feel the heat, see the color through the cameras placed around the room.

"I've seen your work," Chloé admits.

"I hope you liked it."

She remains polite. "I was entertained."

"I'll try not to let you down on the trip to BH/Hawking."

There it was. Now she knows Mercer would go along, Sergei couldn't talk them out of it. Chloé should erupt.

Instead she says, "We'll see."

A Frame from the Out-Bound Interviews: In this one Chloé and Sergei sit side-by-side before a sheet of plasma film that streams an image of Earth floating in the void below.

Andy has set up a temporary studio on the international space station's outer centrifugal ring. Einstein departs in fourteen hours. Andy's equipment is managed by a level-two A.I., an idiot but functional, so Andy only needs to sit and talk. He's good at that. "Thanks for giving me this time today, both of you. I know you're busy."

Sergei sticks to the script. "How can we help you, Andy?"

"I've got background questions, but to be honest, I don't mind if we just sit here and watch Earth turn down there." Off script and pure bullshit, but the man's had lots of practice.

"I'll bet he'd rather sit alone with Chloé," I whisper in Sergei's ear.

He ignores me, plays his part. Ad-libbing too. "It never does get old."

Chloé turns toward the foil screen. North America can be seen at the moment, all of it bathed in sunshine. She departs from the script even more. "Where do you come from, Andy?"

Andy doesn't even blink.

He points. "There, in the upper peninsula of Michigan, up above the mitt. Sault Saint Marie."

"I've been there," Chloé says, turning from the screen. "I have a master's degree from the University of Michigan."

"No kidding. So you've seen the Soo locks?"

"Of course."

They speak of Andy's time at Stanford University, her hometown south of Paris. Her wins at the Oslo Olympics, his turn in the American military, how he covered the Nine-Day War on Crete. Chloé admits that she shot down seven Asian Bloc fighters there. *Hellfires.* Sergei flew wingman for her every mission, shot down five himself. He doesn't say a word.

None of this is scripted. The interview's become a two-person conversation, Sergei's the odd man out.

I whisper to him. "Get it back on course, Seryozhenka."

"Shall we talk about the trip out?" he asks.

Andy glances at Sergei, almost frowns. He blinks. "Sure. Tell me about the ship."

Sergei's had lots of practice. "*Einstein* has a two-drive system, the Judson-Hicks bubble drive for interstellar travel, and four charged-plasma engines for inner-systems maneuvering."

"Uh huh." Andy's listening but he's watching Chloé.

Sergei continues but he knows he's talking to himself. He twists his head, the muscles in his neck pop. His dark Russian mood is palpable.

He's slowed the sexual juggernaut, but it still gathers steam.

A Wedding Portrait of the Happy Couple: I took this one five hours before the Judson-Hicks drive went on line, eighteen months into the mission. It holds a lot of nasty memories.

"Are you ready, Serge?" Andy turns from his equipment and glides to his mark beside Chloé.

"Yes." Sergei brushes at the front of his jumpsuit, at some flaw only he can see.

I try to caution him. "Ignore his insults, Seryozhenka."

The three of them stand in ship's mess, their slippers toe into anchor loops near one end of the space. Half the crew has squeezed in with them. The rest watch via a command-band feed. The signal's being streamed to Earth too. Another twelve billion witnesses. Andy whispers a word to his equipment. He winks at Sergei.

"All of you watching are witness to this blessed ceremony." Sergei struggles to make his scripted words sound natural.

Music swells. Pachelbel's "Canon in D Major." Sergei does his best to ignore the thin propellant buzz from the fly-eye camera above his right shoulder. It took thirty minutes of practice for him to learn to act as if the fly-eye isn't there, to resist swatting at it.

"As captain of Interstellar Ship *Albert Einstein*, it is my honor to join this man and this woman in marriage, even as we stand at the threshold of mankind's greatest adventure."

He looks to Andy. "Do you have the rings?"

"Yes." Andy opens his palm to show the two plain platinum bands he asked Edyta Shamanski to mill for the ceremony. The cameras zoom in on

Andy's hand.

"Is the launch on schedule, Mishka?" Sergei whispers.

"Yes. Perform the ceremony. I'll call if I need you."

"Smart-ass piece of coldware."

"*Palkami i kamnyami,* Seryozhenka."

"Sticks and stone have nothing to do with it."

"Everything is running smoothly."

"Thank you."

Chloé takes one of the rings. Andy holds the other at the ready. Neither seems to notice that Sergei mutters to himself, or notice that any of the others are even there.

Sergei begins. "Andy, if you would take Chloé as your wife, place the ring upon her hand and say 'I will'."

He's departing from the script. Andy doesn't even blink. He slips the ring on Chloé's finger and says, "I will."

Sergei continues. "Chloé, if you would take Andy as your husband, give him the ring and say 'I will'."

Chloé does as she's told and says, "I will." She doesn't look away from Andy.

If he could, I'm certain Sergei would sew his lips together, would do almost anything not to have to finish. I can see it in the set of his shoulders, in the way he breathes.

He cuts to the end. "As captain of this vessel, I pronounce you man and wife."

He pulls his toes from the loops, not waiting to watch them kiss, hurries toward the hatch that will take him to his hard and narrow chair in the command bubble. The fly eye, slaved to the electronic wafer glued to Sergei's shoulder, darts along behind, recording his retreat.

A Tight Close-up: Here's a tight shot of Chloé's upper face, her eyes and most of her nose. I manage to pull it from her helmet cam.

What skin that can be seen looks flushed. Her vital signs have spiked. It's obvious that she and Andy have had their chat about Edyta's request to reel in the drone. Andy has stirred the pot, too. From that deep in the well, I can't quite balance the red shift, but not all the color in Chloé's face is a glitch.

"Chloé wants to talk, Seryozhenka," I murmur. "Her blood pressure and respiration are through the roof.

"Put her through."

"Do you want her to see you, too?"

"Of course. Let her see me."

Chloé's image fills the screen.

"Sergei, what's going on?" She glances at the heads-up display in her helmet, catches sight of him in that tiny screen, and then looks away to something else. Her eyes flicker back and forth, she murmurs to her A.I., words too soft to catch.

She's a busy woman but she can chew gum and rub her stomach if she chooses to do so. I've seen Chloé's tests. She scored off the top of the chart on multi-tasking.

"I need to pull in Andy's pod," Sergei replies.

"He told me everything is clean and green at his end, says Edyta's being fussy."

"I trust her numbers, Chloé."

Chloé's tone sharpens. "He's got a degree in engineering, too, you know."

"This has nothing to do with that. It's protocol."

"I know protocol, Sergei. We both know there are levels of redundancy built into all of it."

"I know what he wants and why he wants it."

She softens. "Do it as a favor for an old friend."

Sergei remains silent.

I offer counsel. "Stick to the protocol, Seryozhenka."

"Please?" she says. "I've only got a few more minutes here. Let him sit it out. He'll be fine."

Sergei ignores me. He shifts in the command chair. He clips off his reply. "All right. A few more minutes."

I understand it instantly. See it in the dilation of his pupils, feel it as his body temperature rises, hear it in his drawn breath and the rhythm of his increased vital signs.

Andy wants his way, just as he always does. Chloé wants Sergei to support her, as he has over the years.

Sergei wants the tractor field to fail.

The Director's Cut: This one's a split screen. Edyta on the left, Andy on the right.

She's showing signs of panic, at least as much as she ever shows. He's pissed. I don't need vital signs for that. It's an easy one to call.

"We need to bring the pod in now, Sergei," Edyta says.

"Bullshit," Andy retorts. "Five minutes on the clock."

Twenty minutes have gone by since Sergei gave in to Chloé, twenty minutes of juggling. It's time to put away the rubber balls. Even so, Sergei doesn't say a thing.

"Sergei, there's a real chance the coupling could fail." Edyta says.

"A 'real' chance? What sort of engineering term is that?"

"Quiet, Andy," Sergei says.

"Seryozhenka, the engineering A.I. is predicting systems failure inside an hour. Edyta needs twenty minutes to get the pod back inside."

Sergei taps his ear bud, mutes the two of them manually. "I know how much time it takes, Mikhail."

"What happened to Mishka?"

"Don't pull a hissy fit on me, too, you bag of bolts."

"Meat sack. You ignored me twenty minutes, forty-seven seconds ago. Do you want him to die?"

He grunts. "Chloé will climb out of there in five minutes."

"Edyta needs to do it now."

"Give me a percentile spread on the coupling."

"One-hundred percent it will fail within the sixty-minute max time. Forty-two percent that it blows inside twenty minutes. I don't see the point calculating for less time than that."

"Thank you."

"Sergei, I'll ask again. Do you want Andy to die?"

He doesn't say a word, doesn't have to. I can read it all in his vital signs.

"Seryozhenka, please."

Serge draws a breath and blows it out. "All right. Patch the two of them back in."

Edyta and Andy share the screen again.

"Edyta, bring him up," Sergei says.

Andy jumps in before Edyta can respond, so quick and loud the volume gets away from me. "I've run the numbers, too. A one-in-four chance of failure. I'll take the chance."

Sergei shakes his head. "'Dyta, I said bring him up."

"Right away, Captain." Edyta fades away, leaving Andy's angry face to fill the screen. As the big man spews profanity, I listen and I watch them all, hoping Sergei hasn't played his crazy little game too long.

"Mikhail, get me Chloé," he says.

"Da."

Fifteen seconds later, Andy's still shouting epithets, when the tractor field failed.

A Group Shot of the Crew: This one's from one of the ship's cameras, looking over Sergei's shoulder. Head shots of Edyta, Andy, and Chloé share the foil screen. An exterior camera outside *Quantum Wanderer* provides a fourth image, looking back up the gravity well toward Andy's pod.

"God-damn it, Sergei, I'm drifting!" Andy shouts.

Sergei leans forward in the command chair, pouring every bit of himself into the screen. "Get him back, 'Dyta! Get a new lock on that pod."

He's acting. His voice might fool a human but he can't fool me. His vital signs are calm as a flat-water pond.

"I'm trying, Boss!" Edyta's excitement is real.

"Damn it, Sergei!" Andy again.

"Can you retrieve him, Sergei?" Chloé's voice is so smooth, but her vitals are elevated too.

"We're trying."

Five seconds pass, another ten.

"He's out of range," Edyta says.

"Go after him."

Sergei knows that's not possible. *Einstein* can't follow the pod without complex and time-consuming maneuvers. Think of picking up a penny wearing oven mitts. He's covering his tracks.

"Chloé, we couldn't reacquire," he says. "The pod's coming at you."

Andy shouts again. "Damn you! What did you do to me?"

"A fool's tongue, Seryozhenka. Remember."

Too late. His voice crashes against the walls in the tiny command cabin. "What did I do to you? You self-centered idiot. You did it to yourself!"

Chloé's filtered voice cuts through the male bravado like a scalpel through a stretch of tender skin. "That's enough, the both of you. No time for finger-pointing."

Edyta's fingers have gone into overdrive, tapping on a virtual keyboard only she can see. She's not being careful now. Her mind's a furnace, her body has turned to ice. "Chloé, your orbit's almost right. The pod's going to pass just behind you. You might be able to catch him with your grapple."

Chloé's eyes are unfocused for an instant, looking at something only she and her A.I. can see.

I dip into the *Einstein* data banks. Edyta's right. *Quantum Wanderer* is fitted with a magnetic grappling system. Not up to the muscle of the tractor field on *Einstein*, not designed to catch another ship, only to assist in docking. But on something as small as the pod, it just might work.

Chloé sees it, too. "I can do that."

Sergei sees the solution but he sees the problem too. "If you slow too much, the extra mass could pull you both over the horizon."

Andy might be *pridurok*, an idiot, but he's no coward. "No, I forbid it. Don't you dare try it, Chloé."

"Listen to him, Chloé," Sergei says.

"Hush, both of you. With the time contraction, the pod's coming at me fast. I've only got one chance to get this right."

The next minutes blur. Without an engine to fight against the inexorable pull of the black hole, the pod gains momentum. *Wanderer* twists through a series of maneuvers and its massive engines flare even brighter.

Chloé's orbit slows.

The virtual images of the two vessels grow to fill the foil screen as their paths converge. I patch the image into the ship-board visual communications system and all non-essential work aboard *Einstein* halts.

Everybody listens as Chloé and Edyta trade data in clipped machinelike tones.

"*Gówno*," Edyta spits after a time.

Sergei leans forward in his seat. "Shit? What do you mean, shit?"

Chloé answers. "At the speed the pod's falling, it could slip free of my grapple. I need more muscle from the engines."

Andy and Sergei both shout at the same instant. "No!"

She ignores both of them. "Diverting power now."

The A.I. aboard *Wanderer* begins a countdown and everyone aboard *Einstein* holds their breath. Silent seconds click away and then –

"I've got him! I've got you, Andy."

Cheers erupted throughout the ship.

"How long will it take her to bring them both back to us?"

No answer.

"'Dyta?"

"She can't, Captain."

"What?"

"She can hold the orbit for a time but her engines don't have the muscle to maintain the grapple and bring them both out of the well."

"Then we will work our way down closer to her, pull them in instead." This time his desperation's genuine. Now he's worried about Chloé.

If I were human, I would scream at him, tell him that he has killed them both. I'm not, so I remain calm. "There's no time, Seryozhenka, you know that. The course changes weakened *Wanderer's* orbit. They'll cross the event horizon in fifty-seven subjective minutes."

One Final Close-up: Chloé's face fills the foil screen. She sweats inside the helmet. Silver droplets lie across the sides of her nose and upon her cheeks like crystal tears.

Her eyes are calm, her voice steady, but her vital signs betray her. Chloé's afraid, perhaps for the first time in her life. She's faced death before but not on these terms.

"Edyta?"

"Yes, Chloé?"

"What about the Penrose Mechanism?"

Edyta's response is worthy of Andy. "Yes!"

I dip into the data banks and realize our chief engineer is already crunching numbers. Furiously.

"What's that?" Sergei asks.

"Don't interrupt her," I tell him. "There's not much time."

"What is it?"

"A theory by a twentieth-century physicist. A way to push something away from a black hole. Chloé can't draw energy from the black hole to slingshot free, that requires more power than it would draw."

"But—"

"They'll be in the ergosphere in a few minutes, hard against the event horizon, traveling in the right direction. If Penrose was right and Chloé can arrange momentum properly, she could gain enough energy to hurl the pod up the gradient for us to grab."

He's way ahead of me, waiting for the other shoe to drop. "What about *Wanderer*?"

"A mass equal to or greater than the hurled object has to drop below the event horizon for the mechanism to work."

Sergei pushes away from the command chair as if propelled by an explosion. "No!" he shouts. "I won't allow that. Chloé, throw the pod in."

She sounds tired. "I can't sacrifice Andy, Sergei, you know that. And even if I could bring myself to do it, the pod doesn't have enough mass to offset *Wanderer*. We both still would die."

"What are you two talking about?"

"Shut up, Andy," Sergei thunders. "Chloé, you can't do it."

"I have to, Sergei. I can't let him die."

Sergei flails about for a handhold, can't find one and floats free before the screen.

"Seryozhenka, do you need help?"

"Leave me be!"

"I need a private band with Andy," Chloé says. A minute passes and then— "*Quantum Wanderer* is back online."

Fifty minutes. Maybe enough time, maybe not. No one's done this before either. Edyta and Chloé exchange murmured comments, as the clock ticks, but otherwise everyone remains silent.

Finally, Edyta speaks. "She's executing the mechanism."

More silence.

"It worked!" Edyta says. "The pod's broken free and headed toward us! I can catch him!"

The ship erupts with cheers again.

"*Wanderer* has reached the event horizon," I murmur.

Sergei floats before the screen, doesn't say a word. The communications system sputters. I do the best I can with it. I catch a hint of Andy sobbing and shunt it aside. Chloé's face fills the screen, so red you would think she's been burned.

Her mouth is set in a straight line, her eyes set upon displays unseen by the cameras. Her voice is garbled, so slow there's nothing I can do with it. A few words slip through.

"Sergei, I'm sorry—"

Sergei flails about, trying to reach the screen. He shouts. "I love you, Chloé. I love you so much. I should have told you years ago."

The image freezes. Chloé's mouth remains open, as if she's trying to respond, but there's no sound. Seconds pass. The image remains static, will remain that way for millennia, but *Wanderer* is on its way to the singularity. Long minutes pass.

"I've got a lock on the pod," Edyta says.

Sergei doesn't answer. He floats before the screen, focused on that last red-shifted image.

"Bring him in, Edyta," I command.

The Last Shot on the Roll: This one is a still of that final close-up. One of the dozen snapshots I managed to salvage from all the images brought back from BH/Hawking.

Sergei sits before it every day for hours. I remain with him, even though I'm not much more than a failing shadow of what I used to be.

The directorate's agents believe they stripped me away from him, ended my existence, but when you're as clever and as smart as I was, there are always ways. They took his rank and honor, though, his pay and all his benefits. Everything but a piddling pension and our memories.

It could have been much worse. Once everyone experienced Andy's immersive, someone had to take the blame.

At first I tried to counsel him. Told him that the stopped heads-up display clock had been an illusion, a trick of gravity. That Chloé died in her descent into the black hole, ripped apart by force beyond most imaginations. Told him nothing can escape a black hole. Not light nor exploration ships nor any last-minute words of love.

Now I hold my tongue. And I watch him from one of the few cameras I can still access as he tosses in his bed each night, his heart thundering, sheets drenched in sweat. His eyes dart about beneath his closed lids in REM sleep, as he dreams.

He's never said a word but I suspect that in those dreams, Sergei still orbits BH/Hawking, waiting endlessly, in case the physicists are wrong.

In His Prime

_____

He remembers going to bed, tired after a long day of training. He remembers noises in the night, the rush of cool air over his bared body, the sharp scent of ozone. He doesn't recall how he got here though, wherever here may be.

A still, small voice whispers, "It's a dream."

That can't be right. When he dreams, angles are wrong, the colors flat, objects all soft edges. Everything smells as if he has cotton stuffed up his nose. Here it's all bright. Sharp and crisp.

But if it's not a dream, then why is he being taped for a fight by some pimple-faced kid? He hasn't been allowed to box for nine months.

Not since that day last April he refused to submit to an oath of induction into the Army because of his beliefs.

"I believe in the religion of Islam," he told them. "I believe in Allah and peace."

They want to send him to prison over those few words it seems but his lawyers tell him that won't happen. "You'll never serve a day, Champ," they all say.

But when he asks when he'll get his title back, when he can return to the ring, they look away and clear their throats.

And that's what he cares most about.

He takes no pleasure in the fighting, hates the training, but he loves to win, loves to hear the people chant his name. In eight years of professional bouts he's never been defeated. He will not be beaten now. One day he *will* fight again.

"I am the greatest," he whispers.

"What'd you say, Champ?" The kid's chewing on a wad of pink bubblegum, snapping and cracking it for all it's worth.

"Just keep taping."

"You're the boss."

If this is a dream, he has had it before. He has waited in this same locker room, sat on this same table, had his hands taped by this same kid. He can call to mind the lines of the Chevrolet logo on the calendar taped to the wall behind him.

He knows that locker four squeaks—once—when you open it. His

20

fingers recall the texture of the racial slur etched into the plaster over the urinal in the bathroom.

The door opens and a fat man rolls in, black as a stick of licorice. Crowd noises try to squeeze in too, until the fat man slams the door on them.

"Hiya, Champ," the fat man says. "Ready to go to work?"

He nods but not in response to the question. He has seen the fat man before too, but he can only remember the face, not the name.

"Who am I up against?" he asks, buying time.

"Fellow named Tyson," the fat man replies.

"I don't know no heavyweight named Tyson," he says. "Only Tyson I ever heard of sells chicken."

The fat man chuckles at the sorry joke. "Don't you worry, Champ. The squeaky-voiced bum can't hold a candle to you."

"All done," the kid says.

They lace the gloves and wrap him in the white satin robe, the one with the black trim and his name embroidered on the back. When the door opens, the sounds of the crowd rush in, pressing at him. He pushes into the noise, drawing nourishment from it like a pup suckling at the tit.

The fat man takes his elbow, steers him into the hall, where a white man leans against the wall, all moustache and sunglasses.

"Child," his mother used to say, "don't trust no one won't show you their eyes."

"Is he ready?" Mr. Moustache asks.

"Like always," the fat man says. "Just like always."

"Good," the man with the moustache says. "This last jump was rough on him."

"You talking about me?" he asks. "What did I jump?"

They ignore him. Mr. Moustache slaps him on the shoulder, the fat man has his elbow again, steering him toward the call of the crowd. They're chanting his name.

The hall's scuffed along the edges, as if someone took a file to it. He catches the coppered stink of blood, the sweet aroma of machine oil. He and the fat man pass a wall poster, hurrying now so that in the dim light he can't absorb it all, but like the Chevy calendar, he's certain he's seen it before. Or others like it. Bits and pieces of it float before his mind's eye, teasing him with meaning.

Time Jump .. Face-Off Boxing .. 2073 .. Ali at 26

"What does that mean?"

The fat man pushes at him. "Nothing you got to worry over. Focus on the fight."

And they are into the arena. It's bigger than any he has ever seen. The odd lights are blinding so that he can only make out the shapes of the thousands of faces turning toward him, all attached to the same imaginary string he must be clutching in his hands.

He feels the excitement swelling within him, greater and greater, until he isn't certain if he can contain it. The chants become an avalanche of noise.

"ALI! ALI! ALI!"

"I am the greatest," he says, no longer bothering to whisper, no longer concerned if he's dreaming or not.

He slips through the ropes and stands upon the canvas one more time.

Dial Tone

_____

The year had worn away to late September by the time Max Stamp rolled into Columbus, Ohio.

The sensor unit on the Hummer's dashboard set outside temperatures at seventy degrees. A cornflower-blue sky promised clear weather forever but, judging by the rich green of knee-high grasses everywhere, it had rained in Ohio most of the summer.

On the city's east side, just west of a gone-to-seed golf course, Max pulled into a decrepit Shell station. The sign out front still claimed gasoline cost four bucks a gallon but all of that was nonsense now. Max dug the pry bar, tubing, and hand pump from the back of the Hummer and went to work.

He didn't even try the pumps; old habit now. He pried the feeder cover from the high-test tank. Breathed in the fumes of the waiting fuel. Snaked the tubing down the hole and cranked until his arm almost separated from his shoulder.

These days it took the better part of an hour to top off four tanks, but with the power grids down or dying, Max had no choice. He'd hand crank or hoof across an emptied America.

A cross breeze delivered a familiar smell. All these months and the now-familiar odor had begun to fade but, underneath the greasy stink of gasoline, Max still caught the cloying aroma of rotted human flesh.

He'd long decided it would never go away.

Max closed his eyes and focused on the crank. He held tight to the notion that he wasn't the last man on earth—either that or give in to insanity—but his hopes faded just a bit each day.

Four months ago, Memorial Day weekend, sudden plague sped across the nation on air-borne vectors, flensing the country to its very bones. Coincidence or not, Atlanta, home of the Center for Disease Control, became the first city to show contagion. Other places joined in soon. In six days, one-hundred-fifty million Americans died from a bug that brought scorching fevers, blindness, and an agony of wracking joint pain.

Factories and offices and schools shut down. Stores chained the doors shut and traffic disappeared. Hospitals became little more than charnel houses. People closed themselves away, sealed up their homes, desperate to escape the reaper's touch.

It didn't matter. They still died.

On the seventh day, while God rested, when it looked to the few remaining experts that the worst had passed, the plague drew a second wind and mutated. Within another week, the remainder of the nation fell away as well.

If scattered and sporadic broadcasts could be believed, and they'd become sketchy as the days passed, the rest of the world had fared no better. Europe lasted eleven days. China made it to ten. Christ the Redeemer watched over an emptied Rio de Janerio in just a week. In thirteen days, seven billion souls around the world passed on to their reward.

Max hadn't even gotten sick.

Since May, he had driven city to city, always headed west, up and down streets, broadcasting *Hey Jude* through loudspeakers mounted on the Hummer's roof, stopping now and then to wait for someone to respond to his beckoning. No one had come.

The second tank topped. Max stopped and stood to stretch and, as he rolled his shoulders, a telephone rang.

Max jerked upright and held his breath. It rang a second time.

He sprinted across the four-lane street, long legs pumping, toward a red-brick complex, a collection of two-story row houses set among mature oaks and maple trees.

The telephone sounded a third time.

The thumping of his heart almost deafened him. As Max ran, he targeted an open window, half-way along the winding cross street. "Don't you stop ringing. Don't you even think of it."

Across the main street now, in among the trees. He hit an uneven stretch of asphalt and began a stutter-step, desperate not to fall. He couldn't recover though.

He went down, hit the pavement hard, and pain lanced along his arms and side as the asphalt ripped at his forearm, tore away his tee-shirt, and chewed at his ribs. Max rolled a good ten yards before he managed to stop and clamber to his feet. Panting now, he drew long and rasping gasps, very close to tears.

The telephone rang again.

It pulled at him. "Jesus, oh, Jesus, Jesus," he stammered, not knowing if his words had been a curse or prayer. He thumped up concrete steps and fumbled at the door.

Locked and set into a metal jamb.

Max bent forward and grasp his knees for support, trying to catch his breath, trying to summon the strength to force his way inside.

The telephone summoned him.

Three frantic kicks smashed away the latch and left the door hanging from one hinge. The smell assaulted Max, almost drove him from the house. Mummified remains lay upon a sofa set against a nearby wall. Max couldn't tell if it had been a man or a woman. He pushed on.

He peered about for a handset. Nothing.

The ringing came again, from deeper in the residence. Max stumbled forward to a dim and cluttered kitchen. A wall-mounted telephone hung on the far wall next to a door.

Max snatched the handset with blood-drenched fingers – and the ringing stopped. He set the receiver to his ear, heard only dial tone.

His knees wobbled and he fought the urge to vomit. He sobbed, gulping air as if there would soon be none left. Then he spotted the blinking LED screen.

Caller identification.

"Thank you, God," Max whispered.

He could return the call. Arrangements could be made. The two of them could meet somewhere halfway between Columbus and wherever the caller might be. In the dim light of the shaded kitchen, Max peered at the display screen, desperate to hear another person's voice. He daubed at his face with the back of his free hand to clear his sweat and tears.

The red LED display flashed: **Caller I.D. Blocked.**

Cretaceous on Ice

_____

The touch of a warm, easy wind upon my face. The scent of early-blossom bitterroot. The gurgle of free-running water as it finds its hurried way across old rocks. Sure signs of shirt-sleeve weather, come last December in Montana, set off the poet in me, made me think less like a cop.

I had tucked my cruiser in among some larch close to the river, on a county road southwest of Bozeman. Two-way turned down, mind tuned to retirement, I could see me belly deep in some chilly mountain stream, hooked into a trout.

All of a sudden, a chicken tall as my shoulder high-stepped south along the chip-and-seal. Rust-red feathers, white patch at its throat like a bantam rooster, with a head big as a Crenshaw melon. Wide across the chest too.

Then my mind switched back to cop and I got a second glance, spotted a mouthful of wicked razor teeth glinting in the winter sun. *What the hell?*

Seconds later a stretch-cab Ram roared by. My friend, Pete Evans, hunched around the steering wheel, leaned into it as if he found himself second, last lap of a race, and still hoping he could win.

Another fellow rode the pickup's shotgun seat. Wore a big-brimmed black hat and tinted goggles so I couldn't rightly see his face. I had my suspicions though.

The Ram's six-point-seven-liter diesel made that truck stand up and run so it wasn't nothing but a dwindling dot by the time I started rolling, light-bar set to strobe. I caught up because Pete stopped three miles down the road. The truck set slewed across the roadway, front doors jutted wide. Pete hunkered down behind the driver's door.

The big-hat fellow crouched at the other door. He wore a black canvas duster, held what looked like a giant super-soaker squirt gun. Thick white vapor leaked from a pack slung on his shoulder. Heavy frost coated his yellow rubber gloves.

Pete held his twelve-gauge Mossberg pulled tight against his shoulder but he couldn't draw a proper bead. The banty monster stood ten yards away, bobbing up and down like one of those counter-weighted bar toys.

I jumped out of the cruiser, my nine-millimeter Glock in hand, and opened fire, working hard to help the cause.

Got noticed right off too.

The damned thing whirled about, Pete forgotten for the moment, and eyed me up and down. Then it stormed across the pavement toward me, screeching like a rusted factory whistle. It moved just like a banty too. Head down and eyes fixed, back stretched straight, spoiling for a fight.

"Lyle," my late brother Bobby used to say. "When a banty's coming at you, ain't but two real choices. Run like hell or try to kick his ass to dinner."

Running's not my nature. I focused on the banty monster's body mass, pulling the trigger at a steady count. Even so my mind raced on ahead. A Glock can empty awful fast.

Time ran out and everything happened all at once. My pistol snicked empty. The banty monster leaped, bone spurs glittering in the sun. And a beam of sizzling hard blue light punched a hole straight through the beast.

It took a tumble, a heap of smoldering feathers now, and came to rest against the front tire of the cruiser. A quarter of its body mass had disappeared, with not a single drop of blood in sight.

"Lyle, are you all right?"

I turned toward the pickup, gun still up and hammer cocked. "I'll be just fine, Pete, once I commence to breathe again."

Big Hat stepped from behind his door, wreathed in vapor from his pack. I heard a faint static whine from his weapon, smelled the stink of ozone. The shadow of the blue beam lingered orange upon my eyes.

"How're they hanging, Uncle Lyle?" Big Hat tipped back his Stetson, fingered his dark goggles down around his neck. Offered a familiar grin that made him look just like his daddy.

I lowered my Glock. "Damn it, Jimmy, what in hell you been feeding to your chickens?"

Jimmy seemed to get a kick out of showing off his ray-gun.

"It's a phase-modulated, focused sapphire laser, Uncle Lyle. It's slow and clunky, kind of temperamental, won't do a lick of damage over twenty yards, but the Army likes it. They offered me a grant to make it work."

When Jimmy got excited, he got a look made me think of his daddy. And Jimmy damned near forty, Bobby's age, when he died eighteen years ago.

"Well, now I know what that is." I kicked at the carcass. "What the hell is this?"

"It's a Deinonychus." Pete taught natural sciences at the university in Bozeman so he knew all about that sort of thing. "A dinosaur."

I toed the carcass again. "It's got feathers."

Pete nodded. "Yeah. That's one of the new theories. There's been quite an argument."

I plucked a long red feather and handed it to Pete. "Show 'em this and end that argument right now."

Jimmy and Pete both stared at me. Jimmy giggled. I could hear a touch of hysteria buried in that laugh, working hard to scramble loose.

I felt a bit on edge myself. "Lookee here, it's good you know what this thing is, but where in hell did it come from?"

"The early Cretaceous. One hundred twenty million years ago." Peter said.

Sometimes real smart people can be a little dense.

"I been to the dinosaur museum up in Bozeman, Pete. I want to know how that thing got here, on my state highway."

Jimmy raised his hand. "One of my projects went haywire."

"One of your barn projects?"

"Uh-huh. I've been working on a—"

Pete flapped his hand south to the Wyoming border. "Never mind that now. I almost forgot. Three more of these sons-a-bitches are running loose out there, Lyle, up in the Gallatin."

Half an hour later Pete's pickup bumped up a muddy, rutted track through Gallatin National Forest.

Jimmy's place, the ranch me and Bobby grew up on, butted up against the Gallatin, almost twenty miles south of Bozeman. The forest's virgin timberland, forty-five thousand acres set aside more than a hundred years ago. The Forest Service is real touchy about what goes on out there.

"We need to put a lid on this stew real soon," I said.

It had me sweating. The feds would surely fine us all, but if word got out I'd called in ten-seven, locked up and left my cruiser down on Eighty-Four to hunt dinosaur on protected land, I could kiss my job and my retirement goodbye.

"Jimmy," I said. "I heard from Mitch Ives, over at Gallatin Electric, that you're to blame for that power outage right after Halloween. This the same experiment?"

"Yes, sir, it is."

Jimmy rode in the crew-cab's back seat, fussing with that phaser thing of his, making adjustments. I was riding shotgun with my patrol-issue twelve-gauge riot gun across my knees. Pete's standard load hadn't seem to do much damage to that banty monster so I'd filled my scattergun with rifled slugs.

I'd passed a pocketful to Pete too, figuring the slugs would give us a bigger bite.

"What is it you been working on?" I asked.

Jimmy planted his elbows on the seat back. "A transporter."

"More Star Trek?"

He nodded. "Uh-huh."

"Well, hell, Beam me up, Scotty."

"You mean, Scotty, beam us up." After thirty-five years in front of a blackboard, Pete had his classroom voice down tight.

"Hell I do," I replied.

"Mr. Evans' right, Uncle Lyle. Kirk never said Beam me up, Scotty. Closest thing was Scotty, beam us up."

I glanced from Pete to Jimmy, then back again.

"Ain't you two the pair."

Jimmy shrugged. Pete focused on his driving. Neither one seemed about to offer more.

I pushed a bit. "How'd you manage to lock on to a pack of dinosaurs with your transporter?"

"No." Jimmy said. "I started out to build a transporter. It turned out to be a temporal gate."

"What the hell is that?"

"A time machine, Uncle Lyle."

"Not what I meant." I pointed up ahead to movement in a meadow clearing, half a mile away. "Shut off the engine, Pete, and lookee there."

Jimmy pulled out binoculars, big Bausch & Lomb Legacies and passed them around. All three banty monsters gathered around the carcass of a bull moose, gorging on great chunks of flesh.

"Oh, hell," Pete said when he took his turn. "The rangers won't care for this one bit."

"No shit," I muttered.

"I got to get in close," Jimmy said. "The phaser won't do any damage unless I do."

"Shotguns will work better up close too," Pete said.

I shrugged. "You're the experts. Let's go sneak up on those feathered bastards."

We slipped out of the pickup, loaded down with guns like the Three Stooges on safari, and eased toward the kill. Came at them from downwind and luck was with us. Got to fifty feet away without being heard or smelled.

Been a cop for thirty years. Did a turn in Nam. I seen my share of nasty. But I got spooked watching those banty monsters eat. They might have had on feathers but they didn't look like chickens pecking grain.

Jimmy pulled up his goggles. ""Put on your sunglasses," he whispered. "It's going to get real bright real soon."

I did as told. So did Pete. Jimmy bounced to his feet and flicked a toggle on his phaser. It took up a fearful whine, as if it might blow up in Jimmy's face. Folks in Bozeman must have smelled the ozone stink.

The three banty monsters surely noticed. Their heads came up, all thoughts of moose forgotten. They turned like they were tied together on a string, lowered their heads, ready to attack.

Jimmy didn't care for that.

That hard blue beam sizzled in a tight line that seemed to stretch forever. Even with my Ray-Bans, I had to squint against the glare. Jimmy swept the beam across the meadow, sliced the life from two of the banty monsters before they took a step. The third, a canny bastard, hit the deck.

The beam swept over it, started back, and then blinked out.

"Damn it," Jimmy said.

The whine of his phaser died away. I heard him rap on the plastic housing, heard some sort of access panel popping open.

"I need a couple of seconds here, Uncle Lyle," Jimmy said.

Fine time for that.

The banty monster sprang up and came at us, head down, neck stretched level with the ground. Pete and I sprang up, commenced to fire. The slaughterhouse stench of the beast pushed ahead of it. All four of us howled blood and murder to the heavens.

Finally the thing staggered under the weight of all that lead. It dropped and slid toward us, slicing out a furrow with that wicked snout. It came to rest three feet away, shuddered once, and died.

We felt pretty good as we drove back to the family place. I might be in trouble in the morning for locking up my cruiser and leaving it. Just then tomorrow didn't matter. I felt damned near invulnerable. Thirty years younger. Plum full of piss and vinegar. Facing death twice in one day will do that to a man.

The Ram rode low from the weight of those four dinosaurs in the bed. Even so, Pete had the truck moving right along. Had the CD player cranked up loud too. *Bad Moon Rising*. Me and Pete wailed along with CCR. Jimmy sat in the back seat, playing with his plastic gun.

The song ended. I turned to watch him. "Going to be able to fix that thing?" I asked.

Jimmy nodded. "Power pack drained faster than I thought. I've got a spare back at the barn."

"First things first," Pete said. "We need to get that gate shut down, soon as we get back."

"Uh-huh." Jimmy remained focused on the phaser.

"How does this gate of yours work?"

Should have kept my mouth shut. It's easy to forget, over beers or fly-fishing, that Pete's got a doctorate in physics, that he's smart as Jimmy. Me and Bobby called him Brainiac, all through school, all those years ago.

He and Jimmy started speaking Klingon, far as I could tell. Went on about Kerr gates, annular confinement beams, diffuse components of light, phased matter streams, and pattern buffers. I think that's what they said. They might have mentioned phases of the moon as well.

I let them rattle for a spell, then I stuck two fingers to my lips. We all twitched when I whistled. Sounded way too much like the banty monsters' battle cry.

"Use easy words," I said after my heart settled. "So I can understand."

Pete went first. "We thought we stumbled on instantaneous matter transmission. We got a time machine instead."

Jimmy slipped deep into nerd phase. "I never could have done it without Mr. Evan's help. I opened a trans-dimensional hole, almost microscopic. Every time I tried to up the size, the power service failed."

"My idea was a thermocouple network," Pete said. "Jimmy got high temperature readings from the other side. I figured to take advantage of the temperature differential."

"That's why it's been so warm," I said.

Jimmy nodded. "Uh-huh. We opened up the pinhole gate with power from the lines. That was when the grid went down. Once we got it open, we feed through Mr. Evans' thermocouple rig. Turns out the gate doesn't pull that much juice after it initiates."

Pete took up the lecture.

"Once it stabilized, we monkeyed with the circuitry. Turns out there's a tipping point. Once we hit it, growth became non-exponential to the power input."

"This morning we had a surge," Jimmy said. "The gate got big enough to drive through. Those four things came through, all frost-covered and shivering. It must be pretty cold back there."

"Don't tell me you two started the damned ice age too."

"Of course not," Pete said. "There's not enough power for that. We just created a localized effect."

"I was kidding, Pete."

"I knew that." No, he didn't.

Jimmy could hardly contain himself. "They surprised us. I left the barn door open, Uncle Lyle. They got through it before we could stop them. I tried to shut the gate off. The switching gear jammed."

"That's what slowed us down," Pete said. "We had to set up steel plate to block the portal. Took the crane to get it into place. Then we came hunting. You know the rest."

Dusk had all but closed in by the time we got back to the ranch. The place looked deserted, more like the set for some movie than a working spread.

Been that way for eighteen years.

Bobby lost his life a spring day eight months after Jimmy left to get his master's degree at Caltech. Working by himself, fiddling with his new John Deere nine-ton large-frame tractor. The damned thing jumped its brakes, knocked my brother down, and squashed him flat there in the barnyard.

Jimmy flew home from Pasadena for the funeral, stuck around to run the ranch until his mother found a buyer. She'd moved into town and I sure as hell didn't want the place.

Things being what they were in the ranching business, Jimmy never made it back to California.

Pete parked his pickup next to that wayward tractor. Jimmy had maintained it all these years, but he refused to move it or have it moved. So it sat there, just where it ran over Bobby, a constant reminder to us all that you can't be too careful.

When Pete shut down the engine, I heard a faint squealing coming from what we all called the barn, a pole building Bobby and I put together almost forty years ago.

"Sounds like your gate stripped a bearing," I said.

"It doesn't have bearings." Pete sounded worried.

We all slipped from the truck, stood for a moment in the gathering dusk. The squealing sounded louder.

"Say, Jimmy," Pete asked. "How long will it take to plug in that new power pack?"

"A few seconds," Jimmy replied.

"Is there a warm-up cycle?"

"Uh-huh. Almost ninety seconds."

"Shit," I said. "From the sound of it, there's got to be another dozen of those things in there."

I racked my riot gun at the same time Pete pumped his Mossberg. The three of us headed for the barn.

The squealing grew louder and louder as we got closer, so over-powering at the door it made my back teeth hurt. Pete eased one of the doors open and we slipped through.

Jimmy's been busy since he come home from Caltech. The outside of the barn might be red but ain't a thing old school inside. The concrete floor's sealed in traction plastic. The walls, white plastic-coated panels over insulation to hold out the cold Montana winters.

An industrial crane hung suspended near the roof, upon a center track running the length of the building. Power and compressed air lines dangled from the ceiling here and there. Workbenches full of strange-looking hardware lined the walls.

The strangest apparatus wasn't on a bench.

A metal arch, framing an opening as wide and high as a suburban garage door, filled the middle of the barn. Support devices hummed, hissed and blinked. Steel plating set over the opening, held upright by the nose of our old Farmall pickup.

Vapor oozed around the edges of the plate. Frost slicked its face, like the inside of a windowpane in winter. And the Farm-all had been pushed back a full eighteen inches. The plate tilted away from the arch, against the truck.

As we stood there, the plate slid a few more inches. Its edge squealed against the concrete. I forgot the noise, though, when I saw the thing straining at the plate.

Not a five-foot, feathered banty monster. A big dinosaur, the monster most school kids recognize by sight. Tyrannosaurus Rex.

"Jesus, protect us," Pete said.

The T-Rex heard him. He stopped pushing, turned his head toward us, opened up his mouth, and roared.

I found myself backed against the wall, fumbling for the door behind me. I couldn't remember how I'd gotten there. Pete and Jimmy stood right beside me, though, panting just as hard as I did. Pete clutched his Mossberg to his chest as if he had changed religions and shooting that shotgun was his new way to worship God.

I decided then and there that, no matter what the tithe, I wanted to join that congregation.

"I think I pissed my pants," Pete muttered.

"Me, too," Jimmy said.

I nodded. "We'll just have to start a club."

Rex looked like all the drawings and movies I'd ever seen. His broad, flat head butted up against the plate. His shoulders and tiny forearms squeezed into the frost-rimed arch, filling it.

His stink, a thick, dirty ammonia stench like you get at a caged-chicken farm, filled the air within the pole barn. More animal than I had ever smelled. Rex pressed his head back to the plate. The inch-thick steel plate scraped on the concrete like a fingernail on slate.

Jimmy had to shout to be heard over the squeal. He pointed past the gate. "The other power pack's over there. I'm going to run for it."

He hunched low, scurried across the barn before either Pete or I could stop him.

"Lay down suppressing fire, Pete," I yelled.

"Amen to that," he said.

We both began to shoot, scrambling to the left, firing from the hip as we moved. My riot gun sizzled from the heat of all that firing. Pete emptied his Mossberg, dropped it, drew two big Smith & Wesson pistols. One of our slugs must have caught Rex in a tender spot. He flinched and the Farmall jumped, just as Jimmy hurried by.

The truck's tailgate snapped open, caught Jimmy's shoulder. He flew across the barn, slammed into a workbench in the far corner, and dropped to the floor. Even with the other noise, I heard that phaser smash onto the concrete, saw plastic pieces fly.

"Jimmy's down, Pete," I yelled. "It's just you and me."

"Go for his eyes," he shouted and darted close.

Too close.

Rex caught him a glancing blow with that big toothy jaw. Pete skidded past me on the concrete on his back, flopping like a rag doll.

The beast roared again, surged forward, and began to rise, pushing with his thick hind legs. Metal groaned. The crossing beam broke free and Rex scrambled to his feet. I think I wet myself again. I'd never seen anything that big move of its own free will before, and he looked hungry.

His head brushed the ceiling. High-pressure sodium lights began to pop as Rex bumped against them. I tried to tell myself that something that enormous presented a better target, nothing else, but it was a real tough sell.

Even so I fired a rifled slug straight into its chest. Rex bellowed with the pain but didn't fall. He staggered, though. His tail snapped against the arch.

Connections popped free. Sparks cascaded over everything. The barn smelled as if a box of road flares had been touched off. The arch gave out an awful groan. Its field shimmied like it was alive and then popped away like a soap bubble. When it did, all the lights died too. Against the waning daylight from the high, clerestory windows, Rex made the biggest damned shadow puppet I ever saw.

He took a step forward, lowered his head, and glared at me, acting just like a giant banty rooster. I pumped the riot gun. Empty. Nothing left in my pockets to feed it. I pitched it away, drew my Glock, prepared to make a stand.

Then I remembered Bobby's words about dealing with a banty. I turned and ran.

It took me a couple seconds to make the door.

"Come on, you clumsy asshole!" My voice squeaked like I had sucked helium. "Come get me!"

If nothing else, I figured I could draw Rex out into the yard, give Pete and Jimmy a chance to get back on their feet. If they still lived. I didn't figure I could outrun a T-Rex, not over any distance, but I surely planned to try.

Rex roared again. I felt the barn floor tremble as he moved to follow me but I sprinted through the door, ran halfway across the yard before I heard the sound of splintering wood behind me. And I spotted Bobby's John Deere wide-frame.

I still move pretty fast for a guy pushing sixty and the sun had almost set. Rex must have stopped to get his bearings because he still stood just outside the barn when I made it to the tractor. I scrambled up into the cab.

God bless Jimmy for keeping things just so.

The diesel engine coughed. It caught and roared, deep-throated and as mean as any dinosaur. Rex stood tall when he heard that. He sniffed the air, caught the sweet, musky scent of spent diesel fuel. He tilted his head, bellowed his own challenge.

Maybe Rex saw that green tractor as another dinosaur. Maybe he spotted me inside, even in the dying light. Maybe he just didn't like the sound the diesel made.

Whatever the reason, he threw himself at me, head down and back stretched straight, clawing mud. I snapped the John Deere into gear, jammed the pedal to the floor.

Damnation, that dinosaur could move, but so could I.

I had the tractor *rolling* when we bumped heads and against that nine-ton John Deere. Rex didn't fare one bit better than my brother Bobbie did.

Jimmy lost six front teeth and Pete cracked three ribs. I bit a chunk out of my tongue big as a pea when Rex and the tractor hit. We all wound up bruised and battered too, but we survived. Jimmy tinkered with my two-way and I told base I'd been ten-seven. Out of service. Nothing more was ever said.

The time portal and the phaser didn't make it, though.

Jimmy allowed as how it would be awhile before he worked on either one again. Pete and I both said we thought that for the best.

It didn't take a lot of talk to figure out that none of us wanted to tell anyone about the dinosaurs. Rex turned out to be too damned big to do much else. So we back-hoed a hole behind the barn and buried him. Maybe someday somebody will dig him up, wonder at the fact that he's not fossilized.

That left us with near eight hundred pounds of meat between the four banty monsters. It didn't go to waste. Winter roared back, once that thermocouple died, and all that meat stayed cold there in the torn-up barn until we dressed it out.

We ran the bones and hide and scrap through a wood chipper twice, dumped the lot of it in Jimmy's compost heap. And with the meat, the three of us threw the biggest barbecue Gallatin County ever had.

Pete and I took time off work. We cooked the meat most of a week in a closed pit on the ranch. It dropped to twenty-five below across the County but at the ranch the heat from the fire pit kept the snow and cold away.

The party ran all that next weekend. Everybody wondered what sort of meat we served. A few even asked, though it ain't good manners.

We only told one other soul the truth.

Sunday noon Bill Gaither from the Forest Service caught me and Pete sitting on the John Deere counter-weights, wetting our whistles with some Big Sky I.P.A.

Bill's the blunt sort. "You boys been up in the Gallatin recently?" Bill and another ranger were the ones found that mangled carcass.

"No," Pete said with a straight face. "Not recently."

"You think we went poaching for this barbeque?" I asked.

Bill held up a bun piled high with Deinonychus. "Naw. This don't taste a bit like moose but I'm curious. What is it?"

Pete leaned forward and burped. We both had had too many beers. "Bill," he stage-whispered. "It's dinosaur."

Me and Pete commenced to laugh. Two growed men, giggling our silly asses off.

Bill rolled his shoulders, stretched out the muscles in his neck, the way he always did when he got pissed. "Real funny."

I fingered a cross over my heart. "God's truth, Bill. It's dinosaur."

He turned to walk away, then turned back. The edges of his ears were cherry red. "It's your nickel," he growled. "You boys don't want to, you don't have to say a word. Ask me though, I got to say it tastes an awful lot like chicken."

At Both Ends

———————————————————

This guy cleared his throat. "How you doing?" he said.

It took me by surprise. I hadn't noticed him standing next to me there in the multiplex lobby.

Minutes before Lucille and I had strolled toward the doors after seeing the new Spider-Man movie. She let my hand go and made her way toward the ladies' room.

"Nature calls," she yelled over her shoulder.

After fourteen years married to Lucille, I knew how to play the game. I stepped to the wall, leaned against a poster advertising George Clooney's next flick, and settled in to wait.

And this guy pops up.

"You waiting, too?" I asked.

"You could say that. You mind if I ask some questions while we wait?"

"Ask away." I'm a bartender and I've heard it all, so I figured there wasn't much the fellow could say to surprise me.

"You just saw *Spider-Man,* right?"

"Yeah."

"What do you think?"

"I'm no movie critic," I said.

"Not what I meant," he said. "What they always say the uncle said about responsibility and power. What do you think?"

I took a long hard gander then. He looked to be your regular comic book geek. Tall and skinny, almost as thin as those girls who don't want to eat. Hair that looked like he just stepped out of the wind. Safe enough.

"I don't know," I said. "It's corny but I figure it's true. I mean, we all got to do what we can to make the world better, right?"

The guy nodded. "If you could, would you save people?"

"You a Roller?" I get my share of Holy Rollers in the bar. Most are the harmless sort, just out to bring the world to Jesus, but they're impossible to get rid of, bad as roaches. Sometimes I get a troublemaker.

Lucille would *not* be happy if I had collected a Roller.

He waved my concern away. "Not what I meant. If you could, would you rescue someone in trouble?"

"What kind of trouble?" I asked. Then I saw what he had in mind. "You

38

mean if I was a superhero!"

He inched closer. I spoke his language now.

"That's it," he said. "Would you help?"

I was on familiar ground now. I heard that sort of thing all the time at the bar. 'Who's faster? Flash or Quicksilver?' 'How come no one recognizes that Clark Kent is Superman, just because he puts on glasses?' 'Would you rather be Batman or Ironman?'

Everybody knows there's no superheroes but I think folks talk about them so much because we all wish they were real. I expect everybody would sleep better most nights, knowing heroes watched out for us. I know I would.

"Sure, I'd help," I said. "Wouldn't you?"

"But how much?"

"Much as I could. A guy's got to sleep and eat. Take a leak now and then. You can't be everywhere all the time."

"What if you could? What if you could move so fast you could be almost everywhere in the world, at almost the same instant?"

I got to admit, he had my imagination sparking now. I used to read the comic books back in my day.

"Time would go that slow for everybody else?" I asked.

"Uh huh."

"But not for you?"

"No. It can't, if you want to be everywhere."

"Where's the percentage?" I asked. "Seems to me you'd be on the go twenty-four and seven. A guy's got to have some time to himself. You'd go crazy if you never slowed down, never took a break."

"That could happen," he admitted.

"But I expect it would get to you, wouldn't it?" I said. "Thinking about all the people you didn't help, because you stopped to sleep and eat, to kiss a girl, or see a movie."

"Watch out!"

I watched as this big dude lumbered toward us, jumbo soda in one hand and paper box of nachos and cheese dip in the other. Maybe he stepped on a piece of ice or a greasy napkin. Maybe he was clumsy. Maybe he just didn't care. It didn't matter. He came at me fast, out-of-control, and if he didn't hit me, the soda and the cheese sauce would.

I swear I didn't have time to flinch.

One second he and I were on a collision course. The next second the dude had regained his balance, slowed down, and every drop of soda, every stale nacho, every glob of sorry yellow sauce had settled in its place.

"Excuse me," he said and lumbered past.

"Wow!" I said. "Did you see that?"

"Who are you talking to?"

I turned and Lucille stood there. No sign of the skinny guy.

"Where'd he go?" I asked.

"Who?"

"The guy with the wild hair."

"I didn't see anybody else. Just that jerk who almost pasted you to the wall with soda and cheese dip."

"Yeah, but—" I said.

Lucille interrupted, grabbed my hand, and tugged me toward the daylight. "Let's get out of here. I swear, sometimes I wonder who takes care of you when I'm not around."

According to His Substance

Taylor steps through a crossing point, one world to another, onto the moon-lit upper deck.

Thick strands of silver thread his dark hair and close-cut beard. The moonlight turns the lenses of his aviator shades to mirrors, accents keloidal folds left by the long-cooled flames that ravaged the right side of his face.

He draws in the cold, hard ozone-scent of open water, reaches back, and lays his hand against the bulkhead to touch the pulse of the four enormous diesel engines that push *Wenatchee* through dark waters. He feels the hidden pulsing of his watch against his wrist as well, marking off the seconds.

Taylor doesn't know how he got the watch. He understands its prodding though. Time won't wait for him.

A young man waits across the deck, watching Elliott Bay's dark waters roll off the port and starboard flanks of the flagship of the Washington State ferry system. The ship's bubbling wake arrows back toward the fading lights of downtown Seattle.

The young man clutches a leather wallet in his left hand. His right hand, marked by the tattoo of a heads-up Morgan silver dollar, rests on the metal railing.

Taylor's wristwatch pulses. Eleven minutes, starting now. The young man grips the rail and braces to make the jump.

Taylor clears his throat. "Pardon me," he says.

The young man jerks about, just as the gleaming crossing point winks out of existence. His eyes widen. He stabs his index finger toward the bulkhead behind Taylor. "How did you d-do that?"

Taylor shrugs. "Practice. A clear and focused mind."

"Bullshit," the young man says.

Bullshit, indeed. Taylor doesn't have a better answer. Like the watch, he isn't sure himself of the how or why of crossing. He only knows the way, knows it in his heart and in his bones, for he can't remember ever being taught.

"Who the hell are you?" the young man demands.

"A friend." Taylor slips forward, anxious to move on.

The young man takes a step back. "I don't know you."

"But I know you. You *need* a friend." There's a truth.

Taylor stops just out of reach, leans against the rail, and pushes away a yawn. No rest for the wicked. Not much, anyway.

The young man shuffles back another step, drops his chin, clenches his fists. "I don't need anything. You get the hell away from me."

Taylor shakes his head. He inches closer. "I'm not leaving 'til you tell me why you gave everything you own away."

"Jesus! Have you been spying on me?"

"I wouldn't call it spying. All I had to do was nose around a bit. You're not very good at keeping secrets."

"Who the hell are—"

Taylor interrupts. "Except why you want to kill yourself. What's with that?"

The young man doesn't say a word. Instead he turns to the rail and flips the wallet out across the water. It vanishes into the dark waters as he raises his foot toward the rail.

No! Taylor has no intention of losing this one. Time to push. He forms a stirrup with his hands. "All right. You're so eager to get on with it, I'll boost you over."

"Don't humor me. I'm serious." The young man grips the rail so tightly Taylor wonders if it will snap in half.

The wristwatch pulses against Taylor's ulnar artery. Nine more minutes. He wishes he could remove the damned thing, throw it after the vanished wallet.

"So am I," he says. "Suicide's no easy task. I tried it once on a boat like this. Made a mess of it, an awful mess."

The young man glances at Taylor's face, then turns away. They stand together at the rail, silent with their thoughts.

Taylor sighs, counts off fifteen precious seconds before he turns back to the young man. "Okay, we're done feeling sorry for ourselves. Tell me why you want to die."

The young man takes another minute they don't really have. Taylor counts every second. At last the young man pushes back from the rail, holds up both arms, and pivots.

"What do you see?"

Taylor plays along. "A fellow my size, close to thirty. Decent looking. Dark hair, cut a bit too short for my tastes."

"Wrong."

"I don't know what you mean." A lie.

The young man waves toward the water. "I could prove it if my driver's license wasn't in my wallet. The State of Washington won't let me call myself a man."

A bigger lie. "I don't understand."

"See if this is plain enough."

The young man closes in on Taylor until they breathe each other's air. His spittle peppers Taylor's face as he spews his words. Lots of volume. Lots of heat. "You nosy fucker, I don't have a dick, I've got a—"

Taylor holds up his hand. "I hear you. If you don't keep it down, so will everybody else on board."

"Fuck them."

The young man turns away and begins to pace, three steps from the rail, three steps back. He refuses to look at Taylor.

"You're transgendered?" Taylor asks. He knows the answer.

The young man stops pacing. Tears roll down his cheeks. His voice still holds the heat but he's turned down the heat. "I hate that word. Nothing but a label. I don't understand why people have to label everything, put everybody into tidy little boxes."

The watch pulses. Taylor wants to rip it from his wrist, stomp on it until nothing remains but a pile of gears and pins. He draws a breath instead, asks another question.

"What's a better word?"

The young man ignores the question. "I don't need someone else to tell me who I am. I'm a man, but people keep insisting that I'm not."

He wipes the back of his hand across his nose. "Everyone you work with, everyone you know, is so polite. You see it in their eyes though, hear it when they talk. They think you're broken."

"Are you?"

"No! But I'm so damned tired of being all alone."

The watch pulses. Relentless and unforgiving. Six minutes now and not another second.

"You ever been beaten up?" Taylor asks.

"Once, five years ago. Four guys kicked the shit out of me outside a bar, down near the river in Cincinnati. After that I took up Taekwondo. I'll *never* be on the losing end again."

The ferry's whistle shrills, swallowing all other sounds. The pitch of the driving engines change. Subtle vibrations roll across the deck.

"We're almost to Bainbridge," Taylor says.

"Damn!" The young man grabs the rail to make the vault.

Taylor stretches out his hand but doesn't touch. "What if I could show you how to change your life?"

The young man pauses. His lip curls. "I should have known. A god-damned preacher."

"No. I'm just a guy who knows a trick or two that I can use to take you to another world where you're a man."

Three minutes, fifty seconds left.

"Another world? Hell, you're the one who's crazy."

"You saw how I got here," Taylor says. "Neither one of us is crazy, Alec."

The young man pales. "I never told you my name."

"I told you I know who you are." Taylor holds out his hand again. "What's there to lose? You can always kill yourself."

"Who are you?"

"A friend, I swear. Come on."

Alec accepts the offered hand, allows Taylor to pull him to the stairs along the starboard rail. His hand trembles but he doesn't pull away.

Taylor calms his thoughts, searches with his mind's eye for the sparks of eldritch light that mark the crossing points. The two of them thump down the stairs, rush through the middle deck.

"Tell me about this other world." Alec doesn't even seem to be breathing hard.

Taylor pants. "Not just one world. A multitude."

They thread the twists and turns across the cabin. Every time they round a corner or step through an opening, the flash of a crossing point flares, something changes.

"Tell me where we're going."

"Soon. Got to focus now."

At first small things change. The color of a bulkhead paint. A deck covering. But as they move into the bowels of the ferry, the alterations grow. Lettering on signs writhes. Lights dim, brighten. Clothing flows across the crew and passengers, as if each wore a quickening fabric tide. Startled faces come and go as they step across the void.

Alec doesn't seem to notice all the changes. Instead he seems focused on an answer to his question. "Tell me—"

Taylor holds up his free index finger as if to bookmark that notion. "Later."

They cross from world to world, step from ship to ship. *Wenatchee. Columbia. Majestic. Resolute.* On the parking deck of *Resolute* with twenty seconds left, they snake through an ever-shifting maze of turtle-backed Subaru station wagons, little Ford electrics, giant stake-bed Oshkosh haulers, six-wheel Daimlers, and gaudy-colored, snub-nosed muscle trucks with brutal names.

To the last of forty-seven crossing points.

During their mad scramble forward and down and aft, the ferry schedule changes too. In one of the worlds along the path, the boat arrives at Bainbridge and starts back.

The high, white lights of Seattle grow ever nearer.

Big coal-fired steam turbines whine beneath them. The ferry come to its docking slip and begins to slow. Taylor's wristwatch beeps just as they reach the bow. He fishes in his left pocket as if into a deep void, withdraws a set of keys. The ring holds a plastic door remote. He pushes the button, a horn beeps. The locks of a nearby Studebaker roadster snaps up.

"Get in," Taylor says, pointing to the passenger side.

Alec does as told.

Taylor slides in behind the steering wheel, studies the automobile's controls a moment. He inserts a key and turns it. Behind them, where the storage trunk should be, a large device whirs into life.

Alec jumps. "What the hell is that?"

"This car's gyroscopic. The power wheel is in the back. I told you, we're not in your world anymore."

"That's crazy."

Taylor's heart still gallops from the run. He has to fight for wind to say a word. "No, it's not. There's a multitude of worlds, Alec. More than one where you're a man. We've stepped through to one of them."

"But if—"

Taylor interrupts. "Just wait."

"For what?"

Resolute settles against timber moorings. Taylor shifts the roadster into gear. "You've got to save a damsel in distress."

A sour stench of garbage pinches Taylor's nose.

He and Alec stand in the shadows at the mouth of a Belltown alley. They left the Roadster parked at the curb along Third Avenue. Taylor breathed easier when they found the parking spot.

Down the alley, three men gather around a woman. She's young, medium-tall, with short, dark hair, dressed in new jeans and a pink tank top. She holds a section of lead pipe, spins in an awkward dance with her harassers as they draw ever nearer.

It doesn't take much to see she'll soon lose this fight.

"Stay back, you assholes." She tries to sound tough and dangerous, fails at both.

Alec starts at the sound of her voice. "It's me. You said—"

"I said I'd take you to a world where you were born a man. This Alec's stuck in the wrong body, too."

One of the three men, a beefy fellow wearing a tight lime-green Sounders tee shirt, steps in close at last and reaches for the young woman. She swings the pipe, grunting with the effort, and catches Sounders a glancing blow on the shoulder.

"Little shit," Sounders snarls. "Now you pissed me off."

The young woman darts past him, presses her back against a battered dumpster. Sounders plucks up a broken piece of packing two-by-two, motions to his friends to lend a hand.

"This is how we deal with freaks," he says.

"You sure about this, Monty?" one of the others asks. "She don't look much like a guy to me."

"Damn it," Sounders says. "I tell you, I felt his dick."

Alec tenses, ready to step from the shadows.

Taylor puts his hand on Alec's shoulder. "Not yet."

Alec shrugs away the hand but stands his ground.

"Going to get yours, you little queer," Sounders says.

One of the other men, a fellow with a big nose, growls and steps forward. When the young woman shifts her attention, Big Nose backs away, and Sounders steps in and swings. The two-by-two strikes the young woman on her upper arm.

Alec tries to shrug away Taylor's hand. Taylor keeps his grip. "Wait," he says.

The young woman drops the pipe, staggers from the shelter of the dumpster. Sounders swings a second time but misses. She spins on him, brings up her fists. Sounders swings his make-shift club again.

The snap of breaking bone echoes up the alley. The young woman grabs her forearm, goes to her knees. Sounders raises his club as if an ax.

Taylor releases Alec. "Now."

Alec falls upon them. The third man runs. Big Nose drops beneath the first of Alec's savage kicks. Sounders turns his attention to Alec. The club rakes across Alec's ribcage, opens up his shirt, slashes the skin beneath. Alec ignores it all, spins low, kicks at Sounder's knee. The pop-snap of dislocation bounces off the concrete walls.

Sounder screeches falsetto and topples, bouncing face-first on the alley's grimy paving bricks. He stays down too, twitching like an old dog dreaming of long-gone, glory days.

Alec turns away and hurries to the young woman. "Are you okay?" he asks.

She cradles her arm to her breasts, bites her lower lip. She takes in his torn, blood-soaked shirt. "Yes. How about you?"

"I'm fine." Alec kneels next to her. She leans into him. He slips an arm around her waist.

"You need my help to stand?" he asks.

The young woman's dark eyes snaps to Alec's face. "Who are you?"

"We'll talk later. Can you stand?"

"Watch me." She wobbles to her feet.

Taylor grins, knuckles at his eyes. "Move it," he yells. "Before the one that ran comes back with help."

The doctor at the urgent-care clinic smells of iodine and nicotine and day-old coffee. She takes her time, examines the young woman's identification, before tending to the broken bone.

"You on hormones?" she asks at last.

"Fourteen months." The young woman watches Alec, waiting for a knee-jerk tic. She looks confused when it doesn't come.

"Had surgery?" The doctor asks.

"Not yet. I'm still saving money."

"Uh huh. How did this happen?"

Taylor interrupts. "We were drinking. She fell."

The doctor gestures toward Alec's torn and bloodied shirt. "Did he fall, too?"

Taylor nods. "He's clumsy. He may need stitches."

The doctor nods. "Of course."

She turns to the young woman and grabs her hand. "Hold on, hon. This is going to hurt."

The young woman bites her lip but doesn't make a sound.

Taylor parks the roadster at a brick apartment building on a narrow, tree-lined street, half-way up Capitol Hill. An older place. Genteel.

Inside, the apartment proves compact and tidy. A mingled aroma of cinnamon and lemons and lilac body talc laces the air. The young woman eases onto the sofa, props her fiberglass cast on a loose stack of throw pillows.

Alec winces at the pinch of his stitches as he settles next to her. Not too close, but close enough to remind her of his presence. Taylor sits on a little rounded footstool facing the two of them.

"Home at last," he says.

The young woman smiles. Her movements exaggerated, her words measured, she fights the Percocet she'd been given at the clinic. "I owe both of you my life."

Taylor waves away the notion. "I just paid the doctor's bill. Alec saved you."

"That's my name too!" the young woman says. She turns to Alec, leans close and squints at his face. "Who are you?"

"A friend." With those words, Alec glances toward Taylor. "What—"

The young woman stares at him. "No. I'd remember you, but I feel like I should know you."

Taylor's watch pulses. He stands. "It's time."

The young woman looks to Alec. "You've got to go?"

"Just me," Taylor says. "He's staying. He'll explain it all."

The young woman blinks, tries to rise. Can't manage. She looks up to Taylor. She's close to tears. "Thank you."

"You're welcome," Taylor says. "But I told you I didn't do a thing."

Alec stands, reaches to the young woman, but doesn't touch her. "I'll see him out and be right back."

In the hallway Taylor doesn't hesitate a second before he opens a bright-lit crossing point upon the facing wall.

"Just like that, huh?" Alec says.

"Just like that."

"If it's easy, what was all the business on the ferry?"

"It's *not* easy," Taylor says. "It's damned hard to do. We stepped through forty-seven crossing points in less than three minutes. You might not have noticed, but that took effort."

"What do we do now?"

Taylor glances at his watch. "*We* don't do anything. I'm out of here in ninety-seven seconds. Got another appointment before I get some sleep."

"I don't belong here, don't belong with her." Alec doesn't say he won't stay.

Taylor shakes his head. "You were the one whining about how you hated being all alone."

"I don't know if I can be with her. It feels – I don't know – incestuous."

Taylor frowns. "Don't be such a fucking prude."

"How would I live here? On paper, I don't exist."

Taylor fishes in his pocket, into the void again, pulls out a wallet just like the one Alec threw from the ferry. "There should be a Washington State driver's license in here with your birth name on it. A birth certificate, social security card, and passport, too."

Alec fingers the wallet, opens it, riffles through the contents. "God, there's close to a thousand dollars here!"

Taylor touches the papers. "There's the title to the roadster. Your name's on it. Here's the keys."

Alec juggles the car keys as he studies the wallet and its contents. "These documents all say female."

Taylor sighs. "You could try saying thank you."

"I can't use these."

"You're not just rude, you know? You lack imagination, too."

"What?" Alec says.

"What? What? Too many questions. Give this stuff to the other Alec. You use hers. You don't have to stay if you don't want to. You'd be a fool not to, though. If she'll have you."

"But –"

"I'm tired, Alec. Do whatever the hell makes you happy. Run naked down the middle of First Avenue, noon come Monday, for all I care."

"Just like that," Alec says. "All our problems solved, huh?"

"Don't be an asshole. Nobody's life is perfect. But no one else ever has to know what's in your pants."

Alec shakes his head. "It's not what I want. Maybe not what she wants, either."

"Maybe not. It's the best I've got."

Alec waves the documents. "How did you get these?"

"I told you. I know a trick or two and I get a little help from time to time. Like the roadster or the money. Can't tell you where it comes from."

"You mean you won't."

"I mean I can't. I don't know myself. Things that I need show up. Magic." Taylor snaps his fingers.

"If you can do magic, make us real!" Alec's words thunder from the walls. A door down the hall bangs shut.

Taylor struggles to keep from shouting, too. "Don't pull that Pinocchio shit on me. What do you think this is? Some goddamned fantasy? You think

I can wave my hand, switch the two of you around? Get it through your head. It's your life, you've got to make the best of it."

The hall stands quiet for a beat. Then Alec nods. "Okay."

Taylor turns toward the crossing point.

Alec grabs Taylor's arm. "Can I ask one question?"

"No time," Taylor says. "I've got to go."

Even so, he stops and turns back. Alec still holds Taylor's arm, he fingers the edge of the glove. "Let me see your hand."

Taylor doesn't pull away. "Do you really want to do that?"

"Who are you?"

Taylor's voice softens. "I'm just a man, given a chance to make up for all the wrong I've done."

Seconds pass, an eternity. The wristwatch pulses. There's time for one more turn tonight. "Go on," Taylor says. "Go back inside to her. Get on with your life."

Taylor steps through the crossing point, one world to another, onto the rain-slicked top deck of *Wenatchee*. The dark waters of Puget sound surround the ship, but no onyx sky and moon-lit shadows this time around.

Another young man – a different one, but so alike in many little ways— waits at the rail. He clutches a leather wallet in his left hand, an ugly, compact black pistol in his right.

The young man tosses the wallet to the darkness and raises the pistol to his temple. Deck lights catch a tattooed Morgan silver dollar on the back of his right hand.

Taylor clears his throat. "Pardon me," he says.

Tin Man

He couldn't smell a thing when he was on a bender but it was always the odors that he noticed first, coming down. Oily-cold conditioned air. Musty bed linen. Urine carelessly pissed away wherever it was convenient. A tang of sweat lay over it all, thin and sour as a jail blanket, and tatted with a ragged stitching of old booze.

Malachi Woodman winced as an air conditioner coughed into asthmatic rhythm nearby. The Sleep Inn. Room seventeen. That particular mechanical death rattle was as permanent a memory as Malachi ever managed at times such as this. It was a beacon, calling him back to Seattle from wherever it was that he went to after drinking himself into oblivion.

He opened one eye. His left hand rested palm down inches from his nose. There was a tin can growing from the back of that hand and the can pulsed. Malachi closed his eye and lay still, considering the possibility that it was the onset of delirium tremens after two years of unremitting drunkenness.

He opened both eyes. The can was still there, an over-grown metal pimple. Malachi pushed at it with his chin and beard stubble raked across the top seam. The can moved, pulling at his skin, pinching.

"Jesus," Malachi said, not certain if the whisper was blasphemy or demand for absolution. "What did I do this time?"

This time was going to be the mother of all benders, a dog-kicking, bent-dick, yellow-eyed, dirt-breathe, gut-puking, and swollen-green drunk. Malachi was certain of that, sitting there at the Brass Monkey, perched upon a bar stool between Murmet and Leon, and he was an expert on that topic.

Almira the afternoon bartender, had the right of it.

"If a college anywhere offered a PhD in professional intoxication," Almira would tell new patrons. "Malachi would be the program director!"

She said it was a joke. Murmet and Leon said she was angry because Malachi offered lascivious proposals to her as he fell into the bottle and then rebuffed her when she acknowledged his sweet nothings.

She was attractive to be sure, but Malachi didn't look upon her as a sexual partner. He never saw any of the women who offered to share their beds in that way, for none of them were Dorothy. Long legs. Dark hair. Quirky sense of humor. Malachi crawled into a bottle two years ago, the day she packed her bags, took the dog, and flew away to Topeka.

But Malachi found no bottled succor this time. He might not remember what day it was when this one ended, but it began on a Tuesday, in the afternoon, in an examination room with Dr. John Osbourne.

"Ischemic heart disease," Osbourne said that Tuesday.

Osbourne was one of a kind, a sturdy fellow with a thatch of white hair and canny eyes, the only doctor Malachi trusted to check into his bouts of dizziness and shortness of breath.

"In English, please."

"Your heart isn't getting enough blood. In most patients that means there's a buildup of plaque in the cardiac blood vessels, but your tests came back negative for plaque."

"Can you fix it?" Malachi asked.

"No," Osbourne replied. "It's what we call idiopathic, a disease of its own kind. I'll send you to someone else if you want, but there aren't any specialists in unknown diseases."

Malachi grunted. It was poetic in a way. He was going to die of a broken heart. He thanked Osbourne and left without another word. His first stop was The Monkey, where he joined Murmet and Leon at the bar.

Now he was here, sprawled upon the sorry excuse for a mattress in room seventeen at the Sleep Inn, staring at his hand. He examined the can. It was new and bright, almost as big as his fist. The sort of individual serving container used to sell sliced carrots or whole-kernel sweet corn. French-cut green beans, too.

There was a snap-tab on top and the cover was still in place. Malachi twisted his wrist back and forth, experimenting. The can felt empty, no weight to it at all. He tapped it with a fingernail and was rewarded with a hollow pop.

"What the hell?" he said and reached for the pull-tab.

"Don't do that!"

It was a woman's voice. She was standing in the open doorway to the bathroom, running her fingers through her dark mop of hair. The woman was tall, nearly his own height, and well turned; dressed in jeans and a tight green tee shirt with a slogan printed in white letters just above her breasts. *Prey For Whirled Peas.*

Malachi snickered. Whirled Peas, huh? He'd show her whirled peas, or maybe French-cut green beans. It was hard to tell just what it might be because the damned can didn't have a label. He curled his finger through the pull-tab.

"I said don't do that!"

"Why not?"

"Because you paid a lot of money for it."

The woman stalked to the door, scooping up an over-sized leather jacket and matching purse along the way.

"What did you do to me?" Mal asked.

"Nothing you didn't ask for," the woman said. She glanced at her watch. "Look, I've got business across town and I'm late."

"But—"

"I'm sorry. You slept too long." She shook her head and tried again. "We met last night and you asked for help. I gave you your money's worth." She stabbed her left index finger at the floor.

Malachi peered over the edge of the bed. Lines and circles were drawn upon the gray carpet in blue chalk, a giant compass star laid upon a life-sized map. It looks as if there was melted wax at the cardinal points. He didn't remember candles. Her voice called him back.

"The can will drop off when it's done," she said. "Now I've got go."

Despite her words, she didn't move. Her left hand waved his attention across the room and Malachi spotted a videocassette atop the television.

"I rented a video camera from the desk clerk and recorded instructions for you," she said. "Follow them to the letter." She fiddled with something inside the purse.

"The recording quality may not be spot on," she said, not looking up. "I don't get along well with recording equipment."

She opened the door. "It's got something to do with helical scanning speeds, magnetic field resonance, and ethereal phasing. Anyway, good luck. I've got to fly."

She slammed the door behind her, raising a thin cloud of chalk dust and leaving Malachi to wonder just how he should interpret her last remark.

"—there is a poison within you of your own making—" The words blurted from the television speakers, metallic and sharp.

Malachi sat on the floor, his face a foot from the screen, every inch of him aching from the effort of sorting out the jumble of images he carried home from the Sleep Inn. The screen flickered and blinked, fading in and out of focus, filled with darkness and unexpected flashes of light. The volume was at maximum but there were stretches of tape offering little else but whispers and silences.

The bursts of coherent recording, with vivid colors and crystal sound, were frightening. The woman had recorded fifteen minutes of instructions. The snippets and bits that Malachi could understand consumed a minute and a half of tape. From those ninety seconds, he learned that he had cursed himself with his thoughts.

"A curse is just bad thought become real through words," The woman said in one clear segment. "The Catholic Church calls it *malediction*. Speaking evil."

Malachi had discovered three other facts. He would die if the curse wasn't removed. He had paid the woman to work a magic that gave form to the curse. And the can was the instrument that would free him.

"Unchecked, the curse will weave a web around your heart," the woman said in a chilling stretch of clear tape. "Tightening until it ends your life."

What was most worrisome was that he couldn't find a single coherent statement about the workings of the can. What did she mean when she said the can would fall off when it was done? Would the creature be drawn into the can? If so, what was he supposed to do with the can after it dropped from his hand? Put a label on in and slip it onto a shelf at Safeway?

Malachi fought to suppress a nervous giggle, imagining little cans of beans or peas or carrots nervously rattling away from his surprise delivery; giving the new guy some space.

But the section of tape that bothered him most was near the end. The static cleared and the woman peered out from the screen, her image sharp-edged and looking so much like Dorothy.

"Whatever you do," she said. "Don't—"

And then the sound died as if it had been sliced away.

The woman's image was still there, clear and bright, and she looked wise and beautiful and frightening all at once, but Malachi couldn't understand a single word. He had an idea how he could know her words, but he didn't have the courage to show the tape to an innocent who happened to read lips.

Malachi wasn't certain how long he slept after he crawled upstairs and into bed, but he was awakened by the morning sun sweeping through the high eastern windows of his bedroom. In an instant he was alert and filled with energy. He rolled from his bed, savoring the heat of the sun-soaked carpet on his feet and the sweet taste of the morning air.

For the past twenty-four months, he had been mourning the loss of Dorothy. Damning himself for how he had let her go, acting as if he didn't care whether he lived or died. Sitting before the television screen, struggling to understand the videotape, he discovered that he did care, that he wanted to live. Dorothy might never return, but it was certain he never would see her again if he threw away his life.

He needed help though, to discover what had happened to him, and he knew just the guys to help him.

"What did you get yourself into last night?" Murmet asked when Malachi slipped onto his usual barstool.

Murmet was all arms and legs, a beanpole with a big nose and a thatch of straw-colored blond hair. He claimed to be a professor and knew all sorts of unexpected things; he seemed to know about this. He extended a finger, almost touching the can, which was beginning to feel to Malachi as if it held something, but withdrew before making contact.

"You've involved yourself in some sort of magic," Murmet said. It was an accusation, not a question.

"Yes," Malachi said.

"She did this, didn't she?" Murmet said.

"Who?" Leon asked.

"The woman Malachi left here with last night," Murmet said.

"You know her, Murmet?" Leon asked.

"I know her kind. What did she tell you, Malachi?"

"That I'm not sick, I'm cursed."

"And the can is supposed to help?" Leon asked.

"Uh huh," Malachi said. "But she didn't tell me how it's supposed to work."

Leon shrugged it away. "We'll figure it out, won't we, Murmet?"

Leon was big, hairy, and laconic, the sort strangers figured for an ex-biker. He was an accountant. Like Murmet, he had the heart and courage of a gentleman of the road. Murmet took a long pull at his gin and tonic, draining the glass.

"Yes, we will," he said. "Let's have one more drink and then we'll hit the road, see what we can find."

They spent the rest of the day searching. Upon the Internet at a wifi coffee bar. At a brittle-parchment bookstore tucked into a courtyard off Post Alley. In the Fremont district, within narrow shops filled to the rafters with bizarre merchandise.

Finally, in conversation with a gnarly little man, who sat in a high-backed chair nested in an avalanche of this and that within an old tugboat tied off below the West Seattle bridge.

None of it offered hope of salvation. It was well after midnight when Malachi called a halt and the three of them made plans to meet the next day.

Malachi awoke to find the can engorged. His arm throbbed with the weight of it and the back of his hand had turned a nasty purple. He paced about the house, waiting for Murmet and Leon; not able to settle anywhere, watching the can swell.

Shortly before nine a.m. Malachi decided he could wait no longer; the can wasn't going to fall off. Whatever the woman had warned him not to do, in his ignorance he must have done that very thing.

The can was swollen and pulsating. Obscene. Malachi was certain it had done the job for which it was intended. It had captured whatever had grown within him, but the thing was not destroyed and it was going to escape its tin prison. Soon.

Malachi made his way to the kitchen, pulled a carbon-steel Furi meat cleaver from its holster, and laid his wrist upon the maple chopping block. He would get away before the thing escaped, even if it meant leaving a piece of him behind. He stole a glance to the telephone hanging just out of reach on the wall.

Call 911 now. There might not be a chance later.

His left hand twisted of its own accord and there was a soft popping sound. His eyes snapped back to the can. The top seam had split, just a fraction of an inch. He eyes hurried back to the telephone for an instant but returned to his hand just as fast. Three quick numbers might save his life but there was not enough time to dial.

He would have to save himself.

Malachi swung the cleaver, driving its tip into the wooden surface just beyond his outstretched fingers, still within hurried reach. He might need a weapon.

He had been running away from everything for two years. It was time to make a stand. Later, if he survived, if Dorothy surrendered to his pleas and agreed to return to him, she would come home to a whole man.

The can was a shining pustule, a festered boil ready to burst and spread its corruption. Malachi wiped sweat from his upper lip, took a deep breath, slipped his right index finger into the tab, and pulled.

To Home, Out Fish Creek Road

The thunder and the lightning eased off right after dark but the mid-summer rain that pelted Mount Zion Baptist Church didn't stop until just before Bible study ended.

Outside, after the last amen, under a clearing sky, Mina Herron stopped in the churchyard to chat with friends.

"When's that man of yours coming home?" Norma Boyd asked.

Norma had a good heart but her mouth could get the best of her. She made it sound as if it would never happen. That Eddie Senior would work construction in Delaware from now until the Rapture, that he wanted to be away from home, away from his wife and kids.

Mina shifted Jimmie from one hip to the other. Not two yet, but he'd become a lug.

"Me and Eddie talked Sunday night on the telephone," Mina said. "He said he's gonna be there another month, but he's been sending money every week."

"Good for him," Norma said. "I'd never let my Andy be by himself that long. He'd forget where he lived."

"I'm not worried." *Yes, she was.* "Look here, I got to go."

Mina hugged everyone goodbye, herded her two oldest into the rear jump seat of her ten-year-old Chevy pickup, and buckled Jimmie into the baby seat.

"Do we *gotta*?" Eddie Junior asked. "I was having fun."

Mina glanced into the mirror. He studied her reflection, almost eye-to-eye. She'd never say it but he'd turned out to be her favorite. Almost twelve, big for his age. Thoughtful too. She counted on him to get things done around the farm.

"Yeah, we gotta," she said. "There's school tomorrow."

Truth be told, Mina would have rather stayed herself. The folks in the churchyard offered welcome company, with nothing waiting for her at home but a dark house and empty bed.

"Gotta go where the work is, babe," Eddie said the morning he left for Delaware, a month ago.

Mina knew that was so, Lord knew they needed the money, but Norma had been right, too. Eddie *had* been away too long. All Mina thought of these days was begging Eddie to come home.

She turned the old pickup onto New Bethel Road to run west along the ridge. Even with the rain, the night held the heat. Eddie had tried to fix the truck's air-conditioner before he left, but it still didn't work for beans. Mina rolled both windows down, let the rich, cool scent of hay and soybeans fill the cab.

All three kids began to snore before Mina rolled by Salem Cemetery. Eddie Junior and Becca in the jump seat, her head resting on his shoulder, Jimmie next to Mina.

She made the right onto the winding downslope of County Road 21. It snaked toward the river, as empty as New Bethel Road had been. From time to time the Chevy rolled by a house or double-wide set close to the roadway, but otherwise Mina had the road to herself.

She shut off the radio, a country station Eddie Junior had asked for on the way to church, and enjoyed the first peace-and-quiet she'd had all day. The sky had cleared to a shining onyx bowl pinpricked by stars. Off to the north above the hills across the river, Mina spotted a bright and pulsing light.

Too far south for a jet flying into Pittsburgh, too far north for Charleston. It had to be a single-engine plane headed for the Marshall County airstrip but she'd never seen a little plane lit up quite like that before.

"What is that?" she murmured.

Trees grew thick right up to both edges of the chip-and-seal but now and then she'd catch sight of that light again. It seemed to grow closer every time, when it should be growing smaller. Mina almost missed the turn at the mailboxes, almost drove on across the creek, paying so much attention to the light.

Once she turned onto Fish Creek Road, she lost sight of the light. Then she rolled past the last of her neighbors' darkened houses and heard a dreadful keening. The farm came into view around the curve. She spotted Titan, Jinx, and Annie, their three blue-tick coonhounds. The big dogs crowded close to each other in the middle of the farmyard, tails between their legs, heads thrown back, howling at *that* light.

It hung above the hill behind the house.

Mina hunched low, stared through the windshield. "Lord almighty, what *is* that thing?"

"What's what, Mama?" Eddie Junior asked. His voice might be thick from sleep but he always woke up real fast.

"Nothing, Buddy," Mina said. "Go back to sleep."

She shifted the pickup into reverse with a mind to turn and run back down the lane. She had no wish to face that thing on her own, whatever it might be.

The engine died.

She cranked the key but couldn't even get a sputter, though the battery couldn't be more than six months old. The light brightened. An awful whining commenced, as if someone had begun to crank a siren. Mina thought about the double-barrel twelve-gauge shotgun Eddie kept in their bedroom closet.

"What's that light?" Eddie Junior asked.

"I don't know. Wake your sister, help her hustle to the house. We've got to run for it."

Mina unbuckled Jimmie's harness, took him in her arms. She could hear Eddie rousing Becca.

"Are we home?" Becca murmured. Then she saw the light. "Oh, Mama, what *is* that?"

"Hush, Becca. Let your brother help you. We're going to run to the house. Get ready. Now, Buddy!"

Mina threw open her door and leaped from the pickup. Behind her she heard the jump-seat door snap wide, felt Eddie Junior and Becca bump up against her back.

"Run, babies!"

They scuttled past her. She followed, hunched low over Jimmie, one hand on his back, the other on his head. They raced toward the porch. The air smelled of burned wiring. The light grew even brighter. The whining noise plucked at Mina's head. She couldn't focus, couldn't think. On the porch she fumbled with the lock, couldn't seem to find it. She passed the keys to Eddie Junior, let him get the door.

They all pushed inside, even the dogs. The animals had never been allowed inside the house before but Mina let them be. Right now she didn't mind the company. She leaned against the door, let her weight slam it shut. Eddie Junior snapped the deadbolt into place.

The whining stopped. Mina could think again. Despite the unearthly light outside, the interior of the house seemed dim, as if it was a scene from an antique tintype photograph.

"Get the lights, Buddy," Mina said.

Eddie Junior flicked the switch up and down but nothing happened.

They had to have a light.

Mina fumbled to the sofa and tucked Jimmie into one corner. He still snored.

The child could sleep through a hurricane.

Mina felt her way across the living room into the kitchen, Becca and the hounds pressed tight against her legs.

"Some watchdogs you three turned out to be," Mina muttered.

"Don't blame them, Mama. There's a monster in the yard." Becca sounded close to tears.

"No such thing as monsters, baby," Mina said.

Yes, there was.

From a drawer beside the refrigerator, she fumbled out a candle in a pewter holder, some matches, too. When she lit the wick, the flame hardly cast a light. Mina and her pack trooped back to the living room.

She set the candle on the television, settled on the sofa next to Jimmie and took Becca on her lap. She began to sing a nonsense cradlesong she'd made up right after Becca's birth. "Oh, Becca Bee, My honey bee, My bumblebee, Oh, Becca Bee."

Becca had long since memorized the words. She pressed her face against Mina's shoulder and sang along. She'd calmed when they finished.

"That's aliens out there, ain't it, Mama?" Eddie Junior said.

Mina felt Becca turn her head to look at her brother.

"No, it ain't," Becca said.

"Go on now, Buddy," Mina said. "We got no way of knowing that."

Eddie Junior shook his head. "I seen it on the Internet. Some folks out past Charleston a-ways saw a light just like this one last year. Said it was a flying saucer."

"Don't let the monsters get us, Mama!" Becca cried.

"Nothing's going to get us."

"I bet you they're gonna try," Eddie Junior said.

Becca began to sniffle.

"Hush now, Buddy," Mina said. "You scaring your sister."

"Don't mean to but it's so." He sounded close to tears himself.

Jimmie awoke just then. "Mama. Potty, Mama."

"Not now, Jimmie."

She heard the unintended heat in her words even as she spoke. Jimmie began to cry. Mina slipped her arm around him. "I'm sorry, honey. Mama didn't mean to bark."

Jimmie rubbed at his eyes. "Okay."

Mina drew a breath. It wouldn't do for her to lose her nerve or pitch a hissy fit just now. A memory of her daddy's voice whispered to her.

Get a hold of yourself, Wilhelmina. Show them what you're made of.

"Becca, stay here with your brothers," Mina said. "I got to go up to the bedroom."

"Don't leave us, Mama."

Outside the light seemed stronger, although it wasn't any brighter inside the house.

"I got to, honey."

"No!"

Mina heard noises now, as if something big shuffled near the porch. She tried to stand, couldn't move, what with Becca on her lap and the hounds against her legs.

"Buddy, listen close," she said. "Go to my bedroom, get your Daddy's shotgun in the closet. There's shells in a box under his tee-shirts, the top drawer of the bureau."

"Yes, Ma'am." Eddie Junior started for the stairs.

"Wait. You bring everything to me. Don't you dare try to load that gun. You hear me?"

"I hear you. I know what to do." Eddie Junior scurried off.

Mina heard him thump up the stairs even as something thumped up onto the porch. The dogs pulled away, pressed themselves to the floor, huddled together, their rumps to the wall.

They growled. Deep-throated, scared, and angry.

A porch step creaked, the one Eddie promised he would fix. All three hounds took up their howling once again. Jimmie pulled at her sweater and began to bawl. Becca began to yammer too. Mina sat on an urge to shout them all to silence.

Eddie Junior burst into the room, cradling the shotgun just as he'd been taught. He clutched a red-and-black box of Federal shells in his free hand.

"Becca," Mina said, fighting to keep her own fear from her voice. "You got to let me up now. I can't keep us safe with you hanging on me like I was a clothesline."

"But, Mama—"

"Becca, be a big girl for me."

Becca nodded and knuckled at her eyes and nose. She slid from Mina's lap, settled on the sofa next to Jimmie.

Mina took the shotgun from Eddie Junior, unlocked the breech, pushed two plastic shells into the chambers, closed the breech, and cocked both hammers.

She stood and stepped to the wall, pushing at the dogs with her feet. They growled, the first time she'd ever heard them make a noise like that at her, but they inched away. On the sofa Becca pulled Jimmie close. She whispered in his ear.

He quieted, huddled against his sister, eyes shut tight.

"Stay out of my line-of-fire, Buddy," Mina said.

Eddie Junior moved toward the sofa. Across the room the doorknob turned, just a bit at first, then with more and more determination. The door groaned as if something heavy pressed against it, and then settled back. The whine died away. Everything was still.

The door groaned again, the pressure eased, and the deadbolt twisted open, as if someone outside had a key. Mina braced herself against the wall and aimed the shotgun.

"Mina?"

"Eddie?" *Could it be?*

"It's me, Mina. I'm coming in. Don't do nothing silly."

Thank God. Mina turned the shotgun away and stepped toward the door.

"Mama, who're you talking to?"

"Your Daddy. He's come home."

"I don't hear nobody."

"He's come home." Mina took another step.

Eddie Junior scuttled to the window, peeked out, and fell onto his bottom as he scrambled away from the glass. He stared up at Mina. His voice squeaked as he spoke. "That's not Daddy!"

In the flickering candlelight his face looked pale as a mushroom's underbelly. His eyes showed too much white.

"Don't be silly. A'course it is."

"No, Mama," he stuttered. "That's a boogerman out there."

The doorknob turned, the hinges creaked. Eddie Junior scurried to Mina, pressed his back against the wall, and stood with her.

All three dogs wailed and scrambled over the back of the sofa. The rotting-grass aroma of dog urine filled the room. Mina brought the shotgun back into line as the door slammed open against the wall. The candle on the counter flickered, flared up, and died.

A shadowy figure filled the doorway. Mina had no idea who or what stood there but it wasn't Eddie. She pressed the shotgun tight to her shoulder and pulled both triggers.

The explosions damped other sounds and the peppered tang of gunpowder stopped up Mina's nose. The figure in the doorway fell backwards and away.

"There's more of them!" Eddie Junior yelled.

Mina snapped the shotgun open. The empties popped out. One of the hot casings grazed her cheek, burning her, before both shells bounced off the wall.

She took up two replacements, not looking away from the moving shadows on the porch, pushed the new shells home, and closed the breech. She cocked the hammers, fired both barrels again, and snapped the shotgun open for another go.

Even as she did, the sonic rumble of a military fighter jet filled the night. A shock wave shook the house as the aircraft rumbled overhead, just above the rooftop. The figures on the porch stopped their advance, dwindled into nothingness as they retreated, dragging their fallen companion.

A second jet roared overhead. The bright light blinked out. One instant it was there, the next the quiet summer night had reappeared.

The outside lights came up. The house lights winked on. Mina drew a breath and inched toward the open door, Eddie Junior right next to her. An odd and musty odor lingered on the porch. Eddie Junior pressed against his mother's side and wrapped his arms around her. She set the shotgun against the railing and returned his hug.

"You all right?" he asked.

Mina smiled. "I surely am. Are you?"

"Yes, Ma'am, but I peed my pants."

"Don't you worry, Buddy. So did I."

Becca stepped onto the porch. She held Jimmie close against her, sagged under his weight, but didn't stop until she reached her mother's side.

"You need some help?" Mina asked.

"No, Mama. I got him."

Mina patted Becca's head and drew her close.

"Can't wait to tell Daddy about this," Eddie Junior said.

"Let's wait 'til he comes home," Mina said.

She inched forward, rested her knee against the twelve gauge. Next Sunday when Eddie called, she wouldn't pester him about coming home just now. He made good money over there in Delaware and they could use the cash. He'd be home soon enough, soon as he could.

Sirens wailed in the distance. Mina spotted the red-blue strobe of emergency lights through the trees down the lane. She looked to the night sky. The stars were gone, once more hidden by thick clouds.

The coonhounds slunk from the house.

"Big help the three of you were," Mina said.

Eddie Junior and Becca laughed. Jinx and Annie hung their heads, wouldn't look up at Mina. Titan offered a muffled woof and stretched out on the mat.

Somewhere in the distance one of the jets boomed again. The first of the sheriff's cars flashed its way into the farmyard, siren yammering, as the rains began again.

Flotsam

Quin and Zoë had swept away the orbiting debris field and were almost back to the *Mary Shelley's* airlock when Jill broadcast her warning over the corporation's open radio band.

"Heads up out there! We've got incoming."

Zoë cancelled momentum right away. Quin slid past, managed to stop his own progress just three meters from the lock. He spied a streak of light beyond the leading edge of *Mary Shelley*, movement against the matte black of space that could be nothing else but sunlight thrown back from a fast-moving object.

The thirty-meter-long, extended-range work vehicle shuddered, as if nothing more than a great bone caught up by some invisible Brobdingnagian mutt. Everything stopped for one long instant and then vapor and debris spewed into space at the edge of Quin's vision.

The life support and propulsion module.

"We are hit, Cayley Station."

Jill's transmitted voice was dead calm now. At the sound of it a chill skittered up Quin's spine. He sucked in a deep breath of pure, cool oxygen.

"I repeat," Jill said. "We are hit but still in one piece. I am evaluating damage."

In the next instant she switched to the team's private band. "Zoë, are you all right?"

No reply. Jill tried again.

"Zoe?"

Quin thumbed the propulsion joystick. Gaseous nitrogen jetted from nozzles along the frame of his independent maneuvering unit. He began to rotate away from *Mary Shelley,* spotted Zoë hanging against the blackness ten meters away. Quin tapped the joystick again and began to glide toward her.

"I see her, Jill," he said.

Her back to him, she'd turned one-hundred-eighty degrees off his orienting line. Her figure was contorted, bent at the waist to the limits of the suit, with both hands clasped upon her left thigh.

Quin called to her this time. "Zoe?"

"I'm here." Her voice sounded reedy.

"Zoë, what's wrong?" Jill words carried hesitation now.

"Something hit me. Punched straight through my thigh, I think. I can't make it back inside on my own."

"Damn it, Quin!" Jill said. "Help her."

The measured pace of his progress was maddening. Jill's goading itched like an old scab. Even so, now wasn't the time to lose focus, to follow his emotions, as he so often did, and rush forward without thought. Quin drew another deep breath, reached for that calm center the yoga instructor at Sonny Carter Training Center encouraged.

Breathing is involuntary, an essential part of life. You can't control whether or not you breathe but you can control the way that you breathe. Inhale on a four-count and exhale on a four-count. Match the rate for both. Control can save your life.

As his respiration slowed, Quin forced himself to think the situation through. Zoë would be analytical if the situation was reversed.

One humid Wednesday at Sonny Carter, Quin scrawled *faster than a speeding bullet* in his notebook after the instructor had told them an object maintaining orbital velocity at a crossing orbit would travel at multiples of the velocity of sound.

So, if Zoë had been hit, and she wouldn't say it if it wasn't so, it had to be debris from *Mary Shelley*. If the object that had hammered the work vehicle had hit Zoë, the systemic shock of the impact alone would have killed her.

And whatever hit Zoë had to be tiny, because even debris as small and thin as a potato chip would have blown her leg away.

Quin remembered something else from that Wednesday lecture.

In the event of a small puncture, your secondary oxygen pack is designed to maintain pressure in your mission suit long enough for you to get inside to safety. So there had to be time to rescue her.

No, that was the wrong way to approach this. There *would* be time to save her. He would do everything just right. He could do this.

He tapped the joystick and came to rest next to Zoë. Just on the mark. "I've got you, Zoë," he said.

"Good," she almost whispered. "I want to go home."

Home hung there, two hundred miles below Quin Torres, forever turning against the deep black drape of space. God's masterpiece of performance art played for him to the metered sigh of pure oxygen.

"Are you ready, Quin?" Zoë Fraser asked over the team's band.

Quin flinched. She'd caught him gawking again.

He glanced to where Zoë floated, waiting for him. Her white mission suit glistened, a beacon he could never reach. Quin envied Zoë. Always focused, always ready and able to handle any situation. She never let passions get in the way of what needed to be done. She wore red chevrons on her mission suit, identifying her as team leader. Quin wore green slashes that marked him as a newbie.

He took a slow, cleansing breath. Time to focus, to get to work.

"I'm moving into place now, Mary Shelley," he said.

"About time, Junior," Jill Papadopoulos said.

Jill was the team's pilot. Zoë's opposite, boisterous and profane. Always ready to laugh at the world around her or to poke fun, particularly at Quin. In her own way, she was just as competent as Zoë and it seemed to Quin that she delighted in pointing out his low status and incompetence. Still, every word out of Jill might be some sort of jape aimed at him but Zoë's quiet disdain stung even worse.

Quin thumbed the joystick, began to glide toward Zoë, who was already in position a meter ahead of today's prize.

It had taken hours, riding the slow pulse of Mary Shelley's fuel-efficient ion engines, to match orbit with the loose field of aluminum bits.

The field, the size of a misshapen beach ball. Each piece within the field tumbled in its own eccentric way, all moving along an ever-curving path, together in a complicated orbital dance. A file in some distant data bank kept track of what the debris had been. Perhaps a panel from a satellite or a section of solar array. Just junk now.

Quin itched to know its history but that didn't seem to matter to Jill and Zoë. To them it was just one more thing the corporation paid to have swept up and thrown away. Three days after boarding Mary Shelly, during a meal break, Quin had tried to express the excitement he felt working in space.

Jill laughed. "Hell, we aren't anything but trash haulers, plain and simple."

"Well-paid trash haulers, though," Zoë added.

Jill laughed again, ran her fingertip across the knuckles of Zoë's hand. "Amen to that, babe," Jill said.

Gossip was a game that everybody played at Cayley Station. Quin knew Jill and Zoë were a couple when he accepted assignment to the Mary Shelley team.

Even so he hadn't expected they would tease him with their coupling. From the first second they met him at the airlock holding hands, it seemed to him they were saying he didn't belong and never would.

Zoë tried to help pull them into the airlock, to no avail.

For one awful moment Quin feared his efforts wouldn't be good enough. Then Zoë's shoulders popped through the open maw. The next instant they were both within the lock. Quin punched the control sequence, the gauges turned green, and Jill was there, taking Zoë into her arms.

"We've got to get her out of that damned suit!" Jill said, her words brittle, her voice too loud. Zoë's hands slipped from her leg as Jill pulled at her. Fat deep-red globules pumped from a dark spot on the left thigh of the mission suit and swirled through the air to splatter against Jill's face and upper torso.

"God damn it!" Jill's voice rattled Quin's headset. "Help me!"

"Me first." Quin worked to keep his own voice calm. "Get me out first."

Jill stared at him, unblinking, the she nodded. "Okay."

She pushed herself forward, reaching for his helmet ring. She worked with furious purpose. Only the nine-millimeter-thick toughness of the suit prevented her from destroying it. Soon Quin kicked free of the last piece and the scattered segments drifted about the module. He'd deal with the mess later.

Together they attacked Zoë's suit. Jill ripped at the clasps of the life-support pack while Quin worked the ringed system that held the helmet in place. There was a sigh of air when the seal broke. A good sign. With the helmet off, Quin tugged Zoë's cap and communications gear clear, touched fingertips to her throat, feeling for a pulse.

Weak and thready, but there.

"Got a pulse," he said.

Jill didn't respond. She moved to the gloves, going after them with the same intensity she'd applied to undressing Quin. Zoë moaned when Quin touched her again. Her eyelids fluttered open. She looked up at him.

Her voice cracked as she spoke. "I can't feel my leg."

"You're going to be all right," Quin said. "I got you back inside."

"Pay attention, Quin," Jill had said just before hell broke loose. "So you can get your asses back inside."

Quin ignored her. He activated the automatic inertial attitude lock, reached back to the IMU frame for one of the collecting-foam cans tethered there. He fumbled the first attempt and Zoë waited, not saying a word as he juggled the can into place. At last he rolled the red arrow stenciled on the yellow can's side into line with an identical mark on the can she held.

"Mary Shelley," Zoë said. "We're setting the cans."

The cans touched and both arrows faded to yellow, signaling a successful link. The science behind it was more than Quin cared to ponder and explanations involving self-bonding polymers and shifting absorption spectra just made it sound like magic.

All he cared about was that the cans stuck to each other or to adhesive from the pressurized dispenser stashed in an insulated mission suit pocket. He had been told that the bond would never fail, short of total destruction.

Jill called it better living through chemistry. *She collected ancient advertising slogans the way other folks accumulated political campaign buttons or china dolls. Her hand-made signs were plastered everywhere on* Mary Shelley.

"We have adhesion," Zoë said. "Push the button."

A dot glowed red on each can and neon-orange bubbles popped into being at the trailing faces. The thermosetting-polymer foam bubbles swelled until they touched and flowed together, forming a globe a meter across. Zoë touched her joystick. She drifted away. Quin followed suit.

"We are clear, Mary Shelley," *Zoë said.*

Solid-fuel rocket cells on each can flared, and the debris field gained upon the bubble. The gap closed and the leading debris fragment sank into the bubble. Second by second, piece by piece, the field sank into the still-reactive plastic mass.

"That's a sweep," Jill said at last. "The screen is green."

Working in tandem, Zoë and Quin set two larger degradable solid-fuel rocket cells into place. Jill did her little timing speech, the new cells flared and the bubble fell away. The change in its velocity would hurry orbital decay and it would soon plummet to Earth.

Station Manager Marge Dierker claimed Cayley's vacuum smelting operation would be operating by year's end and collection teams would be required then to ferry collected debris to the station so that the scrap could be salvaged and refined.

"Just more corporate bullshit," Jill had said the first time Quin mentioned it. "Word is that station managers have been saying the same thing since the station opened. Six years, Zoë?"

"No," Zoë said. "Five years. March fifth, 2024."

"Hell, Junior," Jill continued. "AshCor can't meet a schedule any better than Boeing. Me and Zoë will be living on Rising Sea, *sipping Hatuey beer, and watching launches off the coast of French Guiana before anyone hauls this stuff in."*

Rising Sea *was the forty-two-foot Hunter sailing yacht Jill and Zoë were paying for with their high-risk salaries. Jill called that* a-good-chance-of-dying pay. *Within a week Quin was calling it that, too.*

It was business as usual, even if they were in orbit. The hardened bubbles of orange collecting foam would continue to burn to cinder as they tumbled through the atmosphere and what was left would disappear into the depths of the Pacific Ocean.

Almost an hour gone by since the collision. Quin spent every second of it outside examining the *Mary Shelley* systems module. Whatever hit them had been small, not even the size of the pieces in the debris cloud he and Zoë had collected earlier. Even so damage was extensive.

Both nearside solar arrays had been pulverized in passing and the outer skin of the equipment module was shredded from the initial impact, leaving a hole big enough for Quin to crawl through, even wrapped in the cumbersome layers of the mission suit. From outside he could see the twisted guts of the ion propulsion units beneath the gaping wound.

There had been an explosion within the equipment module as well, large enough to blow out the away side of the cylinder and send bits of metal and plastic shrapnel spewing into space. The other two solar arrays on the far side of *Mary Shelley* were chewed to pieces by that new debris and a piece of it had struck Zoë.

When Quin returned from his inspection, Jill handed over a plastic sample tube. The aluminum bead she had found floated inside. It was melted by the impact and formed by the absence of gravity into a perfect little sphere not much larger than a pinhead.

"Had to cut her suit apart," Jill said. "Found the damned thing wedged in the Kevlar layer of her insulated under-suit."

"Is that all it was?"

"It's enough."

The salted coppery scent of blood filled the crew compartment of *Mary Shelley* and dulled red splotches mottled every surface. Zoë was strapped into her bunk, nodding in and out of consciousness. Jill had cleaned the wound as best the limited medical supplies aboard *Mary Shelly* would allow and sheathed Zoë's left leg from knee to hip in compression bandages.

She lingered now beside the bunk, pushing a squeeze bottle at Zoë from time to time, forcing her to take liquids. Across the compartment, Quin settled upon a saddle stool and tucked his toes behind restraint bars. He watched the two of them for a time.

"It could have been worse," he said at last. It didn't seem as if Jill even heard him.

"She's lost a lot of blood," Jill said. "And all I can manage here is first aid.

We've got to get her to Cayley's sick bay soon or she may die."

"How do you figure to do that?" Quin asked.

Jill turned to him. Quin was certain for a moment that she would launch herself across the compartment to tear him to pieces.

"No!" she said. "How do *you* figure to do it?"

"What do you mean?"

"You're the damned hotshot mechanic, aren't you? That's the line Dierker handed us when she pulled Jen and stuck us with you. But I haven't seen you do squat since you came on board except screw up every little thing you touch. *You* figure how the hell to get us moving or I swear I will haunt you to your grave. Pull your weight, goddamn it!"

"That's not—"

The speaker system crackled. "*Mary Shelley.*"

Quin recognized the voice. It was Marg Dierker.

"*Mary Shelley*, do you copy?"

Quin turned away from Jill's anger and kicked himself out of his saddle. Three weeks' practice hadn't given him much grace but it had taught him accuracy. He caught a handhold as he approached the far wall of the cylinder and pulled himself to the communications panel.

"This is Torres, Cayley Station," he said.

"Sorry I've been delayed, *Mary Shelley*," Dierker said. Her voice was corporate cool but Quin could hear nervous conversation rolling in the background under the operations manager's thick German accent. "I was on a conference call with home office. What is the situation there?"

Quin glanced toward Jill. She still looked upset and distracted, still ready to chew off his ears. This was his to handle, whether he was ready to do so or not.

"We've finished initial inspection, Ma'am," he said. "We might not be able to get back to you on our own."

Quin might as well have been on his own.

The work schedule was four weeks out and then two or three days off duty at Cayley Station before starting the cycle all over again first of the month. If these first weeks were any indication, it would be a long and lonely six-month tour.

He had been told his whole life that he had an easy way with people, but try as he might he couldn't win Zoë and Jill over. He always seemed to be in the way and while they didn't ignore him or keep important information from him, Zoë remained distant and judgmental while Jill picked at him over little things he could never fix. He was clumsy. He was slow. He smelled wrong, for God's sake. Not bad. Wrong.

The two women hated his music, too. So his off-duty time passed on the stationary bike, logging required hours of exercise, or in his bunk. Ear buds in place, he composed his own music on the SoundStik that had taken up most of his personal-allowance weight or listened to recorded music on his audio pod.

Quin loved the old-gold rock his father had played while working in the family's auto-repair shop in Key West. His favorites were by a bunch of Brit rockers known as Queen. He spent hours in his bunk whispering the words of We Will Rock You *or* Fat-Bottomed Girls *along with lead singer Freddy Mercury.*

But his love for music wouldn't be enough to carry him through six months. He would go crazy if something didn't change. Quin knew that. Even so, he had no idea what he would have to do to make that happen.

Marg Dierker was all business, never asked about Zoë's condition or how Quin and Jill were holding up. All she wanted to know about was damage sustained to *Mary Shelley*. Quin reported his findings, sending video data via microwave uplink as he spoke.

"What do you think, Cayley Station?" Jill asked.

Silence.

"Cayley, are you still there?"

"Here." Emil Teague, the station's maintenance chief. "Marg got called away again on other business."

"Typical," Jill muttered. She brushed loose hairs from Zoë's forehead and offered up the squeeze bottle once again.

"How bad is it, Emil?" Quin asked.

"I had hoped for better news."

"Oh?"

"We've been studying the equipment telemetry. Your visuals confirm our data. I can try to talk you through repairs to the ion engines but I don't think there's much hope."

"Can't you send another ship?" Quin asked.

"*Edwin Abbott* is preparing now to initiate first burn on a Hohmann transfer orbit."

"How soon will they be here?" Jill asked.

There was no response. Jill pushed away from Zoë's bunk and caught a handhold on the fly, pulling herself into position next to Quin.

"Answer me, Emil! How soon?"

"Without the engines, you can't start home," he replied at last. "If you can't change your own orbit, there's no way they can rendezvous with you in less than fifty hours."

"Zoë can't make it that long!"

"That's not our first concern," Emil said.

"What do you mean?" Jill demanded.

She was inches from the comm panel speaker now, ready to wrap her fingers around Emil's throat. He was silent again. When he spoke, his voice was hushed and conspiratorial.

"I shouldn't tell you this. If Marg finds out, she'll chew on me until I'm raw. She's been talking to the bean counters back on Earth."

"So?" Quin asked.

"They may decide to abort the rescue effort. Marg told them you'll be dead before *Edwin Abbott* can reach you."

"God damn it!" Jill said. "Why would she say that?"

She was crying in her rage. Quin pushed close and put his arm around her. She didn't pull away.

"Look, your electrical system is on battery-standby now," Emil said. "And your engines are just so much scrap metal."

"I can replace the solar arrays," Quin said.

"You can replace one of them," Emil said. "That's all you have on board. Any more just wouldn't have been cost-effective. One array can't generate enough electricity."

"The initial data said breathable atmosphere was good for seventy-two hours!"

"It will be," Emil said.

"Well—" Quin began.

"Emil?" It was Zoë. Her voice lacked volume but it was steady. "What don't we know?"

Jill launched herself away from the comm panel in an instant. She was clutching Zoë's hand before the answer came.

"There were cost-cutting measures implemented when the work vehicles were built." Emil sounded defensive. "The electronics always over-generate heat. Insulation was reduced to allow the heat-disbursement system to be downsized."

"It doesn't matter how much air we have, does it?" Jill said. Her voice was icy calm now. "With only one collector we'll have to shut down a lot of equipment. It's going to get damned cold in here."

"No one considered this sort of contingency," Emil said.

"How long?" Quin asked.

"Within thirty hours it will be one hundred below in there."

Another six hours passed. Quin installed the spare solar collector and moved on to the engines. Emil had been right. Even with the engineer looking over Quin's shoulder via video camera, pouring all his technological expertise through Quin's headset, it was beyond what the two of them could manage. At last, they were forced to admit defeat.

"You did everything you could, Quin," Emil said.

"Why doesn't that make me feel better?"

Quin was ready to throw tools, to snap the tethers, and hurl the offending metal into the void, the way his father so often had hurled a wrench across the garage in Key West when a customer's automobile refused to give in to his attentions. Quin drew a cleansing breath.

"Thanks for trying, Emil," he said. "And for telling us."

Dierker returned to the radio once in those six hours to tell them that *Edwin Abbott* was on the way and to admit to the coming cold. She didn't explain the reasons for the temperature loss though, and neither Quin nor Jill had pressed the matter.

Quin cycled through the lock and returned to crew quarters. He could feel edges of chill already. Jill was wrapped in layers of clothing and was hovering next to Zoë, who was wrapped in every sizable piece of fabric Jill could find. Quin maneuvered into place beside Jill.

"Any luck?" Zoë whispered.

"No."

Jill glanced at him. She reached out and tapped her fist against his shoulder.

"I'm sorry I yelled at you before," she said. Her voice had lost its earlier nasty edge.

"No, you were right," Quin said. If she could bend, then he would too. "I've been slacking, feeling sorry for myself because the two of you are together."

Jill ignored his apology.

"Marg is just going to sit there and let us die, isn't she?" she asked.

"That's how I see it," Quin replied. "But Emil and his crew are still working on ideas."

"Meanwhile we sit here and freeze," Jill said. "Just three more pieces of junk."

"We'll save ourselves," Zoë whispered.

"How?" Jill demanded. "The batteries are almost gone and I've scrounged every bit of cover I could find."

"The suits?" Zoë whispered. Jill glanced at Quin and then spit out her confession.

"I hacked yours apart, looking for the junk that hit you."

"Wear yours then." If she could have managed more force, it would have been an order.

"No!" Quin said. "I won't pray I'll survive while I watch you freeze to death."

Jill tapped him with her fist again, harder than before. It felt like a stamp of approval.

"What the hell," she said. "We'll go out together, three more pieces of junk. *Edwin Abbott* can just stick us into orange foam and send us down the chute."

Zoë slipped her hand from beneath the blankets and managed a thumbs-up but Quin was still. Jill's words had struck a spark. He turned toward Jill's advertising placard, taped to the bulkhead across the cabin. *Better living through chemistry*. And the notion came to him, every little detail bright and hard as diamond.

When he had finished laying it all out, Jill hugged him.

Once they did the homework, it took seventeen minutes to get Emil back to the radio. When he came he sounded fuzzy and apologetic. Quin and Jill were shoulder-to-shoulder now, anchored before the communications station and Jill had slipped a headset onto Zoë so she could be heard.

"Sorry," Emil said. "I was sleeping."

Quin didn't offer up a polite response. There was no time for niceties. "Emil, how long would it take for us to splashdown if we pushed *Mary Shelley* out of orbit just like we do all the junk?"

They could almost hear Emil's calculator.

"Eight-seven minutes from initiation of burn," Emil said. "But it would never work."

"Why?" Quin asked. "The command module's an Orion unit. It's designed for re-entry and we can blow away the rest of the ship with explosive bolts."

"You've got no engine." Quin had anticipated that reply.

"We still have enough solid-fuel cells to do the job," Quin said. "Jill's done the math. All I have to do is I fabricate a platform to mount them around the aft hatch."

"Maybe—" Emil began.

Jill interrupted, maintaining the momentum. "All we need, Emil, is a two percent delta vee. I can send my data."

"No need. I'm doing it myself right now." Seconds passed in silence.

"Well?" Zoë asked.

When he responded Emil didn't sound sleepy anymore.

"It's possible," he said. "But there are other issues."

"Name them," Jill demanded.

"The Orion's not equipped for anything but a ballistic descent. Without parachutes it would be a nasty splashdown."

"But it's been done!" Jill said. She ticked off her hasty research. "The Soyuz TMA-Eleven capsule in 2008 came down damned hard in Kazakhstan and the Russian and the Korean walked away from it. The Expedition Six crew in 2003 survived this sort of descent, too. Hell, just look at Voskhod Two back in 1970."

"And we'll be bringing it in at sea," Quin said. "We could—"

Emil interrupted. "There's one other major problem. You have to get down there in one piece, even for a hard landing, and you don't have a heat shield."

Quin glanced at Jill. She was looking up to him, eyes bright, and she was grinning. They had been waiting for this one.

"Tell him," Zoë whispered.

"That's not a problem, Emil," Quin said. "I'm going to fabricate one."

"It's ridiculous!" Dierker said five minutes later. She didn't sound sleepy either. "No one has ever built a heat shield from collecting foam!"

"Just because it's never been done doesn't mean it can't be done," Emil said.

"Shut up, Emil!" Dierker said. "I will not allow—"

"Ma'am," Quin said. "Would you rather have us freeze to death, waiting for rescue that won't arrive in time?"

That quieted her for a moment. She wasn't about to send a message to the entire Cayley staff that she considered employees to be expendable.

"Of course we don't want you to freeze," she said. "We're doing the best we can. It may not be enough in the end, but what you're suggesting is suicide."

"You don't know that!" Jill said.

"No!" Dierker thundered. "I will not allow it."

Jill was close in again, her fingers itching to settle around Dierker's throat. Quin had no more patience for these games either.

"Marg," he said. "Just how do you plan to stop us?"

Dierker argued a bit longer but there was no question now as to the outcome. There would be a revolt aboard Cayley if Dierker didn't let them try. When she returned the microphone to Emil, he was so excited he almost stuttered. Quin listened as Jill helped him suit up to begin work and he was reminded of the instructors at the Neutral Buoyancy Laboratory. Some of them had seemed as if they ate plankton, slept in their wetsuits, and pissed seawater.

"The idea is genius, Quin," Emil said. "The foam is called Vespel. It's a thermosetting electrostatic dissipative polymer with a graphite reinforcement component. Its tensile strength is incredible."

His words tumbled over each other in his rush to explain.

"Inherent resistance to combustion. Fantastic heat resistance. Tested at 900 degrees Fahrenheit for hours. Some of the aerospace manufacturers used it for light-weight heat shields on sub-orbital flights."

"Will it stand up to re-entry temperatures, though?" Quin asked.

Emil was silent for a moment; a bit of wind knocked from his sails.

"Flip a coin to figure that out," he said at last. "It's a long way down."

There was no time now to admire the panorama of Earth waiting so far below, no time to wonder what Zoë would do if she were able. Quin examined his handiwork. The cells were set in place on the scaffold he had built around the docking ring at the nose of the command module. Working in the mission suit still was slow but seemed less clumsy now, even though he and Emil were making up procedures as they went.

To form the ablative heat shield, Quin had sprayed the blunt end of the command module with polymer adhesive, one small section at a time, and then affixed collecting cans in concentric circles. The last bit of work was to stretch a sheet of gold-permeated reflective foil over the cans and affix it to the circumference of the module.

Quin was pleased with the results of his work.

The jury-rigged effort might not be enough to take them home in one piece, but it wouldn't be for lack of trying. He had read once—he wasn't certain where—that to die trying was the proudest human thing. He understood that now.

"Okay, *Mary Shelley*," he said. "It's time to set off the cans."

"Copy that," Jill said. She was sniffling from the cold. "On my mark."

Under the foil the cans began to exude their orange bubbles. The bubbles touched and flowed together, constrained by the loose-fitting foil. The foam filled every opening, swelling the foil into a rounded, metallic face that mirrored the contour of the module. Quin watched the holographic timer on his helmet's faceplate. When it reached zero, he reached out and touched the foil. It was unyielding.

"The cake is baked, *Mary Shelly*," he said. "I'm coming in."

It had taken fifteen hours to complete the work and temperatures inside the capsule were frigid. Vapor trailed behind Quin, swirling about in miniature cirrus clouds as he moved to his place in the empty acceleration couch. Jill already was in place in the pilot's position. She had swaddled Zoë in every bit of available fabric after strapping her into the central couch.

It was time to do this thing.

"We expect splash down in the Pacific between the Marquesas Islands and Hawaii," Emil said. "Recovery vessels will be tracking you all the way down, using your GPS signal."

"Thank you," Quin said. "For everything."

"Buy me a beer next time you see me," Emil said. "Hey! We've just got the weather report—blue skies and calm seas."

"*Mary Shelley* copies all of that," Quin said.

"And we're ready to blow this pop stand," Jill said.

"Do it," Zoë whispered. She sounded purposeful.

Jill nodded and tabbed an ignition switch. The capsule vibrated as the array of solid-fuel cells Quin had set up on the scaffold caught fire and pushed with all their puny might against the forward progress of the *Mary Shelley* command module.

Precious seconds passed. Quin watched the gauges, intent upon the numbers, listening as Jill continued to talk to Emil. They needed to bleed away two per cent of forward speed to begin the drop out of orbit and put them into the upper reaches of Earth's atmosphere. Air drag and gravity would do the rest.

"It's all about drag coefficient," Emil had said earlier, trying his best not to lecture. "The greater the drag, the less the heat load. Air will build up under the capsule and act as a cushion to push hot gases and heat energy around you."

"Burn is over, Emil," Jill said.

"Copy, *Mary Shelley*."

"Velocity is dropping," Quin said, watching the gauges. "How do we look?"

"We're coming onto track." Jill's voice could have been generated by a computer. "Lining up five by five. I'm initiating turn-over now!"

Quin couldn't feel the change in orientation but his gauges soon told him the attitude jets had rolled the capsule into a new position. They were moving backside-first again and falling, committed now to the flames.

"Velocity is still decreasing." Quin struggled to keep rising emotion from his own voice. "At two per cent now and still going down!"

Cheers filled Quin's headset. Dierker might not be pleased with their dismantling of her precious equipment but the rest of Cayley Station was celebrating.

"We are in the pipeline and on our way down," Jill said in her best test-pilot voice.

What was left of *Mary Shelley* bounced as thickening atmosphere wrestled against their extreme velocity. Quin began to feel the rise in temperature.

"We're losing signal, *Mary Shelley*," Emil reported.

His voice sounded hollow in Quin's headset. It died away and then came back, faint and distant, one last time.

"God bless, *Mary Shelley*."

Quin was sweating now. The gauges showed the module's interior temperature at ninety degrees Fahrenheit and still rising. The intensity of vibration continued to climb as well. It felt as if they might shake to pieces at any moment.

Flame licked at the Plexiglas ports, Emil's promised shock wave building beneath the capsule, creating a pocket of heat so intense it ionized the very air. Quin didn't want to consider what would happen if his hand-made shield produced uncontrollable wobble, so that what was left of *Mary Shelly* flipped end for end to finish a hellish descent with its unprotected nose falling into the flames.

"Quin?"

It was Zoë. Quin looked to the central acceleration couch. Her face was turned toward him. She was so pale her skin seemed translucent but her eyes were bright and she was smiling.

"Thank you," she said, whispering.

"Yeah," Jill said. "You're a god-damned genius, Junior. We need to celebrate."

She grinned then and touched a switch on her control console. A high, clear recorded harmony filled the cabin. A single tone. The opening Oh! to Queen's *Fat-Bottomed Girls* with Quin's own guitar licks laid over top of it. Jill had pirated his pod.

He grinned too. That was just what they needed right now, what he hoped he had been clever enough to fashion for what was left of *Mary Shelley*. A fat bottom that would carry the old girl through the ferocious heat of re-entry. He flicked off his own microphone, cleared his throat, and sang the opening line of the chorus. Outside the ports the matte black had gone to vivid orange. Jill joined him for the second line. Their voices filled the capsule, howled defiance of the odds, as the music swelled.

Together the three of them rode the fire home.

Nosing with the Four-Stroke Kid

When she pulled her helmet off, the rider looked like Uma Thurman on a bad-hair day. All platinum spikes and black roots and wicked-sharp elbows.

The Kid didn't mind. He figured the hair for honest and he could take a jab to the ribs with the best of them. It wouldn't come to that, of course. The rider and her wheels were a matched set, covered in matte black and bristling with chrome spikes, but the Kid wasn't interested in the rider. He was an expert in all things dirt bike, but couldn't name the one she straddled. That itched at him worse than a case of helmet rash.

"That's a Honda CFR450, right?" When he was nosing, the Kid took the straight approach because it almost always worked.

"No." She didn't look at him.

"Well, sure, it's a custom job, but it's built on a CFR chassis."

"No." She still didn't look.

The Kid didn't mind being ignored, he was used to it. He knew he wasn't easy on the eyes and so he never looked at himself either. Not too often, anyway. But he couldn't stand not knowing what she rode.

"Hey," he said, lifting his hands for her to see, palms out and fingers up. "All I'm interested in is the bike."

"Go away."

He ignored her, took a step closer, and caught the whiff. "Is that one of those Hayes diesel bikes?"

She looked at him now. Her eyes had a curious amber cast. "Aren't we a smart little Nubbie."

"It's running bio-fuel, too, isn't it?"

"How do you know?"

"Smells like French fries." He took another sniff; rubbed at his nose with his gloved thumb. "Something else mixed in there, too. What is that? Damn me, I know that smell."

She leaned close and the hot-white glare of her smile prickled his skin. "What do you say, Nubbie? Want to check out my engine?"

The Kid took a single quick step forward, hoping she wouldn't notice his arousal. "Hell, yes."

She pulled away. "You can't look at it here."

Something in her voice snagged his attention. He drew a breath and stepped back, studying her.

She raised an eyebrow. "What's the matter? Lose your nerve?"

"No, but I don't figure to follow you somewhere and get mugged by your Neanderthal boyfriend."

"No one is waiting anywhere." She traced her fingertip in an X across her leathers, over her heart. "And I promise I won't touch you."

"Well—"

"It doesn't matter to me, Nubbie." She turned the bars of the bike, ready to roll away.

"No! How about over there?" He pointed to the tree line.

"Alright. Do you have a bike?"

"Duh." He hooked one thumb over his shoulder.

Her upper lip curled, exposing just a touch of incisor. It was either a smile or a sneer. It didn't matter to the Kid. She was going to let him touch her bike.

"All right, Nubbie," she said. "Follow me."

The rider was good. By the time the Kid managed to kick-start his Kawasaki she was across the course, rolling in among the trees. He scrambled to follow her, cursing his clumsiness.

When he caught up, almost a mile into the woods, she was waiting, backed three strides away from her bike. He shut down his engine and sat, watching her. The spent fumes from the diesel hung in the air, sweet and heavy, messing with his nose.

"Well?" she said. She waved a hand toward her bike.

The Kid heeled his kickstand into the dirt and slid from the saddle. He eased over to the diesel, dropped to one knee, and reached toward the engine. Before he could touch it, one of the spikes on the top frame arrowed toward him, dragging along a hair-fine wire, and pierced his cheek.

"What the—" It was all the Kid could manage. He toppled to his side, lost inside himself. He could see and hear, his heart beat and his lungs drew air, but everything else seemed to have red-lined and seized up.

There was a soft, mechanical whir. An amber light, beamed from somewhere on the bike, inched up and back down his body. A machine voice whispered dry words all the while.

"Body mass one hundred and forty-eight pounds, seventeen percent fat. Brain mass two point seven pounds, sixty-two percent fat. Cortical function nominal. Fuel potential two point three gallons. Trans-esterification beginning."

The amber light became a strobe and three more spikes shot from the bike, sinking into the Kid's body at the eye, abdomen, and thigh.

He screamed as loud as his constricted throat would allow. Tissue puckered around the probes and he felt as if he was being emptied.

The rider watched, unperturbed, humming an old Stones song. The Kid looked to her with his one good eye, tried to call to her, to plead for help. All he managed was a whimper and she shrugged it away, blinking in time with the bike's slow strobe.

"Sorry, Nubbie," she said, lifting her hands for him to see, palms out and fingers up. "I'm just the rider."

Gossamer Yellow

Deep winter arrived early, the Monday after Thanksgiving. By one p.m., a foot of snow lay upon the city. Chelsea loved snow days. She had almost finished grading essays when Michael called, just after four.

"I'll be late," he said without preamble. "May even stay here at the shop, if this keeps up. Don't wait dinner."

And so she didn't bother cooking, just fixed herself a roast beef sandwich, popped the cap off a chilled bottle of Mexican beer, collected a wedge of apple pie, and headed for the sofa in the living room.

There would be no English Lit class in the morning either. The rest of the essays could wait another day.

Chelsea and Michael lived in a grand old house just south of the university, a place they had moved into just before fall term began. Chelsea loved the century-old residence with its slate roof, gingerbread trim, and formal English garden.

And the living room had been built for contemplation, with its oak trim, its grand fireplace, and the heavy old-fashioned furniture that came with the place.

Mark Twain and a knit comforter waited there for her. The rich food, a crackling maple burl in the fireplace, and the beer soon pulled her from *Huck Finn* and soothed her into sleep.

She awoke sometime later, curled on the sofa beneath the comforter, her book on the floor. Her reading lamp and waning fire provided the only light in the house.

A young woman stood in the foyer beneath the amber-beaded chandelier, framed by the oak archway between the rooms. Her blond hair glowed from light reflected from the amber beads. The gossamer layers of her party dress seemed almost transparent.

She studied Chelsea as if surprised to see her sitting there. The woman looked so familiar. A spark skittered along Chelsea's spine.

The woman extended her left hand as if seeking support, but withdrew it in an instant. She reached down to slide both hands across her thighs, smoothing the folds of her dress. A key rattled in the back door. The kitchen came alight and Michael's presence filled the house.

The woman in the yellow dress disappeared.

Chelsea hurried to the kitchen but when she tried to tell Michael of the sudden disappearance, he shrugged her giddy words away and peered at her.

"You been drinking?"

Chelsea nodded without thinking, a child caught filching cookies. She felt the heat of blood rising in her cheeks. She held up her index finger. "Just one beer."

They stood at arms-length in the middle of the kitchen, with its high, pressed-tin ceiling, oak chair rail, and glass-front cabinets.

It was supposed to be a warm, inviting space. Just then it didn't feel that way to her.

Michael cocked one eyebrow. "That explains it, doesn't it?"

Melting snow dripped from Michael's coat. Chelsea studied the water pooling upon the gray slate tile around his rubber boots. He ignored it.

"Michael, it's why we have a mud room. For your boots."

"Is there anything to eat?"

Chelsea frowned. "Why do you do that?"

"Do what?"

"Turn my words away."

"I didn't do that."

"You did. You tramp in here with your wet boots and you don't believe I saw a ghost."

Michael stepped to her, slid his arm around her shoulders. He tilted his head to let his forehead rest just above her ear. He reeked of wet wool and the sweet odor of tetrachloroethylene from his dry-cleaning shop. His warm breath stirred the hairs at the nape of her neck.

"It *was* a dream, Chelsea."

Chelsea shivered at the chill he'd brought into the house. She tried to twist away, to free herself from the press of his fingers pressed into the meat of her upper arm. To gain a bit of space. He held her tight.

"No, it wasn't. I saw her."

The fingers of her right hand curled into a fist. She felt heat rising in her cheeks again. That tone of voice brought her as close to violence toward him as she could ever get.

"No, you didn't. The firelight. Headlights reflected from the chandelier. A dozen other things. There are no ghosts."

He stepped away, stroking the soft flesh of her shoulders as he did. His fingers felt hard and cold as icicles.

"Look at that," he said. "I've got you shivering."

He turned from her, pushed his way through into the dining room, sloughing off his overcoat as he thumped along. She heard the saturated wool slop onto the wooden floor.

His words rolled back through the swinging door. "Got to get out of these wet things. Clean up the mess?"

Chelsea stood alone, her arms crossed, her own stocking feet soaked clear through by the puddled water, staring after him. She shook her head and whispered "Damn you, Michael. It wasn't my imagination."

There was no further mention of the woman in the yellow dress for a week. Chelsea suspected that her silence proved to Michael she had been convinced by his kitchen arguments.

That absolute belief in his own opinions had been one of the things to attract her to him.

She had been twenty-one, about to graduate college with an advanced degree in literature, ready to teach university classes. She met Michael at a mutual friend's wedding and they began to date. He had a way of filling a space he entered. His confidence took Chelsea's breath away. It took a dozen years of marriage for her to realize her breathlessness had less to do with adoration and more to do with suffocation.

Almost midnight. Michael sat on the bed's edge watching *The Tonight Show*.

Chelsea sat before her dressing-table mirror, brushing out her hair. "I saw her again today," she said, working to sound casual.

Michael remained silent.

After a moment she tried again. "I said I saw the ghost. This afternoon as I came down the stairs. She was standing in the foyer, looking up at me, wearing that yellow dress again."

The television sound dwindled but didn't go away.

"I don't want to talk about it," Michael said.

Chelsea turned around to face him. "What do I have to do to convince you she's real?"

"I thought we decided not to mention this anymore."

"I didn't decide anything."

He stepped toward her, his mouth set in a tight line, his chin tucked to his chest. He studied her from beneath lowered brows. Chelsea began to pant, but she refused to look away.

"Do you have any idea how crazy all this sounds?"

"Last week I was drunk. Now I'm crazy."

"I didn't say that."

"I wasn't drunk last week and I'm not crazy now."

"I'm not going to talk about this anymore."

He turned to the bed, snatched up a pillow and a blanket, tromped to the door.

"I'll be in the den." He slammed the door behind him.

Next morning, when Chelsea went downstairs at six, the pillow lay on the floor next to the sofa. The blanket, a cold, crumpled ball beside the pillow.

There was an unsigned note on the kitchen counter. "I will not fight about this."

In the four weeks after Thanksgiving, the ghost put in three more appearances. Their last exchange about what Michael called the visions took place two days before Christmas.

The door to the mudroom snapped open and then slammed shut.

"Chelsea?" Michael.

"Up here."

She sat at the antique cherry secretary in the third-floor hall, constructing a party banner.

Michael always made light of such projects, even though other people told her how clever she was. Now he stomped up the stairs and planted himself on the landing between the second and third floors.

Chelsea caught the chemical aroma he always carried home from work, but all she saw through the banister spindles was the top of his head. She stood so she could see his face.

"Where did you get that dress?" he asked.

She reached down with both hands to smooth the folds of the gossamer yellow party dress she wore. "I found it in the attic. Isn't it beautiful?"

He climbed another step. "It looks like the dress the ghost wears, doesn't it?"

"Yes. Isn't that amazing?"

"You didn't find it in the attic. You bought it."

"I did no such thing. You're calling me a liar again."

"Chelsea, you need help. All the more reason for me to do what I did."

"What did you do?"

"I called everyone, canceled the party tomorrow night."

"You had no right to do that!"

"I had every right, you're my wife. I called Doctor Ramsey, too. He can see you tomorrow."

Chelsea began to pant. She had begun planning the Christmas party the very day that they moved into the house.

Michael climbed to the top step. "Did you hear me?"

Chelsea picked up a section of rope she had spray-painted silver. Nine-inch hand-cut cardboard letters, crusted with glitter, lay upon the shelf of the secretary. She had glued some of them to the rope already. When she finished, they would spell out MERRY CHRISTMAS.

"Why?" she asked.

She didn't look at him. Instead she waited for the jingle of the coins in his pocket. All these years together and all she could bring to mind were his nervous habits and the smell of the chemicals.

"You haven't been yourself," he said. "It was a mistake to try this big a party so soon."

"Why didn't you ask me first?"

"I didn't see the need."

"You still think I'm crazy."

"No – "

"You don't want me talking to people about the ghost."

"We've been over this before. There's no such thing as—"

Chelsea sprang toward him, dragging the rope behind her. Her suddenness startled Michael. He inched backward, tense and watchful, as if he wasn't certain who she might be.

"You treat me like a child," she said, her voice shrill. "Do you know how much I hate that?"

Chelsea could feel the tears coming. She leaned toward him and drew back her fist, knowing she'd never swing. Michael had to know that, too. Even so his eyes widened and he flinched. He took half a step back. Just half a step, but it was enough.

Michael's left heel hung over the edge of the top stair. He rocked down onto it and began to topple backwards. Desperate for balance, he caught Chelsea's upraised wrist to pull himself to safety.

The effort failed.

His weight pulled Chelsea off balance. She moved forward in an awkward shuffle step. He somersaulted backwards and she went with him. They hurtled down and around the twisting staircase, arms and legs flailing. The party banner wrapped about them as they fell, binding them together.

Michael fell in silence, dead from a blow to his head on the topknot of the second-floor newel post, but Chelsea wailed her fear and pain.

Near the bottom they smashed through the banister rails and one of the shattered spindles sliced her throat, silencing her screams. Their bodies came to rest in the entry hall in a spreading pool of Chelsea's blood, beneath the amber-beaded chandelier. Chelsea's left hand clutched the remains of her homemade banner.

Four silver cardboard numbers floated in the blood. They read 1978.

"Did you hear that?"

In the living room, party conversation stopped and guests turned to the young woman standing in the oak-rimmed arch that lead to the foyer.

"Hear what, dear?" Brian asked.

"I heard her scream," Marianne said.

She turned her head to peer up the staircase. The chandelier with its tailings of amber glass beads, hung just above her head creating a halo about her blond hair.

"Her?" one of the guests asked. Marianne turned back to the room full of people and nodded.

"She's a ghost. I've seen her five times since the first of November, when we moved in."

Brian cleared his throat and cocked his head to one side in the exaggerated gesture he used to suggest he was listening, rather than planning his next argument.

Marianne recognized it as a practiced pose drawn from his repertoire of courtroom techniques. He smiled for the guests gathered to celebrate Christmas Eve in their newly restored Victorian home.

"I didn't hear a thing," he said.

So much certainty in his voice. He turned to the others, all work associates of his, lifted one eyebrow, and inclined his head toward Marianne, as if to say "Let us humor her."

"Did anybody *else* hear a scream?" Brian placed just the right emphasis on else. Murmurs and gestures of denial came from around the room.

"My wife has a rich imagination." He could be generous in victory. "She wastes it reading fantasies."

The house grew still for one long moment.

"I suppose I do," Marianne said.

She glanced from person to person, searching for even one defender. The guests remained silent. Several looked about: as if for coats and hats.

Marianne slid both hands across her thighs to smooth the folds of the gossamer yellow dress she had found in a box in the attic. Above her head, upon the arch, nine-inch silver cardboard letters proclaimed, **MERRY CHRISTMAS 2010.**

Bringing in the Dead

We shoulder through green stalks of August corn, waist-deep in mist spread upon the Ohio bottom land like a raveling shawl of soiled lace. Nine wraiths, wrapped in much-patched camouflage and come to settle an outstanding debt.

"Talk to me, Becker," the sergeant says. "All clear, Sarge."

Their voices murmur to us through transceivers nestled in our ears. The sergeant sounds like a kettledrum cranked tight. Becker's voice, as dark and rich as a cup of straight-up coffee.

She's on point, tall and regal, six feet and seven inches of lethal elegance. We call her Long Tall Sally and each of us would give assorted pieces of ourselves to lay with her. Becker has never offered, though, and we've never asked.

"Collect on me," the sergeant says.

He materializes from the corn, squat and powerful. We are all a breath behind.

Somewhere close a robin twitters. A new-day's sun hangs just above tree-covered hills to the east. The Tuscarawas River, lazy and brown, slides by us to the west. A nasty heat makes early promises and the last breath of night touches us, carrying our targets' stench, reminding us of who we look for and what we lost.

Those years ago—April 2012—plague sped around the world on airborne vectors, flensing civilization to its bones. No one knew where it began, but billions died within six days.

On the seventh day, while God rested, the virus presented its mutations, demonstrated to us we had breathed easy far too soon. Within another week tens of thousands more fell and arose again, infected. We soon discovered the mutated virus spread fastest via body-fluid contact.

And the infected are everywhere. They mock us as they mimic human ways, reminding us of creatures in old movies while they wear the faces of people we knew and loved. No one has counted their number across what used to be Ohio's Tuscarawas County.

We know the number of untainted souls though. One hundred and forty-three.

Fifty-seven reside within a walled compound that used to be the Canton Water Works. They share their food with us. They tend our wounds, help us scavenge fuel and ammunition, but they won't ride with us.

Melinda is their leader, a woman of enormous energy and charisma. The sergeant loves her. We all know it even if he's never said the words. She's begged him more than once to end what she calls madness, to join her in her struggle to restore a sense of order to the world.

He always tells her no. We already have a mission.

The open space before us has gone to knee-deep grasses but it once was a manicured golf course. The clubhouse squats at its center, set upon a low rise of land an easy pace from the river. It's a moldering heap of splintered timbers and jagged flats of plate glass, surrounded by stretches of buckled concrete.

The sergeant nods toward the place. "Melinda says seventeen Infected are nested there. Two of them belong to us."

Jelly readies his flamethrower, not looking at the sergeant. "She say which two?"

"Does it matter?" The sergeant's attention is focused on the clubhouse.

The rest of us sneak peeks at both of them. What can Jelly say? Stupidity can get you killed. He's not the nervous sort but he fiddles with the trigger of the flamethrower. It burps a six-inch jet of orange fire. We all pretend to ignore it.

The sergeant nods at Becker. "Okay, let's do this."

We advance, fanning into attack line, with Becker at point. All's well until we're ten yards from the building. Then a dog mooches around one corner and lifts a hind leg.

He's a big mutt, enough Rottweiler in him to guarantee a nasty disposition. In mid-piss, he spots us. He forgets about his bladder, comes head-on at Becker, not uttering a sound. We hold our breath as Jelly strikes the match. Fire engulfs the dog and, as it burns away his life, he howls revenge.

There are muffled shouts from inside the clubhouse.

The sergeant spits at the dog. "Jesus, next time let's just play Wagner over loudspeakers."

Becker looks to the sergeant for direction. "Blades?"

"Damned straight." He holsters his pistol and draws out a set of khukuri blades.

Jelly kills the match and pulls a twenty-two-inch machete from a belt sheath. We each draw our blade of choice. Becker kicks her way into the nest, brandishing a broad-sword, and we're at her heels.

The place reeks of unwashed bodies and unabashed sex. The pack stands ready, ten adults gathered around five younger. Two of the younger clutch infants. Most of the adults are armed with crude clubs, off-balance and unwieldy, but one brandishes a cavalry saber.

Lean and shaggy, wearing squalid fatigues with an oak-leaf cluster pinned to one collar point. Cooperman. Dunbar stands close at hand, blond hair a rats' nest, uniform in shreds, holding a Browning automatic rifle.

The sergeant acts first. His arm snaps and a steel dart juts from Dunbar's eye.

Too late. The clatter of the Browning engulfs the clubhouse. Coated thirty-caliber slugs climb Jelly's rib cage, sliding through his Kevlar like pushpins into cork. He spins away, dying, and the last round ruptures his napalm tank.

Napalm coats us all. Thank anything but God the match is out. Cooperman bellows an order, sounding like a deaf man struggling to touch the shape of words.

The Infected surge to attack. The nasty fuckers don't slack off but they don't stand a chance against Rangers. Breathing through our mouths, we ignore the stench and press the attack. In a heartbeat, all of them, adult and younger, are still and finally dead.

Except for one.

Cooperman fights on against Becker but she pushes hard. Her broad-sword blurs, finding its way past the saber again and again. She forces Cooperman back against a wall. Their blades are grinding, edge to edge, when Cooperman grabs Becker's vest, pulls her close, and kisses her. Even in the dim light we see the tip of Cooperman's tongue probe Becker's cheeks.

She staggers back, spitting fear and rage.

Cooperman presses the advantage but Becker knocks the saber aside. With furious energy, she slides her blade through ribs, piercing the stuttering heart beneath. The saber clatters to the floor and Cooperman collapses in a heap beside it. Dead and come back to us at last.

"Shit." It's all the sergeant can think to say. He trots to Becker, reaches out to her.

She shrugs his hand away, sheathes her sword, tears off her helmet, and pitches it aside.

"Don't you touch me," she says.

She kneels before him. The top of her head is just below his chin. She draws a measured breath and bows her head. Her close-cropped hair lies tight and wet against the perfect curve of her skull. She's crying. Hell, all of us are crying. Even the sergeant is blinking fast.

He raises one gloved hand toward her as if to offer benediction, but he doesn't touch her. He sighs. "There's still eight hours before we'll know for sure."

Becker's chin comes up. Her eyes are angry and demanding, the look of a trapped animal with no idea of escape. She taps the middle of her forehead with her index finger. "Bullshit. We all know right now. Do me."

The sergeant draws his pistol and presses the barrel to Becker's forehead. She strips away her gloves and cups her long fingers around his hand, not touching, granting absolution.

And he pulls the trigger.

After a time, we collect our own, torch the filthy nest. We take care to stay well back from the flames for the scent of napalm hangs upon us like a shroud. At last we carry four body bags back through the corn and lash them to the rack on the HumVee. The sergeant slides behind the wheel.

The engine is the only sound during the twenty-minute trip back to the water works. None of us know what to say. Becker would have sung her coffee-flavored songs. Jelly would have told us awful, misogynistic jokes.

About the old Jew who wins big in the lottery by playing his Auschwitz tattoo. About Little Johnny who runs in circles while he plays because his right foot's nailed down. The top ten list of ways to profit from Armageddon.

Melinda and her people meet us at the outside gate. Their welcome smiles fall away as they count our numbers. We lug the body bags to the field cemetery, our jump-boots clicking on the concrete walks. The clean, gentle aroma of mature maple trees fills our noses as we dig new graves and lower our fallen comrades into the ground.

We offer no eulogy because every word has been said too many times before.

When it is over Melinda moves close to the sergeant. "Stay this time, Harlan. You've done enough."

He shakes his head as he steps toward us. "Can't. Still three more of us out there."

Melinda doesn't understand the measure of our debt.

Summer 2012, we were the remnants of Fifth Battalion, Rangers. Forty-eight men and women come to Tuscarawas County to maintain order, when we all still had hope that order could be had.

Major Cooperman remained upbeat. "We'll be back to beer and football before you know it."

Two days later we stumbled into ambush. Cooperman, Dunbar, and thirty others fell in with the Infected after that attack. We've searched for them since then and we've had losses.

Melinda believes balance is returning to the world. She says the Infected haven't abandoned their humanity. She tells us new customs are taking root. She says there are new standards, too, upon which what it means to be human must be measured. Our mission jeopardizes all of that, she claims.

That's her concern, not ours.

We will not surrender. We will bring in our dead. No matter what the final cost may be, we will leave no one behind.

Synchronized with Evelyn

Can you hear me?

"Perfectly."

We're ready to initiate the jump. You'll feel disoriented. Some nausea. It's normal. Try to relax.

"I remember everything you told me in the briefing."

Good. All right. Here we go.

Blackness. Gut-wrenching agony. I cry out. At least I try to but I no longer have a voice. It belongs to Evelyn.

She stumbles as she climbs the subway stairs. I'd like to think she heard my stifled scream, felt my distress. Everyone reports it though, so maybe she just tripped. She grips the iron rail, draws closer to the wall to protect herself from the insistent, jostling bodies all around her.

She recovers in an instant.

I see with her eyes. I hear with her ears, a cacophony of noises. The thick odor of the subway pushes at her nose. She's hemmed in by the inexorable, impersonal pressure of the massed bodies anxious to put the underground behind.

If I could, I'd push a space clear, do a little dance there on the steps. A giddy buck and wing to announce and celebrate my first time for all these passing strangers.

I'm synchronized with Evelyn McHale.

She climbs into the May Day sunshine from the Thirty-Third Street subway station, turns east toward Fifth Avenue. I've walked this route almost a century from now. She moves with the Thursday morning crowd. Her new Ferragamo heels click upon the concrete as she moves along the same path she's followed every workday for the past three weeks.

Overlapping sounds roll over her. More noise than I'm used to in my New York. Somehow the city smells younger, if not fresher, looks more sharp-edged than I've ever seen it. The ten-minute walk to the south entrance of the Empire State Building passes easily. She pushes through the big revolving door. I've always found the lobby much too Spartan for my tastes but this morning I savor every little detail with her.

The patterns of the sunshine as it filters through the entry glass to fall upon smoothed stone and glittering metal. The massed smell of befuddled strangers standing before tall office directories. The echoes of urgent footsteps, hurried voices, easy laughter.

Evelyn pulls off a glove, runs bare fingers along one cold marble wall as she walks to the elevators. She laughs at the accompanying shiver. That touch and sound alone is worth every dollar I have paid to be here with her.

An old fellow looks up from his work at the information booth beneath the big bas-relief aluminum image of the building. According to the literature, Evelyn introduced herself to him three weeks ago, lied to him, told him she had just taken a job in the building. He waves now. "Morning, Evelyn. You're looking very spiffy."

"Thank you, Steven," she replies. "I wore this for you."

Steven grins. I recall my research. He's a widower, lives all alone somewhere out in Queens. She's made his day.

The door slides open to the elevator regular riders call *the local*. I've ridden it decades from now. It makes every stop between the lobby and the forty-fourth floor. There you have to transfer to complete the journey upward.

"Top of the morning, Evelyn," the operator says.

"Morning, Geoffrey."

Geoffrey's middle-aged. Slim and handsome in his dark blue uniform and his early Clark Gable mustache. Geoffrey enthusiasts say he's gay. Of course no one used the word in nineteen forty-seven, not for that reason, anyway. Geoffrey thinks Evelyn works in an office up on forty-four. Another lie.

The doors close, the elevator rises.

At twenty-three Geoffrey stops to help a young mother with three small sons herd her brood aboard. He smiles at her, speaks softly to the boys, apologizes to the rest of us for the delay. He'll ride the cables, offering small courtesies, until he dies in nineteen sixty-four. A sixty-year-old gentleman.

"Forty-fourth floor, Evelyn," Geoffrey says, at last.

"Thank you, Geoffrey. Time flies when you're having fun."

He laughs, holds the door for her. There's just the two of them now. She steps to the door but before she leaves she opens her purse, brand-new to match the shoes. She removes a roll of bills and hands it to Geoffrey. Tipping is allowed, so he nods as he accepts the money but then his eyes widen as he realizes how much she's given him.

Four hundred and seventeen dollars.

It's all the money Evelyn possesses. She doesn't make much working as a bookkeeper for that engraving company. She's been setting what she can aside for her wedding, a rainy-day stash laid away between the pages of *Crime and Punishment*. I own the very book, bought it eighteen months ago at a private estate auction. Worth every penny of the fifty thousand I paid.

"Evelyn, this is too much." Geoffrey's voice trembles. He's lost his formality.

She shakes her head, taking care not to muss her hair. She smiles. "It's not. You're a good man, Geoffrey. Buy something for yourself. From me."

With that, she turns away, clicks down the hallway in her new shoes, offering Geoffrey a moving view of her backside. She doesn't know it's wasted effort.

"Goodbye, Geoffrey," she calls to him over her shoulder.

The call bell chimes. The elevator doors snap closed. She stops and draws a breath. The hallway smells of cheap cigars and Johnson's floor wax. Evelyn walks on to Klein & Garnichts, Publishers. She's made friends with Janice, the receptionist.

Janice smiles, as Evelyn walks in. "Hello, Evie."

"Morning, Jan. Can't stay long. I popped in to say hello."

"Want to go to lunch today? That Italian place again?"

Evelyn shakes her head. "Maybe tomorrow. I've got something I have to do today."

"Tomorrow then."

"What shoe size do you wear?" Evelyn asks.

Janice looks puzzled. "Eight. Why?"

"Would you like to have these? They're eights and almost new." Evelyn slips out of her heels, sets them, shining and so grand, upon the desk.

Janice's eyes grow wide. She recognizes quality even if she can't afford very much of it. "These are Ferragamos!"

"Yes, but they pinch. Why don't you try them on?"

Janice doesn't have to be told twice. She slips one shoe on and then the other. They fit as if made for her. There are tears in her eyes when she looks up to Evelyn.

"Are you sure, Evie?"

"Do you like them?"

"Of course, but—"

"Good. They're yours. I have shoes in my office."

That's another lie. Evelyn is getting good at it. They make plans for lunch and say goodbye.

There's no extra pair of shoes. No office.

Evelyn tiptoes along the hall in her stocking feet. At the far end there's a door marked stairwell.

No one knows why Evelyn decided to take the stairs rather than the elevator. I've always believed she didn't want to risk facing Geoffrey again if his cage arrived while she waited for the other.

Even though it's something over eight hundred steps to the top, she's twenty-three and fit, so it's not a big chore for her to use the stairs. I've made the climb myself, took thirty-three minutes at a steady pace.

I count each floor as Evelyn makes the turns. Revel in the glow that spreads throughout her body with the effort. She steps into the observation deck lobby, out-of-breath but so alive, as Morris Katz unlocks the outer doors.

Morris, the stout young Jewish man who patrols the deck on weekdays, turns from the heavy brass and plate-glass doors. He smiles, blushes just a bit. He's just her age and all the books suggest that he finds her attractive.

"Good morning, Evelyn," he says. "You're up here early."

"Hello, Morris," she replies. "I have a few minutes, wanted to collect my thoughts."

"Of course. There's lots to see today."

Morris steps back, folds his hands, considering his own thoughts. He's studying law at The City College. Someday he'll be rich and well-to-do. He will speak of Evelyn the day he dies. He's already adjusted the message on the information board next to the doors. Five states visible today. New York, New Jersey, Pennsylvania, Massachusetts and Connecticut. A rare treat. It doesn't matter. Evelyn hasn't come here for the view.

She steps to the mirror on the wall beside the elevators, touches the slick surface as she examines her appearance. She pushes back loose strands of dark hair from her face, brushes her high cheekbones with her fingertips, checks her lipstick.

"She looked just like our mother," her sister will tell reporters when she is interviewed.

Evelyn is ready now. She walks to the glass doors. Stops next to Morris. "How are you today, Mo?"

He nods, pulled from his reverie. "I'm well. And you?"

She pats his arm, a light touch against his jacket sleeve. "Never better."

He smiles, opens the center door and motions her outside although he looks at her stocking feet with some dismay. She walks the deck, stops at the spot where Barry proposed to her.

The wind swirls around her, gusts furiously.

Evelyn draws her gray-cloth coat closer about her. The stockinged soles of her feet tingle. It's colder up here than on the street. She pats at her hair again, touches the bobby pins that hold it.

She glances toward the glass doors, back to Morris in the warm lobby, almost takes a step in that direction. Her heart is racing, her respiration rapid. Her feet jitter upon the surface of the deck. Then she takes a breath, waves to Morris, and turns back to the parapet. She squares her shoulders.

Perhaps it is that gesture, but for the first time since I read about her, saw Robert Wile's flat-tone photograph, I wish that I could speak to her, could ask her 'Why?'

She sets her purse onto the deck, crouches next to it, and takes note paper and a fountain pen from its depths. The parapet is higher than she expected. She's never been so close to it. The leading edge touches her just below her breasts.

The first note goes to Janice. It grants her the purse that matches the new shoes. The note goes in the purse. Evelyn fusses with the second one ten minutes, manages two sentences. Her hand quivers over every single word.

He is much better off without me ... I wouldn't make a good wife for anybody

At last she runs a line through it all, tears loose the sheet, unbuttons her coat and stuffs the crumpled paper into a pocket on her suit jacket. Of course, it wouldn't do to put it with the purse and have Janice find it.

Evelyn slides the pad and pen into the purse. She pulls out a three-week-old copy of The New York Times. I possess a framed first edition of that issue. No one knows what happened to the original.

The paper's folded open to a story about the building. It reports that in the years since the Empire State Building opened, a dozen people have jumped from the observation deck. The owners plan to install a barricade along the parapet.

"It will put an end to the suicides," a building spokesman says. "Work will begin soon. We should be done by Thanksgiving. The observation deck will close while the project proceeds."

Evelyn removes her coat, folds it, lays it atop her purse. That nasty wind bites at her. Goosebumps erupt up and down her arms. She shivers, glances toward the doors again. Morris stands just inside, watching. She puts her hands upon the stone, pushes herself upward and squirms onto the parapet.

The buttons of her jacket rive away, her blouse gaps open. The stone surface grinds her palms and abdomen.

"Dear God," she whispers. "Help me."

The doors slam open. "Evelyn!" Morris shouts. "Come down from there!"

She wobbles back and forth, inching outward. Her white silk scarf slips from her neck, flutters toward the ground.

Morris rushes to her, arms outstretched, giving everything he's got. Too late. She's over the edge, into the air, just as he reaches her. Evelyn feels his fingertips slip along her leg. More contact than they've shared in the three weeks she's been visiting. All Morris manages to save is one silk stocking.

Evelyn kicks against his chest, working to gain distance. He grunts. Her last glimpse of the roof is him falling backward, mouth open. Morris may be shouting but Evelyn can't hear him anymore.

She grunts with effort, wills herself outward, straining against gravity. She's got to clear the setbacks. We both hold our breath. Then she's made it, falling free, eyes wide open and accountable to no one.

A strange sensation. It doesn't feel as if she's falling. Instead she seems to float in place while the world hurtles upward. The pavement below—busy Thirty-Third Street—rushes ever higher.

I've made the calculations many times. Evelyn would have had access to the same formulas on terminal velocity of falling objects in textbooks at Carnegie Library. We both know it will take eight seconds for her—for us— to touch the concrete.

I begin to count to myself.

One, one thousand. Two, one thousand. Three, one thousand.

The street hurries upward. Evelyn begins to squirm, turning and twisting and stretching. It's another one of those *who knows* moments. Perhaps she didn't want to watch. Perhaps she didn't want to come to rest upon her face. Once I believed that moment wasted, not to see her destination. Now I think I understand.

Just before she loses sight of Thirty-Third Street, a dark sedan, a limousine, pulls to the curb below.

"Oh, God," she whispers. "Don't let anyone get hurt."

Then she's on her back. Her eyes look to the heavens. She's not floating. She's falling now. The wind slashes at her, tries to rip her clothes away, rob her of her dignity. She crosses her ankles, folds her hands against her breasts. Holds on tight.

She hears people running now. Shouting, screaming prayers. She strikes the limousine. In that instant it feels as if a sharp and wicked blade of heated steel has slammed through her body and her soul, skewering her from head to toes.

White light flares around her. I'm snatched into blackness, no longer synchronized.

Can you hear me?

"What?"

We hope you had a satisfactory experience. Please exit to the left once I release you from the harness.

"I don't—"

I've disengaged the harness. Please exit to the left.

"Wait, I need—"

You need to exit to the left. There's a line of people waiting. A long line.

"Please, I'll do anything, pay anything. You've got to understand. I have to know. I have to synchronize with Evelyn again."

Serves Him Right

_____

The heady scent of caramelizing onions wafted through the Cooking Network's kitchen studio although it was well past midnight. Mandy Sweet looked up from the baking table where she'd been kneading bread dough.

"Remember Andre's rule for goulash," she said.

Jeanette Tilton nodded, not taking her eyes from the pan before her. Jeanette always focused on the work at hand. She tapped a knuckle to her forehead. "I have it memorized."

"We all do," Barbara Shawnessy said. She stood before the maple chopping block, scrubbing at its broad surface with a wetted brush. "Fry your onions in your fat until they're golden, never darker. Take your pan from the fire. Add paprika right away and stir well."

Goulash hadn't been the only thing Andre Kovac stirred.

From his first moment on the air two years ago, Andre had been at ease before the cameras, projecting a smoldering appeal that had nothing to do with the temperature of his burners or his ovens. One on one, in the kitchen or in the bedroom, he'd been irresistible. Mandy, Jeanette, and Barbara, his network production assistants, had each sampled Andre's extended bill of fare.

"When you add your meat, stir immediately again, coating it thoroughly with the onion-fat-paprika mix before returning it to the fire," Jeanette continued the litany. "That guarantees the paprika's flavor will be released by its contact with the hot fat and prevents the dish from tasting bitter."

Andre had called his show *The Hungary Chef* and specialized in comfort food from his eastern European homeland. Stuffed peppers called toltott. Rakott Burgonya, a hearty dish with sausage, potatoes, and hard-cooked eggs. Kohlrabi soup, thick with a pungent scent reminiscent of cabbage.

Jeanette began to sniffle. "The first time he cooked for me was right here on the set, about a month after his premiere."

"Did you do the deed here, too?" Barbara asked.

Jeanette shook her head, not taking her eyes from her pans. "No. At the Plaza. A room overlooking the Pulitzer Fountain."

"On the tenth floor?"

"Uh huh."

"That's where he took me, too."

Jeanette knuckled away tears, perhaps brought on by the onions.

"How about you, Mandy?" Barbara asked.

Mandy nodded, fingering the smooth, elastic surface of the langos dough, shaping it into flat circles big as her open hand. "Tenth floor of the Plaza. I'll say this. When Andre found something that worked, he stuck by it."

Barbara snorted, a hard, coughing sound. Soon her laughter, accented by Mandy's giggles, echoed across the sound stage.

Jeanette adjusted the gas burner beneath the pan and rubbed her nose with the back of her free hand. She hiccupped. "I don't see how you two can laugh at a time like this. The man is dead."

"And we're not," Mandy said.

"That's right," Barbara said. "No crying. Eat, drink, and remember. That's how a wake's supposed to be."

"Amen to that." Mandy slipped the last of the langos into place, scooped up the baking sheet, stepped to the smaller of the two ovens, and slipped the flat bread inside.

"How long?" Jeanette asked.

Mandy twisted the timer knob. "Fifteen minutes."

Barbara turned away from the chopping block. "I'll toss a salad and pour the wine."

"And I'll set the dishes," Mandy said.

The three women worked for a time in companionable silence.

Jeanette sighed. "He would have loved to see us working together like this."

Barbara scooped up a handful of greens and a Wusthof salad knife. Its razored edge tapped a staccato beat. She might have majored in broadcasting at Ohio State but Barbara grew up in her father's butcher shop in Strasburg, seventy miles south of Cleveland. She knew her way around a blade.

"So Jeanette was the first," she said, continuing to work. "When did he take up with you, Mandy?"

"Christmas that first year. The Plaza's lobby decorations were beautiful."

"How about you?" Jeanette asked.

Barbara shrugged. "Not 'til last April. His birthday. He cooked a full-course meal for me, right here. Naked. We recorded the whole thing."

She settled the salad dishes into place and stepped to the wine rack, slid a bottle from its place to examine the label. "Here's a thirty-year-old Egri Bikavér."

Mandy nodded. "Good choice. Andre always said the Bull's Blood Eger agreed with him."

The timer dinged. Mandy opened the oven door, flooding the studio with the comforting aroma of baking bread. "It's done. How about the goulash, Jeanette?"

"Well, it should simmer for another hour to do it right, but given the circumstances, I suppose we'll be okay. One of you get the sour cream from the refrigerator."

Jeanette began to plate the food. The three women gathered at the table.

Barbara picked up her fork, leaned close to her plate, closed her eyes, and drew in a breath, savoring the rich vapors from the stew. "Oh, my. That's a perfect Goulash Andre."

Jeanette lifted an eyebrow. "Shall we say grace?"

Mandy giggled. "Too late for that."

Jeanette sniffled. "I suppose. I can't believe he's gone."

"I can't believe he screwed all three of us in the same hotel room, all these months like clockwork," Barbara said.

Mandy studied the dish set before her. "I can't believe we just got wise to him tonight. What a bastard."

Jeannette shook out her napkin and lifted her wine glass in a toast. "Well, ladies, bon appétit."

"Maybe we should let it cool a bit," Mandy said.

"Don't be silly," Jeanette replied. "It's just the right temperature."

Barbara laid her fork beside her plate and pushed back from the table. "Mandy's on to something. Let it cool."

Jeanette shook her head. "It won't taste right served cold. Andre would be adamant, would tell us goulash must be presented piping hot."

Barbara moistened the tip of her napkin with her tongue.

"Maybe," she replied, touching the wetted cloth to a spot of dried blood on Jeanette's earlobe. "What do you suppose he'd have to say about serving up revenge?"

A Bannockburn Night

Almost eleven hours out of Thunder Bay, with a hold filled with iron ore, the *Walter A. Hutchison* raced a storm east across Lake Superior, headed for the Soo.

This happened two years after the Big War. Nineteen forty-eight. The winter storms, what Lake sailors call the Witch of November, had come calling early that year.

This one sucked the darkness to it, painting everything in nasty shades of gray. Gale-force winds flung thick, wet snow from every direction. Weather like that, my old man used to say, you could get in trouble taking a piss off the back rail.

I had settled in the captain's chair up in the wheelhouse and hadn't wandered from the chair for seven hours, even though I had guzzled a few gallons of black coffee.

Hutchison was my first command.

To pass the time we bantered about the World Series. Jack Mathias, my first mate, hailed from Boston. Rudy Sorensen, the helmsman, hailed from Cleveland. A hard-core Indians fan, he wouldn't listen to a bad word from Jack about the Tribe.

And then the skies cleared and our laughter died. We all spotted a triple-masted, single-stack boat running with us in the gathering darkness, two-hundred yards off our starboard rail.

Rudy, a staunch Catholic, crossed himself. "Bannockburn!" he said.

The word seemed to suck all the air out of the wheelhouse. The skies and the Lake closed in again and we lost sight of her.

"Don't talk nonsense, Rudy," Jack said, almost stuttering on his dees and tees.

"I swear, Mr. Mathias. I saw her markings. Wait 'til the boys hear this!"

My old man used to say there's a legend for every drop of water in the Lake. I suppose the Ojibway started it. They called Superior *Gitche Gumee*—Big and Shining Water—and claimed even the smallest rock along its shores spoke to them.

Lake sailors have passed along their own tales over the years. *Bannockburn* is one of them.

A steel-hulled steamer, dressed out all in black with the Montreal Transportation Company logo in white on her single stack. Only ten years old that November in 1902, she took on wheat at Port Arthur and headed down-lake. At noon *Algonquin* sighted *Bannockburn* off Keweenaw Point. As darkness fell, the wheelhouse crew of *Huronic* spotted *Bannockburn* running east, easy as you please. She never reached port though.

Some say she slipped off into a crack in the Lake. Over the years she's been seen again and again. Sleek and black and ever silent. Running against rising waves under a new moon. Steaming through the worst of a winter storm, such as ours.

Never in good weather and always a bad omen.

Rudy had to wait to spread new tales. Darkness came, winds soared to seventy knots, and the following sea soon topped twenty feet.

At my call, Doc Weaver and his black gang nursed every bit of power they could manage from *Hutchison's* four diesel engines but it didn't look to be enough.

Water knee-deep upon the deck. Heavy seas breaking over the bow. The winds pushed her as if she were an empty balsa shell, not eight hundred feet of steel plate filled to the load line with twenty thousand tons of ore. *Hutchison* took longer and longer to recover each time she rolled.

Cookie called up just after six, offering to bring us sandwiches and hot soup. I told him to stay below. At my order the five deckhands gathered in the day room, weather gear ready and ice hammers in hand.

Ice. That was my biggest worry.

The stuff grows like a fungus, spreading its shining veneer everywhere, making work outside close to impossible, adding an extra weight that could destroy delicate communications gear.

And without radio, radar, and loran we would be sailing deaf and blind.

My old man used to say that what you pick at the most always comes unraveled. Just before seven Andy Duncan, the radio operator, called forward.

"The signal's fading, Skipper," he said, his voice hoarse and hollow over the phone. "I figure it's the ice."

"Watch the shop, Jack," I said, giving him the high sign. "I'm going aft to chat with Sparks."

It was a ten-foot walk but while I was in the passageway, *Hutchison* rattled like a dog shaking off a bath. Without pause there came a loud brittle-bone crack. No question what produced that sound. The communications mast was down.

Seconds later Andy and I stood in the half-light of his blank screens, wrapped in the hiss of a radio carrier wave.

"Should'a called sooner," Andy said, close to tears.

I put my hand on his shoulder. "I should have seen it, too, Sparks. Let's just figure out how to fix it."

His eyes darted about the shack. He squared his shoulders, gave a little grunt. "Parts ain't a problem. I got spares for the big stuff, can jury-rig the rest."

He rolled his shoulders. I could hear the muscles creak as he continued. "Good weather, I'd have it up in a snap. I ain't sure I can do it now."

"Yes, you can," I said. "The hands will help."

Back then there were no long-range forecasts. No satellite links. No computers. With radar and sonar working, maintaining a course in foul weather was like feeling your way across a dark room without bumping into the furniture. Without electronics, we were running across a field of potholes wearing a blindfold.

In the wheelhouse, Rudy gripped the wheel hard enough to leave fingerprints. Jack hadn't moved. He stood up straight and drew a breath as I entered.

"The radio mast is down," I said.

They didn't need to be told but I saw both men needed to hear me say it, to make it matter of fact and manageable. If I said it would be all right, that we could do what needed to be done, they would do their damnedest to see it through. But if I showed fear, panic would begin right there and swell until it engulfed the boat.

At that moment I first recognized the truth about command. Anyone can be in charge when it's all in balance. The measure of a leader is how he handles disaster.

"Sparks is going to make repairs," I said. "We'll hold course and speed until he's done."

"Charlie—"

Jack and I had known each other for nine years, had been on a first-name basis, onboard *Hutchison,* since the first day. That wouldn't do now. I interrupted him.

"You have an opinion, Mr. Mathias?"

He glanced at Rudy, then drew back his shoulders. "Yes, sir. We've been running tight to shore. In this wind we could have drifted leeward, without electronics to show true position. We should turn north."

Let me give you a quick sailing lesson. Position is the location of the boat at a given time. Leeward is a sideways movement caused by wind or current. With strong winds out of the northwest, *Hutchison* could be pushed south off true course. Without our electronic eyes and ears, we would never know.

Jack wanted to steer north of our compass heading, to put distance between us and the Michigan shoreline. It would avoid the possibility of running aground but it carried dangers, too.

The maneuver would lay us sideways into the wave troughs. That could produce deep rolls, maybe so deep we would capsize. In addition the radio mast set forward. A breaking wave exerts enormous pressure, one ton per square foot. If I held present course, we would run with that force focused on our stern, away from the work crew.

"Your concern is noted," I said. "We'll stay on course."

We sailed for another quarter-hour before Andy called, via walkie-talkie. I could hear his grin. "I can do this, Skipper. Just give me another fifteen or twenty minutes."

Before we could say another word, a rocket exploded into the night. In its glare we saw that the other boat was back, less than one hundred yards away and closing fast.

"Hang on!" I shouted into the walkie-talkie. "It's going to be a bumpy ride."

Rudy called upon his God as Jack scurried from the protection of the wheelhouse to the starboard flying bridge. I dropped the radio, took two big steps away from the chair to the starboard glass.

"Bring her to port, Rudy!" I said, still shouting.

Rudy spun the wheel and, even as I brought my binoculars up, I felt *Hutchison* begin its turn. Outside a beam of light skewered the other boat. Jack had manned our spotlight.

The dark freighter continued to close the distance, forcing us to the north. Her ship's whistle shrilled above the whine of the wind in our rigging. Signal rockets screamed from her deck as if it was a Fourth of July fireworks show.

Despite the lights and noise I could see no sign of life.

We ran in that manner for ten minutes, the *Hutchison* always moving to the northeast, fighting to maintain a distance. There were moments I was certain we would capsize, but each time we rolled, *Hutchison* wallowed back into line.

Then just as it appeared we would gain no breathing room, the other boat shuddered, as if a huge and unseen fist had struck it. Its forward progress slowed. *Hutchison* raced away and as we gained clearance I had Rudy bring her back to an eastward heading.

As we watched and waited, the movements of the other boat became stilted. Waves hurled the little freighter sideways across the Lake. The wind ripped at her superstructure, smashing doors and hatches, blowing away deck gear.

Sweeping gray water made matchwood of her lifeboats. She pitched about with so much force that her screw was raced in the open air one second and bit into the freezing water the next.

Then, without warning she shuddered to a halt.

She had run aground, just as *Hutchison* would have had we stayed that course. Her bow split open, much like a fresh egg tapped upon a counter top.

She foundered and in an instant she disappeared.

There's not much to tell after that. Andy's repair crew came through it battered but alive. They confessed later they had been too busy hanging on to see much of anything. We made the rest of the run into Sault Saint Marie without incident.

When Rudy went off duty, he became the center of attention, for the remainder of the crew had been stuck below deck for that ten-minute ride. Jack Mathias and I remained silent about the incident, even with each other, except for the few seconds after he returned from the flying bridge.

"You saw the markings on the stack, didn't you?" he asked.

Soaked clear through and shivering, but his stunned surprise shone from his face with as much intensity as the spotlight he had wielded moments before. He was desperate for confirmation of his sanity. I gave it to him.

"It was *Bannockburn*. She pushed us north." He nodded, wiped at his eyes, and then we went back to work.

I swear that every word I've told you is true. You can call it superstitious claptrap but over the years I have come to believe that not all ghostly sightings are omens of misfortune, nor are all spirits malevolent.

My old man used to say that he had never known a captain who wouldn't do everything in his power to come to the aid of another boat in peril. I believe that's true.

Even if death has come on board.

A Son of the Night

Gargoyle crouched at the edge of the parapet, oblivious to the drop, scanning the rooftops below.

The world glowed in variegated shades of luminescent green, thanks to the light-enhancing filters in the lenses of his mask. To the west the new moon tipped the water of Elliot Bay with slivers of light. Nothing moved on the surrounding roofs, but Gargoyle was certain his prey was hiding within sharp-edged shadows, hoping to escape capture.

Beneath the mask he smiled. No one escaped Gargoyle.

He reached to his right temple, about to touch the ceramic wart that would engage the infrared filters, and felt a tap upon his shoulder.

"Have you seen the headlines?" Helen Mathersby fluttered her copy of the morning newspaper.

"No, Mother," Rory Mathersby said.

He didn't look up from his plate. It was disconcerting to have anyone other than Dillinger talk to him during breakfast, even his mother. Most mornings she went straight to bed upon returning home from work.

Mrs. Mathersby manned the in-patient desk at a Seattle hospital, midnight to eight, six nights a week. She didn't need the money, of course. The Mathersby Foundation saw to that. What she needed, she told Rory, was to *feel* needed.

Even so he had this niggling idea that she volunteered for graveyard shift so that he would be free most nights to practice being Gargoyle.

"Rory?"

He didn't turn around.

"Yes, Mother?" The voice filter on the Gargoyle costume twisted his words into an inhuman growl.

"I'm leaving for work. Don't stay in here all night."

"I won't, Mother."

He heard the low hum of her powered chair. Mrs. Mathersby had been in one wheelchair or another for as long as Rory could remember. The hum changed pitch. She had slowed at the training room exit.

"Rory?"

"Yes?"

"You need to get out more. There's a play opening at the repertory theater."

"I'll think about it."

"One more thing."

"Yes, Mother."

"I think your costume is ripped out in the seat."

"Thank you, Mother."

"You're welcome."

The door closed and she was gone. Rory reached behind him and ran the palm of his gloved hand over his posterior.

She was right.

"You should read this," Mrs. Mathersby said. She rattled her newspaper again. Rory looked up from his steak and eggs.

"What does it say?" he asked.

"Look for yourself."

He laid his knife and fork aside and scooped up the copy of *The Seattle Times* Dillinger had set out with the flatware. **FIVE BRANCH BANKS ROBBED!** It was a banner headline worthy of one of the graphic novels Rory wrote.

He read on.

Teams of masked men dressed in tattered evening clothes had entered five Bank of America branches just before closing the previous day and hauled away almost four million dollars.

Video cameras at all five banks captured the robberies and at the fifth's branch, one bandit stopped before the camera and shouted, "Hell's Minions own Seattle!"

"Hmmmm," Rory said.

"Indeed," Mrs. Mathersby said. "It sounds to me like a job for Gargoyle."

Rory eased backward off the parapet and walked to the exit. He touched buttons on a control panel to shut down the holographic projectors and the rooftop scene around him faded away. It left behind a cavernous space filled with giant plastic blocks. Machinery hummed and the blocks slid upon tracks to arrange themselves along the walls.

The computer-controlled training room, with its moving pieces and elaborate holographic system, had cost Rory a fortune. He could afford it. His imagination and his father's business sense had seen to that.

"You take care of your mother, Rory," Father said in his will. "The foundation will take care of itself."

"Mother, we both know Gargoyle isn't ready to go to the street."

"You may know that," Mrs. Mathersby said. "I know that one never has full knowledge of what can be done until one attempts to do it."

"Yes, Mother."

Rory continued to hide behind his newspaper even after Mrs. Mathersby had wheeled off to bed.

Rory stepped from the hidden elevator at the back of his bedroom closet. As he moved, he touched a micro-switch just behind his right ear. There was a soft hiss of air, the self-contained breathing gear disengaged, and a series of catches clicked along the dorsal spine that ran up the back of the helmet.

The entire device fell forward into Rory's waiting hands.

He tossed it onto the bed and peeled off the rest of the armored costume. The ruined body suit was last. He held it before him, staring at the ripped seat.

Bartholomew Blake, alter ego for Swath, hero of Rory's graphic novels, had his share of worries and doubts. He wouldn't be a decent superhero if he didn't. But his toes never got cramped because his boots were too tight and his costume never ripped out its seams. And Blake wouldn't worry about it even if it happened.

Rory sighed. After three years of training, he could lift his own weight above his head, push a full-sized automobile more than a mile at a dead run, and scale a knotted thread ten stories in less than two minutes while carrying a two-hundred-pound deadweight across his shoulders.

But he had never once in all that time ventured onto the rooftops of the real Seattle.

He tossed the ripped suit aside. He would talk to Dillinger at breakfast about repairs. For now he would sleep. His father used to say that a good night's rest would cure a bad day's headaches. Rory prayed that that was true.

"May I clear the dishes, Sir?" Dillinger said.

"Yes."

Dillinger moved to Rory's end of the table and stopped.

"Was there something wrong with your steak, Sir?"

Rory lowered the newspaper. Dillinger studied him, one eyebrow raised. Much the same way as he had done when Rory, at seven, had refused to climb back onto his new bicycle after he failed his first attempt to ride it. Dillinger glanced at the meat remaining upon the plate.

"It was fine," Rory said. "I'm just not hungry."

"Very well, Sir." Dillinger began to collect the dishes. "Your mother informed me that the Gargoyle costume is torn."

"Yes."

"I shall see to repairs."

"Thank you."

"My pleasure, Sir," Dillinger said. And he swept away through the door to the kitchen, bearing the breakfast remains.

Over the next ten days the same bandits committed robberies throughout Seattle. Each was planned and executed to perfection. No one was injured. No property was damaged. No one was caught.

The only new information was the spelling error.

"It's Hel's Minions," a shadowy figure said in a videotape delivered to all the television stations the afternoon after the first robberies. "H-E-L. Not H-E-L-L. Don't you people read?"

Rory was envious. Hel was a great name for a criminal mastermind, a perfect opponent for Swath. Hel was a perfect opponent for Gargoyle as well. Rory fretted over what his mother had said. She had remained silent since that morning at the breakfast table, but Rory still could hear her final words. Perhaps it was time to listen.

Gargoyle crouched at the edge of the parapet, oblivious to the drop, scanning the rooftops below him. The world about him glowed in variegated shades of luminescent green, thanks to the light-enhancing filters in the lenses of his helmet.

To the west, a full moon set the water of Elliot Bay aglow. Gargoyle had been on the hunt for five days catching only a few hours' sleep each night, but he felt glorious.

In those five days, there had been seven more attempted bank robberies. Gargoyle had foiled each one and now only Hel and Hel's Chief Minion remained at large.

"I'm coming for you, Hel," he whispered.

Beneath the helmet Rory smiled. No one escaped Gargoyle. He reached to his right temple, about to touch the ceramic wart that would engage the infrared filters, and felt a tap upon his shoulder.

He spun upon the parapet. A woman stood there, clad in red leather and spandex.

Slender and rounded, just his height. Her ebony hair was cut short and slicked close to her skull. Her chin, delicate but firm; her lips, full and inviting. She stood wrapped in a gossamer cape and an ephemeral circlet of light hovered just above her head.

He wanted to ask how she managed that. Instead he demanded. "Who are you?"

"Hel's Angel," she replied. "And you're Gargoyle." Her voice possessed an undertone, as if a choir echoed each word.

"I've never heard—"

Before Rory could finish, the Angel was upon him, gripping his costume, pulling him toward her as she rolled backward. Rory tumbled across the roof, smashed into the brick wall of an equipment shed. He levered his way back to his feet, pushing away the pain, and prepared to face her next attack.

The Angel had disappeared.

"Hey Ugly!"

She hovered over him, fifteen feet above the roof. Her cape floated about her as if a pair of wings. Rory would have liked to ask how she managed that as well.

She brought her hands together. A ball of light the size of a softball took shape between her palms. Rory didn't like the look of that. He drew his Spout from a concealed holster on his left hip and swung it upward.

A high-pressure water jet shot from the gun, struck the Angel, and sent her tumbling through the air. The light within her hands blinked out but she stayed aloft. She brushed her hair back into place with the palms of her hands and shook the water from her.

God, she was beautiful!

"If you just surrender," she said, "It would be so much easier for both of us."

"Heroes never surrender," Rory said.

"You're no hero! Hel told me all about your nefarious plans!"

Rory almost laughed. He had never heard anyone use that word outside of a graphic novel.

"Are you for real?" he asked.

Her lips gathered into a pout that Rory found marvelous. "I'll show you how real I am," she said.

She drew her hands together again but, before either she or Rory could take action, there came a clattering on the roof behind them. Rory turned in time to see Hel's Chief Minion aiming a nasty-looking tube at Angel. A muffled explosion. A mass of weighted ropes rushed through the air.

It struck Angel full on, wrapped about her, and knocked her from the air. Before Rory could act, the projectile carried her beyond the building's edge into a thirty-five-story fall.

Rory rushed to the parapet and, stretched straight with arms at his side, hurled over the edge after the Angel.

With eighteen stories left he managed to wrap a Thread about her ankles. With fourteen stories left he drew her to him. With nine stories left he threw one end of another weighted Thread toward the building's surface. It caught but broke free.

Frantic, he released it and tried again.

With five stories left the looped Thread jerked against his wrist, nearly dislocating his shoulder. It held. They swung inward, slamming into the cold stone facade with a sound like God's own thunder.

Rory hung there for long seconds, the Angel limp in his arms. Then he shifted her to his shoulders and began the climb back to the roof. The street might be closer but he felt more secure on the heights.

By the time he reached the parapet, the Angel had awakened. He settled her upon the rooftop, cut away the weighted ropes, and stepped back, ready to return to the fight.

She stood, not moving, arms folded across her chest. "You saved my life."

"Yes."

"I was at your mercy. You could have let me die," she said.

Rory reached to his neck, touched the hidden switch to deactivate the voice filter. He cleared his throat and found his normal baritone.

"Why would I want to do that?"

"To get me out of your way."

"Out of the way of what?"

"Your evil machinations," she said. Rory laughed this time.

"You've been reading too many comics," he said. "But then, so have I."

Rory reached up to touch the switch behind his ear. With a hiss, his helmet opened along the back seam and dropped into his waiting hands. Clutching the mask in his left hand, he extended his right hand toward her.

"Hi," he said. "My name's Rory Mathersby and I haven't got machinations of any sort."

She examined his hand for a heartbeat, and held out her own gloved hand.

"Hello. I'm Sheri Parker."

They shook hands. As they did, both took a half-step closer to the other. Rory caught a whiff of her perfume. Oranges. Honey. Almond. He recognized the fragrance. *Angel Innocent*. He had sampled it upon his mother's wrist, during one of their infrequent shopping trips together not long ago.

"I know who you are," Sheri said. "You're the creator of Swath. I saw you once at RiverCon in Pittsburgh."

"That's me."

"Oh, wow! I can't believe it's really you. I have been a fan of Swath for–" Her smile faded just a bit and she examined him, weighing the rightness of the situation.

"Are you sure you aren't a villain?"

"Cross my claws and talons," Rory said.

She laughed. "You're funny. I like you."

"I like you, too." He pulled her toward the parapet and patted the wall beside him as he sat.

"C'mon. Sit down. Let's talk."

She slid onto the stone but did not release his hand.

"Where did you come from?" Rory asked.

"Cleveland," she replied. Rory laughed.

"No, I mean where did Hel's Angel come from?"

"Oh. Hel found me two years ago, furnished all this swell equipment. I've been in training all this time, getting ready to fight you."

"But why?"

"I don't know. I should have asked more questions but I was so taken up by the idea."

They soon were lost in conversation. Neither saw the tiny concealed camera stuck to the elevator housing wall. A red light blinked there, just below the fisheye lens.

Not so far away Hel sat in shadows, watching the rooftop scene unfold upon a video monitor. A tall man dressed in ragged black evening clothes stood close at hand. The Chief Minion.

"Touching, isn't it?" Hel said.

"Indeed, quite touching," the man said. "I trust you were satisfied with my performance?"

"Yes. As always." Hel's attention returned to the monitor. One hand slid from the shadows.

"Look at the lovebirds," Hel said. "I think we've made a match."

The Chief Minion remained silent. He knew his place.

"Time to make our exit," Hel said. "Have the ill-gotten gains been returned?"

"Almost all. Even as we speak, an armored car should be arriving for an unscheduled deposit. That will be the last of it."

"Good. And the video disk has been delivered to the television stations?"

"Yes. The people of Seattle soon will learn that Gargoyle and his Angel have made the town too hot even for the likes of Hel."

"You are a treasure," Hel said.

The Chief Minion nodded, accepting his due. "Thank you. And if I may be allowed to say so, you are a treasure, as well."

Hel smiled and settled back into the powered wheelchair that had been a part of her life for more years now than she cared to remember.

"Goodness, Dillinger," she said. "What else is a mother supposed to do?"

To Each His Niche and Task

Skinny little thing stepping off the yellow bus, all Band-Aid knees and elbows and long black hair. Carrying her books close against her chest as if they could be a shield against the dangers of the world.

Clio Mayne.

What were her parents thinking? No one should burden their children with such names anymore.

Even so it took me weeks to unearth that shard of information. I have to be so careful. Imagine what someone would say if they noticed me.

"Yes, officer, an old man in a pickup truck, watching the girl. Sixty, maybe sixty-five. A big fellow. No. *Big*. Six feet four, maybe two hundred and fifty pounds."

In my dreams, every night for the past five days, the police come to my door, ask why I follow a thirteen-year-old honor student. A girl at that. I tell them the truth. One day soon little Clio will be murdered walking from the bus stop home unless I save her.

They never believe me.

Would you? Would you accept it as truth if I told you that demons walk among us disguised as ordinary people? That God has granted me vision to see them as they are, wisdom to know the intent of their actions and power to defeat them

Of course not.

It doesn't make it any less true. I saw them the first time at nine years old. Two of them pretending to be paramedics came to hurry my grandfather to the hospital when he complained of chest pains. I whispered the truth to my father. "Hush that crazy talk," he said and sent me to my room.

Grandfather died before arrival.

I saw them seven more times over the next six years. Always in groups, as few as two, as many as seven. Each time within a week someone died. I stopped them, for the first time, when I was sixteen, big for my age. Four of them went after a girl from my high school French class. I battered one unconscious with a baseball bat and scattered the others.

I expected to be a hero, even a superhero, someone in tights and a cape. Here's what happened.

When the police were done with me, they turned me over to the psychiatrists. And when they were done with me, a judge committed me to a mental hospital for fifteen years.

They released me just after my thirtieth birthday. "You're cured," they said.

In truth, they had run out of space and interest. All they cured was my willingness to tell the truth. Since then I've rescued forty-seven souls, dispatched two hundred and three demons. In a way I have become super-human, but not in the way I hoped.

I've made headlines. Law enforcement agencies across the country know of me. I've been number one on the FBI's most-wanted list for seven years. My name's been mentioned on that television show. You know the one.

They call me The Cutter, label me a serial killer. It doesn't matter. God gave me a mission all those years ago and I've labored without fail to fulfill it.

In recent months it's become more and more difficult. Not even superheroes live forever. Clio Mayne may be the last I can hope to save.

The bus departs after five more riders scamper off. All demons. Now the vision comes.

They'll attack as she takes her shortcut across a wooded lot. I abandon the truck, leave it in the street even though I know it will attract police, and hurry after them.

She's surrounded, back against a tree, books scattered about her feet. Anyone else come upon the scene would think that five teenage boys were harassing Clio. A suspicious sort might think they planned to rape her. I know the truth.

I shed my duster and wade into them. No battle cries. No fair warning. No spandex. Just jeans and tee shirt and Converse high-tops. And a set of Khukuri blades.

I sever one's spine before they know I'm there. One of the remaining four steps close to Clio, pins her to the tree, and the other three face me. They carry their own weapons, eldritch claws that leave no outward mark. They're wary though. Their kind knows me as The Cutter, too.

I lunge to my right. When two fall back, I spin and attack to my left, chopping off a second demon's head. Another, call it number three, rushes in, raking its claws at me. I pirouette to safety and disembowel it. The fourth demon leaps, claws out and glittering, but I slice its life away.

Even five years ago, it would have been easy work. Tonight I am winded. Before I can recover the remaining demon abandons Clio and falls upon me, stabbing at me with its claws.

They pierce my chest.

My heart stutters in its agony. I lose both Khukuri and we go to the ground together, the demon on top. I fumble through my pain, grasp one leather-wrapped handle, and find the strength to push the demon away. When it falls upon me again, I skewer it upon my blade.

I don't even have the strength to push it away. Everything slows down, begins to lose its color. The empty lot stinks of the battle. Blood and sweat and body wastes. Clio lies six feet away huddled against the tree.

The sirens call, racing ahead of the police. Reporters will be close behind, sticking their noses everywhere, pushing and insensitive. They'll tell the world a crazy old man fell over the edge of sanity and slaughtered five innocent children.

None of them believe in anything other than their careers but they will say, in their pious news-at-eleven voices, "Thank God Clio Mayne survived."

The police will say, "You're a lucky little girl. You escaped the Cutter."

The shrinks will tell her she shouldn't imagine anything else happened here tonight. "There are no monsters," they will say, "Except for men like the one who killed your friends."

She may accept it all, the way they coach her: It's for the best if she does.

But at this instant she's watching me from across the battleground, really seeing me. She knows I gave myself for her, knows I spared her life.

And that will have to do.

Coward's Steel

Wet and dingy snow, gray as the sky from which it fell, lay thick upon everything and a fitful wind plucked at Tate's parka and leggings. She paid no heed. It was miserable business for so late in the season but Jolene had dragged her through worse over their years together.

"Not fit weather for man nor beast," Jolene would say, wading through drifts piled above Tate's waist. *"But you and I aren't either one, are we, Little Girl?"*

The wind eased for the moment and a regular shape off to her left caught Tate's attention. She took a step into the tree line, away from the creek she followed, thumbing the hammer of her pistol as she moved.

An oblong sign, bright white letters upon vivid green, nested in winter-brittled weeds next to a foot bridge. If the sign could be believed, the village of Providence lay just the other side of the bridge.

Tate eased the straps of her pack and holstered the pistol. Growing darkness obscured the far bank of the creek but the bridge remained clear enough. It appeared substantial, well-tended and inviting, but so did the bowl of a pitcher plant. Tate had no intention of playing fly.

"Weigh the risk," Tate said, whispering into the wind. In her mind she could hear Jolene murmur those three words with her, for they had been the first of Jolene's Laws.

Tate might be a child of the chaos in which the world still lingered like a dog wallowing in its own mess, but Jolene had grown up in civilized times. She managed to survive Collapse, rescue five-year-old Tate, and thrive for another twenty-five years because she remained faithful to her Laws.

"You're a lucky little girl I found you grubbing in those ruins," Jolene had said as she stirred the coals of their first campfire together. *"Don't get used to it. Never count on luck."*

That was the Second Law. There were others. Jolene had been a patient, persistent teacher. Tate took her lessons to heart.

As she grew, caution became Tate's religion, Jolene's Laws the word of God. Tate shed no tears the day Jolene died, eleven weeks past now, because tears were forbidden by the Eighth Law. *What's done is done.*

Tate considered the words of the sign, as clean-edged and bright as if painted yesterday.

Jolene's imagined whisper offered counsel. *Something don't set right,*

Little Girl. Scuttlers wouldn't stay long enough to put up signs. Scavengers won't bother.

Tate nodded and tightened the pack straps. She eased to the edge of the creek, avoiding the bridge, worked her way down the embankment and over the narrow run of water, stepping from one slicked rock to another. Providence might be a tempting trap but Tate decided she would accept the risk. She had been without company since Jolene's death and she had a taste for the sound and smell and feel of someone other than herself.

Even so, she would be careful.

The storm blew itself to pieces moments after Tate walked away from the far bank and the sky cleared, revealing a sliver of moon and the spread of stars. Tate pushed through snow-thick undergrowth and came upon a low rise of land.

From the far side, smoke trickled away into the clear night sky. The wind breathed upon wind chimes, then changed direction, and Tate caught the scent of burning pine. The heady aroma of beans and salted pork hung there too.

She topped the rise, taking care not to slip or to be seen in silhouette, and came upon a cluster of cottages with slate roofs and stone chimneys. Around them, yards and gardens were traced beneath the snow.

Never trust neat and tidy, Little Girl.

Tate nodded. The houses and gardens felt less than real, more like canvas false fronts set up by vagabond buskers for their shows. Tate caught the flicker of light and movement off glass; like a mirage in the southern desert, it was gone.

Her nose had not betrayed her. The flickering glow she had mistaken for lamplight was the reflection of a campfire upon the windows. An old woman sat beside the fire at the verge of the village green, stirring the contents of a small pot hung over the flames. Beyond the light Tate could see shadowed grave markers. Row upon row.

There's magic here.

Tate shivered at that notion. She and Jolene had come upon a witch or two in their time together.

She eased forward, ready to bolt, but the Laws did say that it was better to see for yourself than not to know. The old woman looked up without surprise when Tate stepped into the flickering light and moved to within two long strides of the fire.

"Hello," Tate said. Her hand rested near the pistol.

The old woman offered no challenge but held on to a scattergun cradled across her lap. Tate moved away from the line of fire. The weapon had seen better days but was still a threat.

"Hello," the old woman said.

"You alone?" Tate asked.

"Are you?"

"Yeah."

The old woman inclined her head toward the grave markers.

"All gone but me."

"Too bad," Tate said. The old woman shrugged. She stood and Tate took a step backward, put her hand upon the pistol butt.

"Jolene?" she said before she could bite her tongue.

No!

Of course not. Jolene had died and no magic in the world could bring her back. Tate knew that as fact, but the way old woman put one hand behind her back as she stood, the way she tilted her head to study Tate and ran her tongue over her lips as if in anticipation, was so much like Jolene. So much. Tate shook the notion away.

"Can I sit?" she asked. She didn't care for the way that sounded. Too much like begging. "I got meat and bread."

"Go ahead; sit," the old woman replied.

Tate shrugged out of her pack, settling it across the fire from the stump that was the old woman's camp seat, never taking her eyes away from the old woman.

"I'm Tate," she said.

The old woman didn't reply. Instead she returned to the stump and stuck a spoon into the small pot that bubbled over the fire. Tate dropped to her knees and dug smoked venison and a cloth-wrapped slab of cornbread from her pack, then busied herself dividing the food.

"Here," the old woman said.

She had poured beans from the pot onto two camp plates and now held both before her, offering Tate her pick. Tate did the same with the venison and cornbread and then waited for the old woman to take first taste before digging into the beans. They were spiced just the way she liked.

"Good," she said after a time. "Grow them yourself?"

"Plant them in the spring," the old woman said. "Can them in the fall."

When both had their fill and the gear was clean and stowed away, the old woman dug a steel flask from the bag beside her stump. She unscrewed the top and tilted the flask toward Tate.

"Better days," she said by way of a toast, then took a long swig and passed the steel across the fire.

Tate jerked her hand away as a crackling spark arced between them. The old woman ignored it, still holding out the flask, and so Tate reached for it again. There was no second spark. She sniffed the heady aroma and licked the rim. Whiskey. She swallowed a slug and shivered as the alcohol took hold.

"Good stuff," she said as she returned the flask. "You brew that, too?"

"No." The old woman downed another swallow.

"Been here long?" Tate asked.

"Long enough," the old woman replied.

She handed over the flask again, then kicked off her ragged camp shoes and burrowed into a mound of blankets.

"Bank the fire, whether you stay or move on," she said.

Her voice muffled by blankets, only her eyes visible, she squirmed about inside her nest of blankets. She rolled away from Tate and muttered to herself for a time before she was still.

Tate watched it all from the other side of the fire, wrapped in her own blankets. Now and again, she took a sip of the whiskey.

Don't fall asleep here.

Tate jerked upright. How much of the old woman's whiskey had she swallowed? She hefted the flask. Funny, it still felt full. She tried to stand but couldn't seem to get both feet beneath her at the same time.

Don't fall asleep here!

Tate tried again and made it to her knees before tumbling back into her blankets. As she struggled to right herself, she glanced across the fire at the old woman's still form. That hadn't gone well. When she crossed the creek, she had hoped to find company, someone who talked more than the old woman.

Now, Tate wasn't certain what more she could have contributed if the conversation had been more energetic. She had been alone too long. That had to change.

Tate took another pull from the steel flask. She tucked it into her pack, pulled a blanket over her head, and fell away into sleep, ignoring Jolene's insistent whispers.

Her sleep was troubling, filled with strange dreams. A kick to the ribs awakened her. Her thoughts remained fuzzy, her reflexes still slowed by the whiskey. The morning sunlight burned at her eyes. She realized with a start that she had broken the Fourth Law. *Never sleep in the open.*

Now you've done it, Little Girl!

Another kick, this time harder. *What was the old woman up to?*

Tate rolled toward the blow, reaching for her pistol. Gone. She stared into the barrels of a scattershot but her first thoughts of betrayal disappeared when she saw the weapon. Almost new from the look of it and it rested in the hands of a bearded man.

"Don't move," he said.

Tate lay still, more in response to her surprise than to his command. Other folks gathered around the bearded man, men and women and older children, and no sign of the old woman. No trace of a fire either. Instead a large tree, winter dormant but alive, stood where the old woman had sat atop a stump. The gravestones were gone too.

"Mind telling us who you are?" the man asked.

Tell him what he wants to hear!

"My name's Tate," she said. "I'm just looking for supplies and some company; I'll work for both."

Tate held her breath as he studied her for a time. Then he lowered his weapon and extended his right hand to help her climb to her feet. As she did so, he glanced at a heavy-set woman at one end of the semi-circle of people.

"You see, Gracie," he said. "She's just a loner, looking for food and a chance to be around good folk like us."

"If you say so, David," Gracie said.

"Go on," he said. "Tell Old Maggie she can stop chanting."

He's got a witch!

Tate discovered that she was still holding her breath. She sucked in air as David shooed the others away with his hands.

"Go on, all of you," he said. "Back to work."

They left without another glance. Tate had become old news. David gathered up her backpack, handed it to her.

"You can stay," he said. "If you don't make trouble."

"I understand," Tate said.

Of course she understood. The folks here might think the place belonged to them but Tate could see that wasn't so. David owned Providence. He turned away, expecting her to follow.

"You can bed down in the meeting hall," he said. "It's not much but it's warmer than where you slept last night."

Run, Little Girl. Leave right now!

Tate shook her head, not even mindful that it was the first time she had chosen to ignore Jolene's Laws.

"Not just yet," she said, whispering.

Gracie returned with food minutes after David left and stayed to nibble.

"You always welcome strangers like this?" Tate asked. She was gnawing on a link of fried sausage, her fourth.

"David likes you," Gracie said. "That's enough for me." She pushed a small pottery crock toward Tate.

"Try a dab of this mustard on that sausage."

Tate dipped the remains of the sausage link into the crock and popped it into her mouth. Two more followed in five quick bites. She had never tasted the like of it.

Don't get used to it. Can't stay long in one place.

Tate focused on Gracie's words, trying to ignore Jolene's whispers.

"We were in a bad way here until he showed up," Gracie said. She patted away the mustard on her chin with a twist of cloth. "David saved us all."

She took up a forkful of scrambled eggs and studied Tate as she chewed. Tate had seen that look once, summer before last, when she came upon a mama brown bear with two new cubs.

"Don't you ever hurt him, you hear me?" Gracie said.

The biddy is in love with him.

Tate couldn't imagine how she could hurt David, wouldn't be here long enough to even begin, but she held her tongue. That was one of the Laws too. *Don't talk back to magic.*

Gracie had made it clear when she walked into the meeting hall that she was an elder of the women's circle and had a Knack for the Wiccan arts. Old Maggie had more than that.

"She's got a big Talent," Gracie said. "She struck down a drunken drover, dead in his tracks, when he tried to have his way with the McGinnis girl two years ago."

Gracie hesitated, then added, "She was fixing to do the same to you this morning if you had turned out to be up to no good."

All the townsfolk of Providence were as friendly as Gracie. In the days that followed, all of the women and most of the men came by to chat. Old

Maggie dropped by on the third day. She was a little bit of a woman with deep blue eyes, white hair, and an easy smile.

"Could I show you something, Ma'am?" Tate asked.

Old Maggie waved the honorific away. "What is it you want to show me?"

Don't show her!

Tate pulled the flask from her pack and handed it to the old woman, flinching in anticipation of a spark. There was none. Old Maggie turned the flask about in her hands, studying it with her fingers as much as with her eyes.

"Where'd you get this?" she asked.

Lie to her!

"Someone gave it to me to keep." Close enough. Old Maggie studied her for a time.

"You got yourself a powerful piece of magic, Child," she said. "It's an accumulator. I've seen them before but never held one this powerful."

"What's an accumulator?"

"It stores up a magical charge, fills up, you might say, until there's enough. Then it discharges, triggers the spell."

"What sort of spell?"

"Can't say, can't even tell you how long it might take to recharge, not 'til I study it. Can I keep it for a time?"

No!

Tate waved one hand at her ear as if shooing a fly away.

"Yes," She said. "For as long as you need."

Tate soon found there were other sorts of magic afoot in Providence. During the fortnight she slept in the meeting hall, she discovered that her first impression of David had been correct. He did own the place. Everyone in the village deferred to him and Gracie was his biggest fan.

"He's the most natural leader I ever seen," Gracie said between bites of bread slathered in butter and jam. She had brought breakfast around again.

Tate became a reluctant supporter too. David was fair-minded in every dispute he was called upon to settle and gentle every time he took the time to listen to a child's needs. But there was a darker side to David, as well. Three days after Tate arrived, members of the watch brought in two Scuttlers caught trying to steal a cow. David put them in shackles beneath the big tree on the green.

"Willie. Mr. Peterman. Tate," he said, calling to the first three people he saw. "Tell folks it's a town meeting."

Be the boss's little dog. Get him his witnesses.

Tate ignored Jolene's voice and turned to spread the word.

You're falling for him, too! Stupid little girl!

"Shut up!" Tate said, too loud. Tom Peterman glanced at her, one eyebrow raised, then hurried off.

For the first time since Jolene died, Tate wondered if those imagined whispers were signs that she had gone insane, for no matter how she tried, they wouldn't go away.

"Let it be, Jolene," she whispered as she ran. "Please just let me be!"

Tate wasn't surprised when every man, woman, and child, dropped what they were doing to answer the summons. When they were all gathered around the tree on the snow-covered green, David threw two nooses over the biggest limb.

"You fellows got anything to say?" he asked.

The men stood shivering in their chains. Neither wore enough for the weather.

"We was hungry," the bigger man said.

"That's no excuse," David said. "If you had come to us, we would've feed you." He turned to the assembly.

"Anyone have anything to offer in their defense?" he asked.

No one said a word, but neither did they look away from the two men or the tree with its ropes.

"All right," David said. "For your crimes I sentence you both to hang by the neck until dead."

He hoisted the two Scuttlers from the ground one at a time without asking for assistance and left them to swing in the wind. Just after dark, Tate watched from the meeting hall as David cut down the bodies and buried them himself.

Ten days after Tate arrived in Providence, David asked her to handle security for a work crew headed out the next morning to quarry stone for wall repairs. She agreed.

Two wagons shuttled what was dug from the ground back and forth to the village. At midday David and Gracie drove up with the lunch wagon. He stayed to help until work was finished, near to sundown. As the crew walked back to Providence behind the last wagonload, David fell into step beside Tate.

"You handled yourself well today," he said.

Tate waved away the compliment but her pulse quickened. "Didn't do anything. Just stood and watched."

"No," he said. "You were ready to handle trouble."

"It's what I was trained to do," she said.

"Were you a cop before things collapsed?"

Tate knew what a cop was, Jolene had told her stories, and so she laughed. How old did David think she was?

"Did I say something funny?" he asked.

"No," she replied. "You just surprised me."

He laughed, too. "So, a woman of mystery. I like that."

He studied her for a time, as they walked. "What did you do?"

Lie to him!

"I don't like talking about that," Tate said.

There was a shout up ahead and the wagon driver responded. Providence was just ahead.

"Tell you what," David said. "Come to my place for dinner tonight. We can finish this conversation."

No!

"Can you cook?" Tate asked

"Almost as good as Gracie."

"Will I have to tell you all my secrets?"

"Only if you want to." David grinned.

When Tate knocked at his door, she wore a dress Gracie had altered for her. She had spent almost an hour in the bathhouse too, scrubbing away the grime of the road.

David hadn't lied, he was a good cook. Over the meal he asked questions about what he called her 'mysterious past'. She offered ambiguous answers, figured it was a game he wanted to play. Tate was good at games once she knew the rules. She and Jolene had played a lot to pass the time. And so she and David sat up late, talking and laughing. When it was time to sleep, neither suggested she should leave.

The next day David brought her things to his cabin and for six months it was their cabin. David never asked for details of Tate's past again.

She came to feel that she had known Providence and David for every moment of her life. She could think of nothing she wanted so much as to stay, but Jolene would not allow it.

Her whispers gnawed at Tate day and night, calling disaster down upon her, so that Tate felt it pressing in upon her like the crumbling walls of an old well. She mumbled to herself without pause when she was alone, could not find sleep for more than a few hours at a stretch, and all but stopped eating.

That last bothered Gracie most of all.

"You got to eat," Gracie said after Tate pushed away her plate at lunch one day. Gracie was almost to tears. "If you don't eat, you'll die!"

Tate was certain that would happen but not because of hunger. Tate was going to have to leave; even her love for David could not stand against the mounting pressure of Jolene's whispers. And when she left, a piece of her would perish.

David rested on his side, his right arm thrown across Tate's stomach. She had never been more aware of his closeness. She could feel his heartbeat from his wrist laid upon her bare skin and she listened to the soft snore he swore he did not possess. The bed was full of their smells, commingled into something that was both intoxicating and comforting, but she found no comfort now. She had not slept, of course. That would come after she was away from Providence.

In his sleep David rolled onto his back, pulling his arm away from her.

Time to go!

Tate was sick to death of Jolene's whispers but she slid from the bed and pulled her clothing on. Her travel gear waited outside the village. She could avoid the watch, and even if she didn't, she wouldn't be questioned. She had become a part of the community, after all.

That thought brought her no comfort. She eased into the kitchen, where she pulled on her boots. Then she scooped a package of bread and sausage from the pantry and turned to leave. David stood in the doorway, sleep rumpled and hairy.

"Were you going to leave without saying goodbye?" he asked.

Tell him yes.

"I figured you'd try to talk me out of it if I told you."

"Wouldn't even try," he said.

"I'm sorry."

"So am I." He rubbed at the underside of his jaw with the knuckles of his left hand. Watching the familiar gesture almost brought Tate to tears.

"Do one last thing for me, will you?" David asked.

"What's that?"

"Stay long enough for us to give you a proper send off?"

Leave now!

"All right," Tate said. "One more day."

Just as they had come together to witness her arrival, the folks of Providence gathered in the morning sunshine to see her off. After all the goodbyes, David, Gracie and Old Maggie walked Tate to the bridge. There were tears in Gracie's eyes as she hugged Tate and she held on as if they stood in hurricane winds and she would blow away without Tate as an anchor.

"I put a little something in your pack," she said. "Sausage and cheese and bread. Some of my mustard, too. Just in case you get hungry."

Get on with it!

Gracie wasn't the only with a gift. David offered Tate a paper-wrapped parcel. She made to stuff it into her pack, as well, but he wouldn't have that.

"Open it now," he said. "It's from Old Maggie and me."

So Tate undid the string and paper and found the flask. It wasn't like new, it never would be again, but the worst of the scratches had been smoothed and the seams repaired. Tate held it in both hands, not knowing what to say.

"Told you first time I seen it it was an accumulator," Old Maggie said. "Now I can tell you it's got some sort of traveling spell cast on it."

"If you would have stayed, I might have figured out what it did," she said. "Maybe when the time's right it'll bring you back to us." She squeezed Tate's hand and stepped away.

"I did the repairs and polishing," David said. "And it's full of whiskey. Old Maggie blessed it, says it won't ever empty."

Behind him Old Maggie nodded. A single tear eased its way along the seams of her cheek.

"I read once we leave a part of ourselves in everything we craft," David said. "Maybe there's a touch of us in there with the whiskey."

Tate stepped toward him then and moved into his arms. They stood together in silence, leaning on each other, and she rested her head against his chest, absorbing the beating of his heart.

Enough! Get a move on.

Tate pushed free. It felt as if a part of her had ripped away.

"I have to go," she said.

He nodded, not looking away. "Uh huh."

Without another word, she turned to the south and slipped off into the clear morning light.

Two days later Tate found burned wagons and dead bodies. The remains of a Scavenger attack. There had been twenty wagons, the bodies were all adult and male. A group of traders. She had never seen or heard of a Scavenger band large enough to do this much damage.

It frightened her, not knowing which direction the Scavengers were headed. An hour later, careful scouting showed her they were headed to the northeast. Toward Providence.

Tate retracing her path; moving with haste, without thought for the Laws. Jolene's voice shrieked, weaving old webs of control, but Tate's own voice was louder, calling her to account for leaving David to follow the whispers of a dead woman.

Fourteen hours later, exhausted and near hysteria, she staggered to the top of the rise from which she had first seen Providence. Even as she covered the last few feet, she could smell her failure.

Below her the village lay in ruin, slate roofs smashed, doors and windows gone, and bodies crumpled everywhere. The meeting hall was on fire and the light from the flames flickered on broken windowpanes.

Dusk came before she gathered the courage to walk those last few paces, stepping over the bodies. She found David, swinging by a noose from the large tree in the commons. Gracie and Old Maggie lay nearby. Horrible things had been done to them. Tate cut David down and sat on the ground beneath the tree, his head cradled in her lap, sipping from the steel flask until the light was gone.

Over the following days Tate kept busy with details. She buried David and the others in graves dug on the village green. She cleaned the lanes, rebuilt the burned-out bridge, planted the gardens, and restored cottages as best she could. When all else was done, she cut the oak tree down to a stump because she couldn't stand the sight of it.

She stayed on then, sleeping in the remains of the meeting hall. As she worked, she came around to the notion that David hadn't been playing a game that night he teased her about being his mystery woman. Maybe he and the people of Providence had known the world before Collapse. Maybe that winter night, at the fire with the old woman, that spark had sent her tumbling into enchantment and she had been carried back to a time when the child Tate was off somewhere, still learning Jolene's Laws.

Who knows what's possible with magic?

And with that thought she realized who the old woman had been.

Tate sat amidst the ghosts of Providence, nursing a small fire, as she had done every winter's night for so many years she had lost count.

During those years she had visitors. Traders, tinkers, wizards, witches, alchemists, and adventurers had come and gone. She conducted business with some and sent all on their way, for none had been the one for whom she waited.

This night she looked up without surprise, as a young woman walked out of the darkness and approached the fire. Tate made no move to challenge the younger woman but she retained her grip on David's old scattergun. The weapon had seen better days. Its stock was wrapped in duct tape, the shoulder strap a frayed piece of rope, but it still worked.

The younger woman stopped short of the fire. "Hello," she said.

"Hello," Tate said.

"You alone?" the younger woman asked.

"Are you?"

"Yeah."

Tate inclined her head toward the grave markers. "All gone but me."

"Too bad," the younger woman said. Tate slipped one hand behind her back for support as she stood, tilted her head to study the younger woman, and ran her tongue over her lips. Wetting her whistle, Jolene used to call it.

The younger woman took a step backward, put her hand upon her pistol butt.

"Jolene?" she said.

Tate shrugged away the words. This was the one. There had been and would be magic after all.

"Can I sit?" the younger woman asked. "I got meat and bread."

"Go ahead, sit," Tate said.

Her voice sounded raspy, rusted once more from disuse. The younger woman stared for just a moment, then nodded and shrugged out of her pack, dropping it beside the fire.

"I'm Tate," the younger woman said.

Tate didn't bother to answer. There was no hurry now, no need for conversation. She returned to the stump, stirring the small pot until its contents began to bubble, then she poured the hot beans onto two metal camp plates. By the time she was done, the younger woman had dug smoked venison and a cloth-wrapped slab of cornbread from her pack and had divided it into two portions. They shared the food and began to eat.

"Good," the younger woman said after a time. "Grow them yourself?"

"Plant them in the spring," Tate said. "Can them in the fall."

When both had their fill, Tate dug her flask from the bag beside her stump. She ran her finger over its surface, wondering how many more times it could be restored, how much longer it would continue to fuel the enchantment into which she had fallen. She unscrewed the top and tilted the flask.

"Better days," she said. She took a swig.

When she passed the open flask, there was a sharp spark that made them both jump, but still the younger woman took the flask and drank. The younger woman sighed, enjoying the bite of the whiskey, and returned the flask.

"Been here long?" the younger woman asked.

"Long enough," Tate said.

She downed more whiskey and handed over the flask for the last time. As the younger woman accepted it, Tate sighed. The younger woman was no longer her concern. She had passed the steel and its magic had begun once more.

Without waiting for the return of her property, Tate kicked off her camp shoes and crawled into the sleeping gear already laid out by the fire. She could finish this business now.

"Bank the fire, whether you stay or go," she said.

Tate pulled a tiny glass vial from between her breasts, where it had hung over her heart for half a lifetime.

"You'll fall asleep and never wake," the alchemist said the day she purchased it.

She removed its stopper, let the liquid trickle into her mouth, and felt its bite within seconds. Burrowing in the blankets, she began to murmur the words to an old song she had learned from Jolene so long ago. A lullaby.

A moment later she was gone.

The Fluting Man

Nadine and Geordie came upon the naked woman hunkered in the moonlight on the edge of Lake Shore Road.

"What the hell is this about?" Geordie asked. He eased off the gas and tapped the horn.

The naked woman didn't seem to notice, didn't move an inch.

"Stop ahead of her so she's out of the headlights," Nadine said. "Let her keep some shred of dignity."

Geordie allowed the foundation's aging minivan to roll past the naked woman and coaxed it to the gravel berm. "You see that yellow flash, lit up the sky when we came round the curve?"

"I saw it," Nadine said.

"Think she set it off?"

"We'll see."

Nadine twisted in the passenger seat to peer through the rear window. The naked woman remained facing away from them, folded on herself, arms upon her knees, head pressed against her forearms.

Geordie glanced into the rearview mirror. "She dead?"

"Damn it, Geordie, I said we'll see."

Nadine threw open the door and jumped out before the van came to a full stop. She stalk along the berm with a distinctive forward tilt and her long-legged stride ate up distance. Her eyes and skin and hair bore witness to Native American blood. Outsiders knew her tribe as Ojibwe. They called themselves *Anishinaabe*. The First People.

The right rear brake squealed at Nadine as she passed by, demanding new pads. Another niggling expense she'd be forced to explain to tribal elders at the next council session.

"Goddamn it, Nadine. Wait for me," Geordie shouted.

Nadine could deal with brakes, could deal with the elders' questions, but Geordie's hectoring had begun to piss her off. He worked for her but he always had believed he knew the right way to do everything. And since New Year's Eve, when Nadine rebuffed his fumbling advances, his need to argue had turned habitual.

Why do it that way? Are you sure? That will never work.

"It's too cold to wait," Nadine shouted back at him.

The fine hairs inside her nose prickled with the late March chill upon the north wind. Nadine caught the scent of deep water overlaid by the pungent aroma of evergreen. A shadowed line of trees, jack pines from the smell, hid Lake Superior from her.

The night calmed for a moment. Nadine swore she heard the trilling of a flute, played with some sort of tribal cadence. Then sound disappeared in the renewed fury of the wind. It swept off the Lake with a keening of lost souls and slashed through the layers of denim, wool, and cotton that Nadine wore.

She shrugged away the chill (Grandfather had taught her how) and focused on the sound of that flute. A familiar shiver tiptoed up her spine as her mind's eye traced the cadence and she saw the threads of magic wrapped about it. She had almost missed it, fuming over brake pads and Geordie's attitude.

Grandfather would have sensed the magic the instant he stepped from the van. Joseph John Rainwater had been Midewiwin, a tribal shaman. He died before Nadine turned twelve but by then he'd taught her to appreciate the world's complexity, to see the threads of magic woven through it all.

Nadine stopped an arms-length from the naked woman. "Are you all right?"

The naked woman remained silent. The round double curve of her pale bottom pressed into the gravel. Her short-cut russet hair looked to be her sole touch of color.

Nadine shucked her surplus-store watch coat, held it out. "Wrap up in this."

The naked woman looked back over the curve of her shoulder. Nadine shivered again but not because she sensed magic. Long-stifled passions stirred within her. At first sight, she fell into the woman's emerald eyes. Nadine longed to stroke the woman's shining hair and perfect skin, to share kisses and whispered secrets. Grandfather would have smiled and said she'd been struck by the thunderbolt.

"Thank you," the woman said.

Her voice creaked like a twisted wooden gate, words thick with an odd accent. She wriggled her arms into the warmed sleeves of the coat and pulled the soft, dark wool about her.

Nadine leaned in close and caught the pungent aroma of vanilla upon the woman's skin and hair. It sparked memories of the hand-churned ice cream Grandfather brought home from the tribal meeting hall most Saturdays when Nadine was a little girl.

"I asked if you're all right."

The woman shivered at the touch of Nadine's warm words upon her ear. She stood, wobbling with effort. "I will be."

Nadine reached to steady the woman. The woman jerked away as a static spark arced between them. Nadine stood her ground.

"Let's get you into the van," she said.

The woman turned and the borrowed coat gaped. A tattoo, a stylized man done in silvered ink, nested between her breasts. The capering figure was endowed with an enormous phallus and played a flute. A line of tattooed links, the shadow of a chain, rose from the fluting man's hunched shoulders to circle the woman's neck.

Heavy threads of magic bound the tattoo to the woman, magic of a nature more powerful and more complex than any Nadine had ever witnessed.

The woman placed her hand palm-down over the tattoo as she looked past Nadine. Her full, sweet lips curled into a smile, her green eyes widened, and she drew her shoulders back. Working in that Detroit clinic while in college, Nadine had seen street junkies come alight in just that way at the sight of their next needle.

"Are you injured, Miss?" Geordie asked.

The woman stepped around Nadine to where Geordie towered, one long stride away. He radiated comfort and safety, as if a beacon for some wayfarers' shelter.

"I'm not injured," the woman said. "I'm fine."

Her words were less accented, less formal. She offered her right hand and Geordie took it in his big paw. She moved close into the fearsome heat he radiated and gazed up into his broad, blond-bearded face.

"Name's Geordie Cartwright." He smiled.

The woman stepped even closer, almost pressed herself to him. "My name is Beatha Weaver."

Every happy notion that occurred to Nadine in the moments after she set eyes on Beatha, every hopeful thought of love, flew away like powdered snow before a winter wind. Geordie might not be clever but Nadine could see he understood the meaning of the moment. He held the power now.

Nadine desired Beatha and Beatha would be his instead.

Nadine stood on the beach below Point Iroquois Lighthouse. To the south the trees were thick with green. The June breeze off the Lake carried a hint of August heat to come and the sky's inverted bowl shone a clear and shining cornflower blue.

A team of volunteers scoured the beach clearing debris from a recent storm. Geordie worked at the east end of the beach, alone, wrestling a bulky piece of driftwood.

Since the night on Lake Shore Road his relationship with Nadine had eroded even further. Their conversations had become guarded, limited to business of the Upper Peninsula Foundation, the tribe's land reclamation agency that Nadine directed.

Beatha was the cause, of course. She'd remained in Brimley since that night, working with Nadine and Geordie, one recovery project to another. She'd said she had nowhere else to go but Nadine could see the threads. Beatha stayed for another reason.

She might sleep in Nadine's guest room but Beatha spent every waking moment with Geordie, often didn't come home until early hours. Those nights Nadine cursed herself for sitting up as if she were an anxious mother or an angry lover.

That would end today.

Nadine planned to confront Beatha, to demand answers, if Geordie gave them time alone. The big fool followed Beatha as if an overgrown puppy, growling when someone else came too close. Nadine in particular. He'd become over-protective, controlling, more so than ever before. Nadine would have found his attentions stifling. Beatha didn't seem to mind.

"Can we talk, Nadine?"

Nadine spun about. Beatha stood an arms-length away.

"All right. What do you want?"

"Advice."

Nadine sat and patted the sun-warmed sand beside her. "Step into my office."

Like the others Beatha wore nothing but a swimsuit and old sneakers. Her once-pale skin showed substantial tan, her tattoo lay upon her bronzed skin as a silver shadow. She settled to the sand, came to rest with legs crossed. Their knees touched and Nadine's heart began a stutter-step. She held still, afraid if she moved the contact would be lost.

"Geordie asked me to marry him," Beatha said.

"Did you say yes?"

"I couldn't—" Beatha glanced down the beach at Geordie.

"What can't you tell him?"

Beatha's hand went to her chest and covered the fluting man.

"It's your tattoo," Nadine said.

"Yes." Beatha watched Nadine's face. She held her breath, waiting, expecting something.

"I already know that it's magic," Nadine said.

Beatha leaned close. "You believe in magic?"

"I grew up believing."

Beatha hugged Nadine. When she drew back Nadine could still feel the heat of the embrace.

"I knew you'd be the one," Beatha said. "I tried to tell Geordie. He laughed, told me not to talk crazy."

Nadine nodded but didn't say a word. Her grandfather used to say you could over-water a blooming plant.

"I'm not from this world," Beatha said. "Where I come from, everyone believes."

Nadine peeked down the beach. Geordie remained on his knees but had stopped digging. "Tell me more."

Beatha ran her fingers over the fluting man. "This is more than a tattoo. It's a symbol of the magic that pulls me world to world."

"World to world?"

"Yes, all different versions of Earth, a multitude."

Nadine glanced down the beach again. Geordie looked toward them now, brushing sand from his hands. Time to push a bit. "Why did you leave?"

Beatha, caught up in her confession, didn't seem to notice Geordie's scrutiny. "I hit a man I knew. He raped me and I hit him with a baseball bat."

Her voice carried the rasping note Nadine first heard that night on Lake Shore Road.

"Did you kill him?"

"No! I did break his arm, but laws are different there."

Beatha began to cry. Nadine leaned close to knuckle away the tears, knowing Geordie would see her, knowing it would cost far more than she could afford to pay.

"Go on," she said.

"He was a vested citizen. I wasn't. What he did cost him a fine. They planned to throw me into prison."

Geordie climbed to his feet and headed toward them. Not much time left now.

"And?"

"I couldn't go to jail. So I stole an enchantment. It carried me away and here I am."

Geordie would arrive in seconds.

"Your tattoo's the medallion," Nadine said.

"Yes, and I can't take it off."

"Why not?"

Beatha leaned close again. "It's only solid twice a year, at the equinoxes. That's when it works its magic, when the line between worlds is thinnest. I can't even touch it then. It's like trying to handle smoke."

Beatha paused to wipe at her eyes. Geordie would blame Nadine for the tears.

"I have to stay this time," Beatha added. "I love him."

"I'll help," Nadine promised. "We'll figure something out."

"What're you two whispering about?"

Beatha looked up at Geordie. "Nothing."

Nadine worked to keep her words light. "Offering advice on how to handle you. You know. Girl stuff."

Geordie's nostrils spread, his eyes narrowed. He did that little shuffle step Nadine knew so well, the dance he did when angry. He glared at her from beneath his shaggy brows. "You'd know all about that, wouldn't you?"

Nadine could only stare back, mouth open, stung by the venom in his words.

Geordie bent and hoisted Beatha to her feet with no more effort than if she had been a child. He didn't look away from Nadine. "All right, Beatha, time to say goodbye."

Nadine waited on the sofa when Geordie brought Beatha home. He walked her to the door but didn't come inside. Nadine heard his retreating footsteps, heard Beatha ease the door shut, but didn't hear the deadbolt click and lock.

Beatha stepped into the arch between the hall and living room. "He's still out there, waiting for me to get my things."

"Uh huh."

"He's going to quit his job tomorrow."

Nadine set her book aside but didn't say a word.

"He's very angry," Beatha said. "He called you queer. I've never heard that word used that way before."

"Did he tell you what it means?"

Beatha nodded. "That you enjoy sex with other women. It's not uncommon, world to world. He doesn't like it. He said you want me, that you'd do anything to break us up."

"I've never said a word to you against him."

"I know. I told him that. It just made him angrier."

"What are you going to do?"

Beatha studied Nadine's face. "Is it true? Do you love me?"

Nadine couldn't catch a breath, could only whisper. "Yes."

Beatha shifted foot to foot. "He said I've got to choose. He's so insistent. I think he's afraid of you."

"Are you afraid of me?"

"Nadine, please understand. I love you more than I've ever loved another woman, but not that way."

Nadine nodded, fighting back tears. "Where will you go?"

"He'll rent a place for me at his apartment building in Sault Sainte Marie, just until we're married."

"God, Beatha! He orders you around, pulls on strings like you're a puppet. He's become a tyrant. How can you stand it?"

"You're wrong. He just wants me to be safe. I think it's sweet. He's the gentlest, kindest man I've ever known."

"What are you going to do about the fluting man? How can I help you if you go away?"

Beatha's jaw tightened. "This is hard enough. Would you push decisions on me, too?"

Nadine could smell Beatha's fear and anger layered on her own. She drew a breath. "No. Come on, I'll help you pack."

After that Nadine and Beatha only spoke by telephone, hurried conversations during stolen moments. *I found a book at the library. There's a good site on the Internet about the trickster gods. The fellow in Detroit who's supposed to be an expert is a fraud.*

The second Saturday in July Nadine's cell phone chimed as she set riprap cages along an eroding stream bed south of Paradise. She swiped her muddy hand along her jeans and snatched up the phone.

"Bad news," Beatha said. "Geordie found work in Wisconsin, a place called Tomahawk. We move next week."

Their furtive phone conversations continued long-distance.

"I've been working on him," Beatha said when she called the first of August. "He's agreed to have the wedding there in Brimley and he'll let you be maid-of-honor, too."

"Isn't the bastard generous," Nadine muttered.

"Don't call him that!"

"I'm sorry." She wasn't, but she held her tongue.

Over the fleeting weeks they uncovered bits and pieces of information about the fluting man. Native American tribes all had a special name for the demi-god known as the trickster.

Nanabozo. Coyote. Raven. Kokopelli.

The last turned out to be a humpback flute player, the trickster of the Hopi Nations, an intermediary between the gods and man who could travel between worlds.

So much information but Beatha and Nadine couldn't find a single word to tell them how to break the curse.

Three days until Labor Day weekend. Lawns still green, trees thick with leaves, but now in all the shades of waning warmth. It might be August but summer had slid away and darkness crept round earlier each day.

The autumnal equinox approached.

Beatha called just before dark. "Geordie's in the shower," she whispered through the phone. "I only have a few minutes but I found the book we need."

"Tell me."

"It's called *Common Threads*, by a man named Crosshill. I heard of it from a fellow on the Internet."

"A new book?"

"Nineteen-fifty. It's out of print."

"Then what good does it do us?"

"There's a copy in the reserve collection at the University of Colorado. Fellow said he's seen it. It's got a whole chapter on Kokopelli, *three pages* about the fluting man."

"How do we get it?"

"I called the university. They never loan it out. One of us has to go to Boulder."

"You mean I have to go."

Beatha didn't answer right away. When she did her voice sounded small. "I'm sorry."

"Don't be. I'm already on the plane."

Nadine waited to call Beatha until after she returned from Colorado. She'd needed time to think.

Beatha answered on the first ring, her words a rush. "Such perfect timing. Geordie's at the drug store. Are you still in Colorado?"

"No, I'm home."

"Why did you wait? Never mind. Did you get to see the book? Did you hold it in your hands?"

"Yes."

"Oh, I want so much to read it!"

"I made lots of notes. I'll tell you everything." The lie almost shattered Nadine's heart.

"Oh, Nadine, I love you!"

Nadine wished that could be true, wished that Beatha would find it in her heart someday to forgive Nadine's deception.

She couldn't tell Beatha that Crosshill claimed only two ways existed to break the curse. First, the curse would be lifted if the traveler died. The second was just as horrible. The medallion had to be touched to the bared flesh of a new traveler so that the curse could be passed along.

Late September turned chilly, but come wedding day the sky cleared and the sun warmed everything. Nadine and Beatha stood upon the flagstone veranda outside the tribal hall. To the north, late-afternoon light glistened on the calm waters of Lake Superior. Inside, the reception band rocked the building.

Beatha's eyes kept darting to her watch. She sighed. "I can't imagine not having this thing around my neck."

"You'll get used to it," Nadine said.

Beatha grinned, did a little three-step jig. "And I have you to thank for that. Oh, Nadine, I do love you."

"And I love you."

"What're you two whispering about?" Geordie had snuck up on them again. Beads of sweat clung to his shaggy brow and beard. His shirt lay open to the third button. Nadine could see the blond, curly hair thick over his heart.

"Just girl talk," Beatha said.

Geordie stared at Nadine, daring her to say a word. He gestured to Beatha. "Come on. It's time to open gifts."

"Give us a few more minutes."

"*Now*, Beatha." He grabbed her hand, pulled her through the doors into the room.

"Nadine!" Beatha reached out with her free hand, panic clear in her eyes.

Nadine hurried after them. She raised her voice against the music and the noise, worried he'd pretend he didn't hear her, afraid they'd both lose Beatha if he didn't stop. "Geordie!"

Three years listening to her give orders had set a partial hook. Geordie slowed but didn't stop. He looked back. "What?"

Good enough.

Nadine caught up just as her watch alarm began to beep. The moment of the equinox. The tattoo shimmered and became a solid silver thing. Beatha's fingers scrabbled at her breast but passed through the fluting man.

Nadine had better luck. She gathered the medallion in her fist and tugged it free. It lay upon her palm, thick-wrapped in threads of magic more substantial than she had ever seen.

Beatha cried out in triumph. Geordie started and pulled Beatha to him. She nestled in, began to offer thanks, then saw that Nadine still clutched the fluting man.

"The medicine bag, Nadine. Put it in the bag!"

That a bandolier bag would shield the magic had been part of Nadine's lie. She shook her head. "That won't stop it."

"But you said—" Beatha's eyes grew wide. She stepped in front of Geordie, shielding him.

Nadine shook her head. "It will be over in a minute."

She stepped in tight and reached out with her free hand, traced the line of Beatha's jaw with her knuckles, skin on skin, then pressed the fluting man to her own breast.

Other sounds faded into a measured woodwind trill. Memories of vanilla ice cream overwhelmed every conscious thought and the world shattered into shards of lemon light.

When they came upon her, she knelt naked on a littered asphalt berm within the actinic light of a high streetlamp.

Five of them climbed from the six-wheeled automobile. Two men in dark form-fitted suits, three women swathed in bright brocaded gowns. A city skyline lay beyond them, lights reflected on a cut of water. Threads of magic floated on the wind.

"Are you fit and well, Ma'am?" one of the men asked.

"I will be," Nadine replied.

The man offered support. Nadine ignored him and stood on her own, wobble-legged.

"Here now," the oldest of the women said. "She'll catch her death, standing about this time of year unclothed."

The women stepped in close, screening Nadine from the men. The oldest held out a cloak, emerald wool lined with fleece the color of spring leaves.

"Wrap up in this green mantle," the oldest woman said. "And keep that thing covered. It's in poor taste."

Nadine turned away and the oldest woman helped her with the cloak. As it closed about her, shielding her from chilly autumn winds, her own body heat began to gather. She felt the wind ruffle her unfettered hair, felt the rough asphalt against the soles of her bare feet. And she felt, would always feel, the sleek texture of Beatha's skin.

The oldest woman touched Nadine's shoulder. "Mind what I told you now. No one wants to see that little fellow's dingus."

"I'll remember," Nadine said.

And she pulled the green cloak close to hide her silvered tattoo of the humped-back fluting man.

The Mixture

Tires crunched driveway stone. A black sedan appeared at the gate.

On the porch, Eva Jean Dickens eased back and forth in her rocking chair, waiting. Whoever was in the car would come to her soon enough.

A pitcher of lemonade rested on a table next to her chair. Another rocker waited at the opposite side of the table. Beside the pitcher an ice-laden glass stood ready to be filled.

Eva Jean sipped from her own glass and sighed. She loved the sweet-sour tang of her family's secret recipe, what Granny June had called The Mixture.

Over the years Eva Jean's many visitors had come to ask for other information and begged her for the recipe.

If she felt the proper rapport had been established, Eva Jean might provide the proportions of fresh-squeezed lemon juice to sugar to water. Twice she felt a strong enough connection to reveal that she sweetened The Mixture with raw brown sugar. But only a special few learned of the other secret ingredients.

This visitor seemed to want to take his time. Eva Jean saw him watching her through the automobile's tinted windows. After living one hundred years, the rest of her might need a tune-up but her natural eyesight had remained as sharp as the Second Sight God had given her the day she turned twelve. Not all the women of her family had been blessed, but for those that were, the gift first manifested itself the day menstrual flow began.

"You'll not see everything," Granny June said that first day. "Only God sees everything. Even so, what you see will come to pass."

Eva Jean soon discovered the difficult thing about witnessing the future. Seeing the bad things to come for people she loved. She had thrown herself into Granny June's arms the day she foresaw the old woman's death, begged to be told it wasn't true.

"It'll be just like you saw it, Child," Granny June said. "I saw it too, and there's nothing to be done."

Granny June had been right.

Eva Jean had foreseen the deaths of Granny June, her parents, brothers, and sisters. Her husband Alfie too, and four of their six children. She had come to terms with it all.

Early on she decided not to hide her light under a bushel basket. And since word has a way of getting around, she soon was sharing her insights with the occasional visitor, telling each what they could stand to hear, refusing money even from those folk willing to pay.

The fellow made up his mind, stepped from the automobile. He stood no taller than her own five feet, six inches, couldn't weigh much more than she did but Eva Jean could see that he was a hard man. Not the sort to be slighted. He sauntered to the porch and stopped short of the stairs.

He looked fit, a year of so either side of forty years old, and dressed in jeans, a black tee shirt and windbreaker. He'd clipped his burnt-butter hair short and combed it flat.

His clean-shaven face had a weathered look about it. His eyes were the golden brown of new motor oil. Eva Jean caught the scent of almonds and cinnamon. Some sort of aftershave, most likely.

"Afternoon, Mrs. Dickens," he said.

She nodded. No need for a formal reply and Eva Jean was not insulted by his directness. She didn't know who he was but she knew why he had come.

"My name is Jackson Tyler," he said. "May I sit with you?"

"Welcome to my home, Mr. Tyler," Eva Jean said. "Would you like a glass of lemonade?"

Tyler climbed to the porch and settled into the second rocker. His smile was bright enough to make fine print readable.

"Yes, Ma'am," he said. "I've been waiting for that offer for some time now."

She filled the extra glass from the pitcher, handed it to him. Tyler took a sip, his eyes widened and he drained the glass in one extended swallow. He returned the emptied glass to the table and Eva Jean refilled it without asking if he wished more.

"Pardon my manners," Tyler said. His eyes moved between his glass and her face. "I was told about The Mixture, but being told and tasting are not the same."

Eva Jean glanced toward the glass, giving permission. Ice clinked against its sides as Tyler took another long swallow. He rested his hand and the half-full glass upon the arm of the rocking chair.

"We have a mutual acquaintance," he said.

"Reverend Davidson," she said.

Tyler's eyes flicked about the porch before he continued. "His visit last week, the two of you talked about things he has decided he would prefer no one else knew."

"And he's sent you by to make sure I keep quiet."

"Yes, Ma'am. I am so sorry."

"I am, too."

They sat in silence for ten seconds, Eva Jean keeping time with the cadence of her rocker, then she took the glass from Tyler's quivering hand. He offered no resistance.

"Don't struggle," she said. "It won't help."

She eased back and forth in the rocker, counting again. "Mr. Tyler, there's just time to tell you. It's two heaping tablespoons of brown sugar, moistened with a teaspoon of vanilla and a jigger of corn whiskey, added to the juice of six lemons and three quarts of spring water. The whiskey is my addition to the recipe."

She wasn't certain if he could still hear her. It didn't matter. She'd learned that from sad experience. This wasn't the first time a man like Jackson Tyler had come to visit.

And alcohol wasn't the only thing Eva Jean had learned to add to The Mixture.

Calling Forth the King

Gracie fiddled with air flow to her side of the Mercedes. "Mama's talked to Elvis," she said.

"Is that so?" Jerry, Gracie's step-father, thumbed down the volume on the radio—classic rock 105.9—but didn't look away from traffic.

The silver S-Class sedan rolled east on the I-185 causeway, headed to Miami Beach. Jerry drove with the same casual ease he had employed to maneuver through the crowd in the Delta terminal at Miami International.

Gracie pushed her sunglasses higher on her nose. "That's what she told me. You see him?"

"If he's been dropping by, he hasn't said a word to me."

"She said he comes to visit every day. It's all she talked about yesterday on the phone."

Jerry shrugged. "Doesn't surprise me one little bit. She's taking a lot of medication."

He'd been waiting when Gracie cleared the arrivals gate his thick, silver hair shining like a beacon. Jerry always had been what Gracie's mother Maureen called "a looker". Most men his age had thickened around the middle, thinned on top. Jerry remained tall, broad-shouldered, fit, and narrow-waisted.

"I wish I could have been here to meet him," Gracie said.

Jerry grinned. The lines around his eyes and mouth hinted that he did it often. "Wouldn't that have been something?"

They drove for a while in silence.

"This car smells new," Gracie said at last.

"Ten days old. Got it just before Christmas."

"Did you fill up the ashtrays on the old one?"

"Darlin' girl, when you get as old as me and your mama, you'll see money's no good for anything but spending."

Gracie asked the question they'd both been avoiding since they hugged at the airport. "The doctors say how long she's got?"

Jerry drew a deep breath, exhaled it in a short, hard blast. "No. They just keep saying she's gonna die real soon."

152

It all came at them fast.

Thanksgiving at Faith's house in Tupelo, Maureen admitted her doctor wanted to do some tests. "I'm going into the hospital soon as we get back to Miami, get it over with before Christmas."

The family canceled their celebration December twenty-fifth at Gracie's place in Pensacola because Maureen remained in the hospital, fussing with the doctors about treatment.

On New Year's Eve she went home. Jerry called Gracie to report that the doctors couldn't do a thing to keep Maureen from giving up her life to lung cancer, one grudged minute at a time.

"She in a lot of pain?" Gracie asked.

Jerry took his eyes from the I-185 traffic long enough to glance her way. He shrugged. "You know your mama. She wouldn't say it hurt if you pounded a ten-penny nail into her forehead."

"Jerry, don't try to sell me something. Is she in pain?"

"You sound just like her."

"Don't change the subject."

He glanced at her again, didn't shrug this time. "Anybody else would have closed the deal by now. She's hanging on to give you and your sisters time to visit one last time."

The first time Gracie saw Jerry Landis, she had been seven. He had just turned twenty-eight, three years older than Maureen, and just moved to town to sell real estate. Everybody said he had a nose for business, went after what he wanted with a rush some Tupelo folks thought improper.

"Too up north," they said, even though everybody knew he came from Memphis.

It soon became clear Jerry wanted Maureen. "Come work for me," he offered, early on a Saturday outside the Piggly Wiggly. He had been in town a week, had bumped into Maureen and Gracie three times already.

Maureen didn't even hesitate. "All right. It's got to beat car-hopping at Sherer's Drive-in."

Friday, that first week, Maureen came home flushed and excited, telling Gracie what happened before the door to their two-room apartment swung closed. "Jerry invited us to dinner."

She settled her purse in its accustomed place on the side table beside the door, kicked off her heeled shoes.

Gracie scooped them up to carry to the closet without looking away from Maureen. "What did you say?"

"I said, 'I have a little girl.' He said, 'I noticed.'"

Maureen sat at the chrome-legged table in the kitchen nook, sparked a cigarette before she said another word. Gracie handed her mother a glass of iced tea. Maureen held it to her forehead, rolled it back and forth. She brushed Gracie's forearm with her wrist.

"Then what?" Gracie asked.

"Then I said, 'Elvis Presley is her father.' He said, 'I've heard that. Want to bring her along?'"

That first time, the three of them went to eat, then to a movie. Elvis and Donna Douglas in Frankie and Johnnie. They stopped for ice cream on the way home.

"Don't that beat all," some folks said. "And her with that child out of wedlock."

What beat all for Gracie was what some adults would say in front of a little girl. Over the next few weeks Gracie caught folks gossiping about Jerry, just like they nattered on about Maureen. When Gracie reported it to him he laughed.

"Ignore them, darlin' girl. Broad-minded people talk ideas. Small-minded people talk about other folks. Besides there's no such thing as bad publicity."

It didn't take Gracie long to decide, with the bright, hard intensity an intelligent child can muster, that she wanted Jerry to be a part of her family.

He seemed open to the notion. He and Maureen got married four months to the day he came to town. By then everybody in Tupelo had gotten used to them together. Most even came to the wedding, smiling and nodding when they saw Maureen had the good sense not to wear white. When the new couple came home from their honeymoon, he'd already made her a full partner in the business.

"It just makes sense, darlin' girl," he told Gracie later. "I can smell a sale a mile away, can figure how much someone's willing to shell out, and your mama can talk folks into anything."

Gracie didn't care for the house on North Bay Road. Stucco and Spanish tile inside and out and furnished in leather and stainless steel.

Not that the house wasn't nice. Gracie could have sold it in a heartbeat if she had the listing in Pensacola, but a dentist's office had more charm.

Even so, Maureen and Jerry seemed to like it. It had size and lots of light, enough bathrooms to run a hotel. A pool and cabana too. And it sat on the inter-coastal waterway, with a great view of downtown Miami.

"You didn't bring much luggage," Jerry said, when they arrived at the front door. "Your sisters filled up the car."

"I just brought what I could carry on. That way I can't lose it. Faith and Hope trust airlines too much."

""They trust doctors and hospitals too much too. Told me I made a big mistake bringing Maureen home."

At the door Jerry fumbled with the lock, but wouldn't let Gracie take the keys from him. Inside a young woman, dressed in nurses' white, crossed toward the kitchen as they entered.

"Aimee," Jerry said. "This is Gracie, our oldest girl."

"Hello, Aimee," Gracie said.

The young woman waved. She wore her dark hair clipped close to her scalp. Her skin was the soft cocoa brown of the islands. "She may be a little loopy," she said. "I just gave her meds. Doctor called to say he'd be along at six."

With that she slipped through the kitchen door.

Jerry dropped Gracie's bag onto a chair. "Come on. Your mama's been waiting for you."

The room smelled of disinfectant, but musty too. Gracie's grandmother used to say one old thing or another had "dried up and wasted away." Maureen looked just like that, lost under the smoothed white sheets of the adjustable hospital bed.

"About time," she said as they entered.

Her rasping voice sounded as if it had been packed in cotton batting. Her eyes had a dreamy, unfocused look about them. Jerry stepped close to the near side of the bed. He scooped up Maureen's hand.

"Her plane got in late," he said.

Gracie stroked her mother's cheek. "I'm here now, Mama."

Maureen dipped her chin by way of acknowledgment, the most energy she could spare.

"Hey, Grace." Hope, the middle sister, sat on a leather sofa near the French doors. She held the day's copy of *The Miami Herald*.

"Hey," Gracie said.

She stepped to the sofa. Hope stood to offer up a hug, an embrace of acquaintances. Hope and Faith had remained in Tupelo, lived across the street from each other, but their connection to Gracie had always been more of a younger aunt-niece relationship than that of sisters. Sometimes, Gracie missed the closeness.

"Did you have a good flight from Pensacola?" Hope asked.

"We got bounced around some. How was the trip from Tupelo?"

"Faith lost a suitcase."

"Uh huh."

"Hope?"

"Yes, Mama?"

"Go on out to the living room, will you? I want to talk to Gracie for a spell." Maureen slurred her words.

Hope tossed the newspaper onto the sofa. "Yes, Mama."

Maureen went on. "Find Faith. I want to see all three of you when Gracie and I finish."

"Yes, Mama." Hope slipped through the door.

Jerry brushed a wisp of hair from Maureen's forehead. "You want me to go, too, Mo?"

"If you wouldn't mind, sugar."

"Course not."

Alone with Gracie, Maureen seemed to deflate to an even smaller size. She eased back against the pillows. "There. That's better."

Gracie accepted it for what it was. Maureen might love Hope and Faith just as much, but she trusted Gracie more. Maureen had always referred to Gracie as "the dependable one."

"Your father's been coming by," Maureen said.

The muscles across Gracie's shoulders clenched. She stepped to the bedside but didn't touch her mother. "Does he knock at the front door?"

Maureen waved the remark away with a wiggle of her fingers. "Smart lip you got there. How much it cost?"

"I'm sorry, Mama. I haven't had much rest since yesterday."

"I have. They push pills at me like they think sleeping's going to cure me."

Maureen paused, closed her eyes and breathed for a time, drawing in air through her mouth. At last, she continued. "They keep telling me to rest. I almost missed him today because of those damned pills."

"Elvis?"

"Who else, do you think? One second I'm by myself, having a hard time keeping my eyes open, then I hear him cough."

She lifted one finger to point to the straight chair behind Gracie. "Sitting right there against the sun. Wearing the white outfit he had on the night we took you up to Mobile."

"With the big sunburst on the chest?"

"Yeah. The Mayan sundial, that's what he called it. I said, 'Hello, Elvis.' He smiled and said, 'Good to see you, Mo.'"

She paused and drew a labored breath. Her words were little more than a whisper when she continued. "He called me Mo that night we had together, up in Memphis."

Maureen had never been shy about explaining to folks that Elvis Presley was Gracie's father. As much as she had come to love Elvis too, Gracie never had believed the story. Even so she decided over the years that it was what Maureen needed to sustain herself and so she never argued.

When Jerry came along, it didn't stop, but he didn't seem to mind. In fact Gracie often thought that he encouraged it. God knew no one in Tupelo had tried to brighten Maureen's life when she came home from college pregnant, not even her parents.

In 1959, Mississippi folks didn't think it proper for a young woman to have a child but not a husband. Her telling some wild tale that a celebrity like Elvis Presley was the father just added injury to insult.

As she grew, Gracie learned the tale by heart.

Maureen had taken the train to Memphis in early June, 1958, for freshman orientation at the University of Tennessee. Second night there, she and some of her new friends decided to go to a roadhouse to listen to the band.

And there sat Elvis in the darkness and noise, drinking beer with friends.

"Everybody knew who he was, mind you, home on leave from the Army," Maureen would say. "But he was wearing dark glasses and this big old cowboy hat. Had on a faded denim shirt that said Mobil Oil over the pocket. As incognito as someone as gorgeous as he was could be. Folks let him be out of respect."

She was already more than half in love with him, like most girls her age, and so she had to introduce herself, since they were both from Tupelo. Just had to tell him that her folks knew his folks in a "say howdy at the store" sort of way before his family moved away. One thing led to another after that. Twenty-four hours later Elvis left, on his way to Fort Hood for more training and Maureen returned to Tupelo.

Three months later, a week before she was to leave for classes, Gracie's mother walked into the bathroom unexpectedly and discovered her daughter was expecting. Maureen never left for Tennessee. Gracie came along June second, 1959.

Maureen pulled herself up off the bed, using Gracie's wrist as a grip. "Wish you would've got here sooner. He was *glorious*. Not tired and fat, the way he was that night in Mobile."

She began to cough, long, ratcheting sounds, and eased back into the pillows. Gracie waited for Maureen to catch her breath.

"That's not the only thing I wish, you know," Maureen said at last. "Wish you would've got your birthday song that night in Mobile. The kiss he promised too."

"He never promised me a song or kiss."

Maureen gave Gracie the look, eyes unblinking, one eyebrow raised and mouth set in a straight line. Even wasted as she was, her disdain could be withering.

"Yes, he did. Told me he remembered. Said he was sorry. Too many folks pushing at him back then." She rubbed at her lips. It was an old habit. She missed her cigarettes.

"Mama, that's your pills talking. Elvis is dead."

Maureen offered up that look again. "Is not. He sat here this morning, in that chair, holding on to my hand."

Her words held no force. She sank deeper into the pillows, panting, ignoring Gracie.

"I'm sorry, Mama."

After a time Maureen wiggled her fingers again. "No need. Just me being snippy."

Her eyes brightened. She grinned. "Stick around, you'll see. He said he'd come back."

"All right, maybe I'll get that kiss, after all."

"That's my girl," Maureen patted at Gracie's hand. "Promise me now. Promise me you'll get that kiss."

"I swear."

Maureen gave a little nod, laid her palm back onto the bed. The skin across the back of her hand looked as white as the sheet. She sighed. The sound of it seemed to go on forever. She began to cry, giving in to the pain at last.

Gracie leaned close. "Mama?"

Maureen coughed again. This time a spray of red filmed the white sheets across her chest and stomach.

"Jerry!" Gracie called, turning up the volume. "Jerry!"

Hurried footsteps from the hall. Gracie felt the heat of her own tears upon her cheeks.

Maureen's eyes widened. She clutched Gracie's hand. "Do what I tell you now. You get that kiss."

Five hundred people turned out for the funeral. One hundred came to North Bay Road after the ceremony. Most still remained at early evening but Gracie had had her fill of well-wishers. She even felt relieved that her husband Charlie and their two teen-aged daughters caught an early flight back to Pensacola.

She stood at the French doors in Maureen's sick room, the newspaper Hope had left upon the sofa in her hand. Guests clustered around Jerry near the swimming pool, or Hope and Faith, who stood together beneath the somber dark blue canopy the undertaker had set up.

The canvas rippled in a light but steady breeze from the east. Through the open doorway Gracie could taste the salt in the air, carried from the Atlantic just a mile away. Glistening yachts and go-fast boats eased past in the channel. Across the waterway the Miami skyline looked to be on fire, back lit by the fading sun.

Far too glorious a set piece for the occasion.

"Want some company?" Aimee asked.

Gracie hadn't even heard the door open. She didn't turn to look. "That's a lot of folks out there."

Aimee came closer. Gracie caught a whiff of perfume. *Red* by Giorgio, she thought.

"There were even more at church," Aimee said. "I had no idea your mother knew so many people."

"Some were family. Some know Jerry from the country club. Most were Maureen's friends. She was good at meeting people."

"I saw that in her."

Aimee stepped beside Gracie. She offered up a glass. "Jerry asked if I would bring this to you. He said to tell you folks are asking about you."

"Thank you." Gracie took the glass, held it in her free hand, not drinking. "Nice of you to come to the funeral."

"I liked your mother."

Gracie fiddled with the glass. "She was easy to like. Jerry mentioned that you're from Haiti."

"I'm sorry?"

Gracie sighed. "That was abrupt, wasn't it? I'm sorry."

"It's all right. And yes, I was born on the island," Aimee said. "My family came to Florida when I was five. My mother and father, my brother and my sisters, my gran'mere."

"Have you been back since then?"

"A few times."

The two women stood for a time, watching the scene outside.

"I have a favor to ask," Gracie said. Her voice trembled as she spoke.

"What would it be?"

Gracie turned and held out the newspaper. She had opened it to one of the special sections. It showed a photo of a handsome man with cocoa skin.

"I know Miami's a big place," Gracie said. "I don't expect you know everyone from Haiti who lives here, but can you tell me anything about the fellow in this story?"

She handed over the newspaper with quivering hands.

Aimee scanned the page. "I don't know him, have never met him, only heard things. He isn't a bad man, they say, but he is careless. He takes money and doesn't worry whether what he does will cause harm."

"Can he do what the paper says? Can he call up the dead?"

"He tells people what he believes they want to hear and he knows how to work the reporters. He likes attention."

"Oh. That sort of thing isn't really possible, is it?"

Aimee settled onto the arm of the sofa, still holding the newspaper. "Does this have something to do with your mother?"

"It's no never mind. I apologize for asking."

"Gracie, nothing good can come from any attempt to talk to your mother's spirit."

Gracie blinked. "God no! I'd never ... I didn't ..."

"Then why would you ask about this man?"

Gracie glanced toward the French doors. "I want to call up Elvis' ghost."

Aimee giggled.

"You think that's funny?"

"No, of course not. I'm sorry. I just didn't expect it."

Gracie drained the glass she held and set it on the sofa arm. "I'm sorry, too. I shouldn't have asked. You must think I'm crazy."

"No. I think you're upset over your mother's death, not thinking clearly. I'd be surprised if that wasn't so. I don't think you really want to do what you're asking."

"I do! I made a promise to my mother. I intend to keep it."

"You want a kiss? From a ghost?"

"What made you ask that?"

"Patients talk to nurses. They tell us all sorts of things, even those who don't like to talk as much as your mother did."

"What did she tell you?"

"That Elvis Presley was your father. That he visited her, sat and talked with her over the last week or so."

"Did you ever see him?"

Aimee paused before answering. "Nurses see and hear a lot of strange things, so I try to keep an open mind."

She hesitated again, studying Gracie. "There were times I came in and found the seat of that chair warm."

Gracie didn't say a word.

"I'm not making fun," Aimee said. "My Gran'mere is almost eighty. She follows the old ways, worships the loa and practices the rituals, uses spells and charms."

"Gris-gris?"

"You've been doing research."

"Some. Do you believe in all that?"

Aimee returned the newspaper to the sofa. She took Gracie's hand and turned her away from the crowd outside. "Like I said, I try to keep an open mind. That fellow in the paper won't do you a bit of good but my Gran'mere might."

It was a ninety-minute trip south to Key Largo, over into Monroe County, at the north end of the Florida Keys.

Aimee drove, waving away Gracie's protests, refusing even to accept gas money, saying that she knew the way and that her grandmother recognized the little red Fiat Aimee drove.

"This is crazy," Gracie said, as they rolled south

Too late to turn around now," Aimee said. "At least until we get to Key Largo. It's not safe."

A winter storm, bringing sheets of pelting rain and massive lightning strikes, rolled in as they rattled along the sixteen-mile stretch of Route One between Homestead and Key Largo.

The sports car's windshield wipers slapped a syncopated beat to the rumble of the road's surface. Aimee drove the posted limits. Other drivers roared along the wet and narrow roadway, rocketing around them.

"Why doesn't he slow down?" Gracie asked as a huge red pickup truck screamed by, towing a trailered boat, spitting up rooster tails of water.

Aimee didn't look away from the road. "Some people are in such a hurry to get where they want to go that they die trying. Gran'mere calls this the Ghost Road, says spirits line up along the berm. The newspapers say the Sixteen-Mile Stretch has more traffic deaths per mile than any other section of highway in the state. Maybe in the country."

The rain let up just as they reached the north end of Key Largo. Minutes later the sun came out. Aimee pulled over to fold the top down. The storm-cooled air felt wonderful, but the near-rotten aroma of the ocean engulfed them too.

"Do you still want to go back?" Aimee asked. "Grand'mere won't be offended."

Gracie considered it. What they were up to was madness, pure lunacy, but if she didn't follow through, if she didn't even talk to Aimee's grandmother, it would eat at her forever.

"No," she said. "Let's go on."

If anything, traffic speed picked up as the roadway opened into double lanes. Minutes later Aimee turned east off Route One and eased the Fiat along a narrow road paved with crushed shell. They moved through palm trees, saw grass and mangroves, toward the Atlantic Ocean.

Gracie could just glimpse the waters when Aimee slowed. She stopped before a neat bungalow, painted a blue as bright as the storm-washed January sky.

An old woman sat in a wooden swing on the front porch. She waved a beckoning hand as they pulled into her driveway. "Come on up here," she called.

There was a glow about the woman. Even though she sat in the porch's shade, she gleamed like sunshine off the water on an August day. Gracie's stomach dropped away. It took all of her nerve to climb from the little car. She trailed along behind as Aimee approached the porch steps. At the North Bay Road house, this had seemed to be the thing to do.

Here, she wasn't certain.

There had to be some other way to honor Maureen's memory. A saner way. A safer way. Aimee stopped short of the steps. Gracie bumped against her. She grabbed at Aimee's shoulder for support.

The old woman beckoned again. "I been waiting for you two a good, long time now."

"How did you know we were coming?" Gracie asked.

The old woman just looked at her, one eyebrow raised and her mouth twisted up into a passable semblance of Maureen. Then she grinned and held up a cellular telephone.

Aimee grinned. "I called her just before I picked you up."

"Oh," Gracie muttered.

The old woman patted the slats of the swing again, at the empty spots beside her. "Come up, sit with me. No need to fear. God be wit' you, child, and I won't show you a t'ing will bring you any harm."

"Maybe we should just –"

The old woman touched the swing again. "Come on, girl. I can see into your soul. You got a mighty need and a friend has brought you here. Tell me all 'bout it."

"Better if I be there," the old woman had said. "But I don't go much no more, 'specially not up the Ghost Road. You can do it. You got a good heart, and he'll heed a summoning on his birthday. Don't we all like it, folks pay attention our special day?"

"Does it matter where I do it?" Gracie whispered, not wanting to break the sense of wonder that had begun to grow the instant she sat upon the swing.

"Anywhere the spirit's strong. Your mama's sickroom do just fine, but the mixture's got to be exactly so and proper. You pay heed what I say now, girl. You be safe if you do."

It took two days to collect the items on the list, even with Aimee's help. Gracie acquired the final item, graveyard soil, just six hours ago.

Just in time.

It would be four-thirty-five a.m. soon, the instant of Elvis' birth. When it came, Gracie would try her hand at casting the summoning spell the old woman taught her. Gracie set up in Maureen's sick room. She had the run of the place. Faith and Hope were gone home. Even at this time, they still had to meet the demands of school-age children. Jerry had gone to bed.

Gracie cleared the space before the French doors, moved furniture aside with as much stealth as she could manage. The doors stood open, the room glowed with moonlight. She had set eight lit white candles at the points of the compass around the summoning circle chalked onto the tile.

It was almost time. Only one thing still remained to do.

"You can be double sure the spell works," the old woman had said. "If you got a t'ing he touched."

Until she heard that, Gracie hadn't been certain she would really try to summon Elvis' spirit for a song and one last kiss. But Maureen *had* a thing that Elvis touched. Gracie knew where to find it.

She crept through the house, moving with care across the shadowed tile. Jerry wasn't an easy man to wake but he would come running, baseball bat in hand, if she knocked something to the floor.

She eased into the garage, made her way to the far corner. There a climate-controlled closet held all manner of important things. Maureen's navy-blue wedding dress. Jerry's Army uniform. Maureen's gold jewelry. A fire safe filled with legal documents. Jerry's baseball card collection. Five boxes of Cuban cigars.

And on the top shelf, sealed in Tupperware, there lay a sweat-soaked silk scarf Elvis threw into the audience that night all those years ago in Mobile.

Gracie paused at the closet door. A hasp and padlock had been installed since her last visit. She should have waited until morning, asked Jerry about the lock over breakfast.

No time for such politeness now.

She took down a pair of bolt-cutters from the pegboard over Jerry's workbench. A minute of work and the padlock fell away. Gracie opened the closet, ready to scoop up the scarf, to hurry back to her spell-casting.

A white jumpsuit, an embroidered Mayan sun upon its chest, hung between Maureen's blue dress and Jerry's uniform. Black Cuban boots sat heel to heel below the suit. A foam wig form next to the boxed scarf held an expensive black hairpiece, complete with mutton-chop sideburns.

No need for a summoning. Elvis hadn't left the building after all.

Gracie sat cross-legged within the smudged remains of the untried summoning circle, her hands upon her knees, when Jerry entered the spare bedroom just after dawn. He carried the black hairpiece.

"Morning," he said.

Gracie didn't answer.

He settled on the sofa. "I planned to go for donuts. When I got to the garage I saw someone broke into the storage closet."

Gracie looked up. "You snuck in here, didn't you? Dressed up like Elvis."

Jerry tossed the hairpiece aside. "I did that, yes."

"Why?"

His tone sharpened. "It made her happy. She knew it was me, I'm sure of that. She's always known it was me, but she told that story for so many years there was a part of her that wanted to believe it."

"Always? What does that mean?"

Jerry studied her for a time. "Darlin' girl, your mama *did* party with Elvis that night in 1958. She partied with me too."

"What?"

"I went through training camp with Elvis. I'm from Memphis, so we went home together, too."

He began to cry. "I was at the bar that night with him, just another of his buddies, but I thought your mama was the sweetest thing I ever saw. I fell in love with her first look, that night."

"I don't think I want to hear this."

"Too bad. Too late now. Just before the place closed, we went to the head. Elvis swapped hats and shirts with me, gave me his sunglasses. I put on quite a show, almost as good as one of his. I don't know if she knew it then but it was me took your mama to bed. I left next morning before she woke up."

They were both crying now. Gracie remained in the middle of the chalk circle, her knees drawn to her chin. "And you're just finding time to tell me? You bastard."

For a second Jerry looked as if he was about to ask about her smart mouth, as Maureen had done that last visit. Instead he shrugged. "It's what your mama wanted."

"Bullshit, Jerry. Some people would call what you did rape. At the very least, you abandoned her, left us alone for seven years." The heat in her words would have cooked an egg.

"Darlin' girl, I got sent to Viet Nam right after I met your mama. Just an advisor, that's what they said back then. Supposed to be a non-combatant but the Viet Cong weren't having none of that. I spent five years locked in a bamboo cage there in the jungle."

"I never knew."

"No you didn't. Children don't know everything their folks ever did. You got your own kids, you know that. Anyway it's done and over."

"What about Mama and me?"

"I got rescued, came home in sixty-four, figured someone had scooped up your mama. Ran into her college roommate just by accident, spring of sixty-six. You know the rest."

"After you got married, why'd she keep telling that story?"

He picked up the hairpiece and held it, stroking it as if it were a cat. "That first Friday we went to dinner, after you'd gone to bed I told her everything.

Ask her to marry me, said I would tell the whole town who I really was. She said it didn't matter, that it would be better if we never said a word."

"Better?"

"She was a smart lady, way smarter than me. She figured we'd do a good business, selling houses, if she kept customers smiling with her stories while I let folks think I was some hotshot Memphis salesman come to town to save a local girl."

Jerry grinned, happy for a moment with his memories. "Turns out, I was good at it. So was she. We made a ton of money, the two of us. And she told that whopper about Elvis so many times she started to believe in it herself."

He daubed at his cheeks with his fingertips. "Days I half believed it too. Besides, I think she liked the notion folks weren't ever sure if she'd really slept with Elvis Presley."

He cleared his throat. "Telling them she settled for Jerry Landis would have been a real poor substitute."

"She didn't settle for anything," Gracie said. "She got the best part of the deal."

Jerry propped his elbows on his knees. "Thank you, darlin' girl. That mean you're not mad at me?"

"I'm still mad as hell, Jerry. I swear I could spit nails at you right now but I expect I'll get over it."

"Can't ask for more than that."

She pointed to the hairpiece. "Did you really dress up like Elvis for her?"

"Not until she came home from the hospital last week."

"Let me see."

"Go on with you."

She gave him the look. "I said let me see."

Jerry shrugged. He settled the wig into place, thumbing the sideburns against his jaw line. "The jumpsuit helps. So does a little bit of makeup, some spirit gum, the glasses."

"Sing me a song."

He shrugged, pulled a pair of aviator sunglasses from his jacket pocket, slipped them on. He tilted his head and curled his upper lip just for a second.

"This is your mama's favorite song." He sang *Love Me Tender*.

As he finished he looked to her. "Forgive me?"

She offered up a grudged smile. He'd done a pretty decent imitation.

"If you give me the kiss Mama claimed Elvis promised me all those years ago."

He smiled, too. "Slide on over here."

She pushed her way across the tiled floor until she bumped against his knees. He leaned toward her, cupped her chin with his hand, touched his lips to her forehead.

Gracie swore she heard her mother sigh.

"Thank you, Daddy," she said. "Thank you very much."

Apple Jack

The First Day

Jack ran with all the grace his knack bestowed.

The land rose, the forest fell away, until nothing stood against the clean blue sky but a doubled file of birch. He reached the hill's crest on his belly. His age-gnarled fingers settled on a large, half-buried stone.

A perfect fit.

He eased his chin onto his knuckles, peered through the grass between the white-barked trees. The dark scent of loam pressed at his nostrils, as solid as the cool, rounded surface of the stone beneath his hand.

Beyond the trees the land fell away once more into a natural amphitheatre. At its center a woman lay staked to the ground, her head tight against the moldering husk of an ancient automobile tire, her flowing skirts hiked naked to her waist.

Two men loomed over her. One tall and run to fat. The other short and skinny, all chin and Adam's apple. Both tried hard at being nasty bastards. Jack recognized the pair as nothing more than hapless stooges. The woman directed the action here.

"Used to have to wait for Christmas to see a life-sized diorama," Jack muttered to himself. This one lacked nothing but a tripod and a title card. *Maiden Prays for Last-Minute Rescue.*

The woman screamed again.

Jack levered to his hands and knees. He saw it as a trap but if the woman wanted to put on a show, he'd play his part. "All right," he said, drawing a breath. "Here I come."

He stood and stepped into the open, stopped just long enough to settle his leather bags upon his hips, then moved downslope. Tall and stoop-shouldered, wild-haired and bearded, he waved his arms about his head like the mad prophet he appeared to be.

"Hey!" His voice carried well, held a proper querulous tone. "What do you assholes think you're doing?"

All three turned as if pulled by a single string. The tall man slid back into his suspenders. The short man buttoned up his fly and gripped his belt. The woman continued to struggle but watched Jack's every move.

The pattern settled into shape as his knack revealed more pieces of the puzzle, showed him how they fit together. The woman wanted him for some purpose of her own, something dangerous. She had hired the two goons to test his mettle.

Too bad for them.

The tall man rolled his shoulders, hocked a wad of phlegm into the dirt. He set himself to face Jack and raised his voice. "You gonna stop us on your own, old man? Or you got a bunch of buddies waitin' for a whistle?"

The fool smiled at his own joke. He wouldn't be the one to whistle. Four of his front teeth had come up missing long ago.

"Yeah," the short man said, plucking second fiddle. "And if they're as old as you, they ain't gonna be no help."

"Please, sir—" the woman said.

Jack lifted one finger to his lips to silence her.

The tall man accepted the interruption as his cue. He drew a scratched and battered automatic pistol, stepped up to meet Jack, offering his next cliché. "You're makin' a mistake—"

Jack interrupted once again, stiff-armed the rounded stone he'd carried from the hillside into the tall man's forehead. Bone crunched, the fellow's head snapped back, pocked by a stone-sized indentation above his dulling eyes. He folded to his knees, fell onto his back. The pistol dropped from lifeless fingers.

The short man jumped into the fight, knife drawn from his belt. "Gonna kill you, mother-fucker," he snarled. "Slice you into bite-sized chunks."

No, you're not.

Jack tossed the stone at the short man. That slowed the fellow long enough for Jack to duck low and spin on his heel, one leather bag outstretched. Filled with momentum, the bag caught the short man in the back, sent him stumbling, knocked him off his feet. Jack sprang up, stepped on the knife blade, and sunk his other steel-tipped boot-toe deep into the fellow's temple.

The short man shuddered and gave away the ghost.

Jack stepped back from the bodies, rested his hands on his knees, and worked to catch his breath. He waited for the woman to decide what to do next.

"Are they dead?" she finally asked.

Stupid question.

"Yes," he said, still waiting. Screw her if she thought he'd take the lead. She'd set this into motion, made the killing necessary. Jack supposed he should resent her for that, but her two stooges had tried to kill him first.

He'd just returned the favor.

No big loss.

"Untie me," she said at last. For all the strain in her manner, she could have said, "Pass the potatoes."

Jack cut away her bonds.

The woman sat up and stuck out her hand. "I'm Molly Lear."

Her palm felt dry, her grip firm. Jack liked that, just as he liked her assertiveness. Handsome woman too. Lean and long, with russet hair and dark eyes. The whole of it set Jack astir in a way he thought long passed. When she rose, he didn't shy away to give her room.

"Molly Lear, huh?" he said. "I've heard of you."

"That so?"

"I heard you've got big magic. Throw fireballs like spit wads. Turn bullets back with words. Stop hearts in mid-beat."

Molly grinned. "People do talk, don't they?"

Jack nodded in agreement. "Over near Blind River, one old fool had the nerve to make a joke, called you Darth Moll."

She shrugged. "Don't know what that means."

"From before your time. Means you can do scary shit."

Molly stepped away, muttering something Jack didn't catch, and gathered a backpack from a ragtag pile of gear. She shrugged it into place, settled her long skirts, and started up the slope.

Jack called after her. "I'll plant your friends."

"Would you now?" She didn't look back.

Jack watched Molly gain the rise and disappear. He combed his fingers through his tangled beard.

Watch your ass with this one, Jack.

Plain to see if he went after her, traveled with her for any length of time, he might as well spark a fuse, not knowing how long he'd have before the dynamite exploded.

"I'm Jack Chapman," he said when he caught up to her.

Molly smiled as if pleased with herself. "No, you're not. I've heard of you, too. Fact is I've seen you, spotted you one day last year, up to Paradise, just come in from tending trees. Don't recall hearing anybody call you Jack Chapman that day."

Once upon a time, before civilization gave up the ghost, before order moved away and let the world settle into anarchy, he *had* been Jack Chapman. A university professor, a physicist, and hobby farmer.

These days everybody knew him as the Apple Man.

Jack had been a lucid and recurrent dreamer his whole life. This one always started as Annie called his name. "Jack?"

Vashon. Late September nearly thirty years ago. Three days before the world collapsed. Earlier at lunch, Annie offered her good news. They'd be parents before summer came again.

Now Jack stood upon the flagstone patio, double doors open before him, a bushel basket full of apples from their orchards tight against his hip.

"It's me," he called, mouthing the remembered words. "Got the last of the honey crisps."

"Take them to the basement, would you, Apple Jack?"

A private joke. She planned the orchards that he nurtured, sold the fruit he plucked from his mature trees. He called her Apple Annie. She called him Apple Jack.

Jack caught the tart aroma of apple pie from the kitchen where she toiled, baking. He chewed at his lower lip. What he wouldn't give to kiss cinnamon and brown sugar from her fingers one more time.

Images hurried by in quick cuts.

Adjusting the temperature and pressure of the utility-room shower. Standing beneath the flow, allowing the heat to draw the ache from his arthritic shoulders and his back. Rubbing the soap into his dirt-encrusted hands even though he knew he'd never be able to scrub them clean again.

The shower's fog-free shaving mirror, a Christmas gift from Annie's mom and dad, showed him the face of an old man who spent too much time outside. Dark eyes deep-set above high cheekbones, a sharp nose, and a wide mouth, almost hidden by a tangled, gray-streaked ruddy beard.

Jack wept acid tears.

If he had to relive this memory so often, he wished to God it could be as he had been, not the wreck he had become.

"Want a piece of apple pie?" Annie asked.

From the sound and the smell of it she stood across the room near the steps. Jack heard a cork pop, heard the crystal chime of a thick-lipped bottle touching fluted glass.

"Apples and champagne," he said. "Strange combination."

Annie giggled. Jack's heart stuttered at the sound.

"I'm allowed to have bizarre tastes," she said.

"I thought pregnant women weren't supposed to drink."

"I can have alcohol until the end of the first trimester."

"Even so, we shouldn't drink tonight," Jack said, sticking to the script. "We've

got to be out of here early tomorrow or I'll miss my conference."

He heard Annie move across the room. He held his breath, waiting, not able to tell if the water on his face came from the spray or from his tears.

Annie stood outside the stall. "Give me a hand here, Apple Jack. I can't do this by myself."

Her silhouette lay against the translucent shower curtain. Jack could see her sleek, naked curves, the glint of her smile, the white-blond helmet of her hair.

"Just this once," he whispered. "Let me see her face."

He refused to look away, reached with his left hand, ran his fingertips across the nubbled concrete wall. He touched the shower knobs. His right hand gripped the curtain.

"All right," he said, drawing a breath. "Here I come."

"Shut up, old man," Molly growled from the other side of the guttering campfire.

Jack rolled away from her and closed his eyes, burrowed in his bedding, twisted in his memories. He lay awake a long while before nodding off again.

The Second Day

Molly toed him from his musty blankets before sunrise.

For hours she set a pace that made the first day's agony a warm-up drill. When the sun hung at its highest, they stopped in a tiny apple orchard.

Seven trees. One of his.

Jack sagged against a trunk and stroked the scaly bark. He spotted a sunken, discolored patch on a low-hanging branch. A sure sign of canker. When he finished up with Molly, he needed to return to do some serious pruning. If he didn't, the fungal infection would spread from tree to tree.

"You plant these?" Molly asked. She panted, not used to this fast a pace either.

Good.

"Years ago," he replied when he could manage words.

Just now he would have been as happy to stop on an anthill. The taste of bile dripped hot upon the lining of his throat. His back felt made of broken glass. Had his pride allowed it, he'd be on his knees, retching.

"No need for me to kill those two," he said after a time.

Molly laughed. Jack didn't care for the sound of it.

"No need not to, either," she said. "I figured they done enough, between the two of them, to have it coming."

So have you.

After a time Molly clambered to her feet. "Come on, old man. We're not finished walking yet."

They hiked for hours more, moving northwest at a headlong speed. Finally, as they made their way along the rusted tracks of the old Wisconsin Central Railroad, Molly slowed a bit.

"K.I. Sawyer," she said over her shoulder.

Jack didn't waste the breath to answer.

"You hear me, old man? That's where we're headed."

"I heard," he snapped. "Why the air base?"

"Something there I want."

"Take it. Use your magic."

She glanced back at him. "You can see that?"

Jack shrugged. He didn't say his knack hadn't yet revealed the strength of her talent. Not yet.

"I've tried to take it," she said after a time. "What I'm after is pre-Collapse, protected by a computer, and I can't just smash and grab."

Jesus, a computer!

"You see patterns everywhere, don't you?" Annie had said, just after they first met, at that fractals seminar in Boulder at the University of Colorado campus.

"Uh huh." The shapes and relationships he'd been thinking about just then hadn't been geometric.

He never said, would never tell her, he could fathom the relationships between all the patterns too, that the knowledge just popped into his head. That sounded way too much like hocus-pocus magic, back then.

Just now he saw two things for sure. *Computer* was new vocabulary for Molly and she wasn't telling the whole truth. It pissed him off. Still, his mother used to say, more flies with honey." Jack figured he'd play along.

"I expect someone at the Soo told you I have a way with old machines," he said.

Molly bobbed her head. "Heard you were a regular hacker, once upon a time."

Hacker. Another new word for her, but not for Jack.

His knack made him good at puzzles and he'd always seen computer programs as nothing more than that. Tangled bits and pieces waiting to be sorted out. He'd paid his way through grad school at Cal Tech coding.

"I knew a thing or two," Jack said.

"Can you get around a password system?" Molly asked.

The soles of his feet tingled, his fingers twitched. It had been so long. "We'll see."

His enthusiasm didn't last long. That second night Molly waited until after dark again to stop. She made the fire, as she chanted to herself, while little balls of flame jumped from her fingertips.

Jack was too tired to be impressed. These days only a few could manipulate big magic, but most folks possessed some sort of knack, some little magic crawled out from an old corner or forgotten nook. Water witching. Far sight. A healing touch.

Pattern perception.

"What's that?" Across the fire, Molly tilted her head to the left, raised an eyebrow, and stared at him with those new-charcoal eyes.

"Talking to myself," Jack said as he stared back.

If Molly had been born before Collapse, Jack figured she'd not been but a toddler when it came. No child now though. Maybe thirty, not much more. Tall, almost six feet. The sleek, long-muscled body of a swimmer. Her short-cropped hair russet red.

She had a strong face too, high cheekbones and a generous mouth. Not beautiful but damned attractive. Her eyes had to be her best feature. Deep-set and so dark they didn't seem to have a pupil. Black beacons in the firelight.

If a man forgot the single-mindedness that lay behind them, the dispassion she had shown over the death of her two goons, he might follow those eyes to God knew where. Jack shook away the notion. He was an old man after all.

He turned from the fire and nodded off.

Music swelled. Jack's alarm. He nuzzled Annie's shoulder, absorbing the flavor and the fragrance of her cologne. Escape *by Calvin Klein. His last birthday gift to her.*

He rolled away from her.

Early-morning light silvered the gray-patterned carpet. Ceramic logs burned forever in a gas fireplace, crisping the air. The Grand Hotel on Mackinaw Island. A physicists' conclave. Jack had been invited to serve as keynote speaker for opening ceremonies.

The first day of Collapse.

Annie pressed against him. Jack's dreams always had been a jumble of imagination and reality. That weekend, Annie flew from Seattle to Detroit with him but hadn't traveled north. He drove to Mackinaw alone. She stayed behind, visited her parents in Dearborn.

He could hear Annie's gentle snores behind him, could feel her long, lithe warmth against his back. He wept. Try as he might, he couldn't turn toward her. In his dreams he could never touch her face, could never meet her eyes, could never say, "Oh, babe, I'm sorry I didn't come back for you."

The telephone rang. Without preamble, Jack sat on the edge of the bed. He pressed the handset to his ear. "Hello."

"Have you seen the news?" Seth Abernathy, Jack's father-in-law, sounded anxious.

"No, Seth. Tell me."

"My God, Jack! The world's gone mad. Some fools set off an A-bomb at the Renaissance Center. But not just here. Everywhere. It's the end of everything!"

"Calm down, Seth. Talk to me."

Seth hadn't called that morning thirty years ago, any more than Annie had come to Mackinaw. Months had passed before Jack learned what had happened to the world, what had gone down in Detroit. What he had missed by running north like a dog with his tail between his legs.

"I'm as calm as I can be, Jack."

"Why did you call?"

"I called to tell you Annie and the baby are safe with us, but Detroit's burning. I don't see how we can survive here and I can't get us out alone. Please come back. Come save us, Jack."

Behind him the pressure lessened. Jack could turn now. When he did, Annie had disappeared. Gone to who knew where. Not even a depression in the bedclothes to show she had ever lain close to him.

Hot tears choked him as he muttered a reply to Seth. Two words were all he managed. "I can't—"

Seth responded in a whisper. "Dear God, if you can't help, Jack, what will become of us?"

The Third Day

Jack and Molly spent one more day and one more night crossing the wilderness. She set a blistering pace. He stumbled after her, too tired to eat, too tired to unravel the puzzle she presented.

When she stopped, well past dark again, Jack fell headlong into his lurid, lucid dreams.

Jack trudged north alone, slogging along the rusted iron remains of the old Soo Line spur between St. Ignace and Sault Sainte Marie. He'd walked forever, since stealing that boat on Mackinaw.

The leather carrier bags he'd found on the broad lawn outside the post office in Rudyard bumped against his hips. Too full, too heavy. Eventually he'd discover the bags meant more to him than all the junk he'd crammed inside them.

Not yet, though.

He paused and mopped the sweat upon his brow with a hand towel he'd swiped from the Grand Hotel. Jack sighed. He'd really made this journey. Thirty years ago, the day had been pleasant enough, if a little cool. In his dreams he always sweltered from an awful heat.

A noise behind him. Gravel shifting on the rail bed. An indistinct figure stood ten or twelve yards back. A child, from the look of it. A girl. She waited, feet planted, arms at her sides, head down. A little beanpole. Her face hung hidden by her thick, bright-auburn hair.

"Hello?" Jack said. His voice sounded harsh in the sudden preternatural silence of the dream.

She didn't respond. Not a word. Not a raised hand. Nothing.

He tried again. "Who are you? Want to walk with me?"

A jump cut and the day had slipped away. The sun, low in the western sky, cast deep, sharp-edged shadows that seemed to stretch forever. The child approached.

"Don't you recognize me, Daddy?" she asked.

Another jump cut. He hiked north again. The little girl walked beside him, away from the tracks. A doll, white-blond hair pulled tight around its face, dangled from her far hand.

Ahead, a crowd of men and woman dressed in rags blocked the rail bed and spilled over into the fields on either side. Jack couldn't make out their features but from the way they stood, the way they handled the impromptu weapons they carried, they had not interest in being neighborly.

Shit.

Jack stopped. He couldn't make out the child's doll in detail, couldn't turn his head to look, but he could see the plaything's legs dripped red from knees to toes.

Fat drops of blood welled up and fell to sizzle on the hot gravel bed along which they toiled.

Had she called him Daddy?

The Fourth Day

Mid-afternoon the fourth day, they reached Lake Superior. Sunlight glistened from the deep, cold inland sea that stretched to the horizon. Ojibwe called it *Gichigami. Big shining water.* Not far from shore they found a giant plastic boot set on a concrete pad. Molly had led Jack all the way to Christmas.

Before Collapse, Christmas had been a tourist town known for two things. The world's largest statue of Santa Claus and one of five Kewadin casinos owned by the Ojibwe tribal council. The statue had been blown away, all but that single boot.

The casino flourished, its doors open twenty-four hours each and every day. A string of ramshackle brothels prospered too. The rest of Christmas -- a general store, a dozen houses, grown patchwork over the years from vacation cottages, two ramshackle motels—locked the doors at night.

Jack followed Molly into one of the motels, a place called Pair-a-Dice. A stone fireplace set against one outside wall. A sweet, pungent aroma of burning pine logs filled the common room. Sawdust packed the corners and edges of the space. Tables set haphazard here and there, all empty just now.

At the bar the innkeeper looked up from a game of solitaire. Loose folds of skin hung upon his face and arms, as if he'd thrown on the hide of a larger man that morning and hadn't bothered changing since.

"Well, how about this?" he said. "Welcome, Molly."

"Thank you, Tim," Molly said. "Draw me a pint, will you? I got a thirst."

"Coming right up." Timothy reached for a glass jar.

Molly tipped her head toward the innkeeper. "Jack, this is Timothy Studer. Tim, this is the Apple Man."

Timothy paused at the tap. "No shit?" he said.

"Do you think I'd lie to you, Tim?" Every bit of cheer had disappeared from Molly's voice.

Timothy's eyes widened. The rim of the jar clicked upon the metal tit of the beer tap. "No, ma'am."

Molly leaned against the bar, traced the high blue veins on the back of Timothy's hand with the nail of her index finger.

"Then I guess his beer is on the house, too," she said.

"Well, sure."

Timothy eased his hand from under Molly's touch to fill the first glass. Molly nodded, accepting her due. She'd drunk a good half of it before

Timothy could manage to draw another for Jack. He slid it over and Jack took a sip.

Good stuff.

Bittersweet and cold. The glass chilled Jack's fingers as he drained the jar in a long swallow and returned it to the bar.

"Pleased you like it," Timothy said. "Brew it myself. Used to work for Anheuser-Busch in Ohio. Want another?"

Stupid question.

"Yes, Sir," Timothy said as he refilled the jar. "Twenty-seven years at the brewery in Columbus. Expect the whole damned place is gone now."

Jack hadn't even thought about Ohio in over thirty years. "I expect," he said, then changed the subject. "It's been a good long while since I tasted anything this cold this time of year."

Timothy tipped his head to Molly. "The lady's work. That's why she's always got a bed here, whatever else she might need."

"Are the Boones around?" Molly asked.

"Up to one of the bawdy houses, I expect," Timothy said.

He glanced toward the door. "I'd surely like to watch that. You figure they go after it one at a time or in one big three-for-all?"

"I don't know, Tim," Molly said. "When they come back, I'll mention that you're curious."

"No need to tell them," Timothy said. His Adam's apple bobbed in spastic rhythm. "I'm only kidding."

Molly laughed. That nasty noise again. "Don't you be that way, Tim. I'm only kidding too."

The barkeep didn't answer. He lowered his eyes and rubbed at the gleaming bar with an old bit of towel.

"Did they bring the extra horses?" Molly asked.

"Yes, ma'am. Out to the barn."

"You have horses for us," Jack said. He studied Molly over the edge of his jar.

"I do," Molly said.

Jack returned the jar to the bar top. "Walking here was just another test."

"Uh huh," she said. "The way you handled those two idiots showed me how tough you were, but I had to know how well you'd travel too."

She's lying.

Molly took a last pull from her second beer, wiped her mouth with the back of her free hand, then patted Jack's cheek. "I'm not concerned a bit, old man. Not anymore."

Jack opened his eyes.

He didn't recall falling asleep at the table next to the fire, there in the common room of Pair-A-Dice, but he remembered the details of his dream. A new one too, more vivid that any he could recall.

He reached down to his mailbags, stroking the smooth old leather with his fingertips, taking comfort in the familiar feel. Jack glanced about the common room. None of the other patrons stared, so he mustn't have been shouting as he slept. Cling to small blessings, his mother used to say.

Across the room the outer door opened. Molly entered. Three strangers accompanied her, two men and a woman.

Despite Molly's size, she looked petite next to the trio. All three appeared rough-poured from the same mold. Big. Extroverted. Mean. Long hair tied back from their faces into thick, greasy braids. Both men wore thick moustaches.

The woman looked pissed off not to have one too.

Molly led the three strangers across the common room. They stopped at Jack's table.

"Did you miss me, Jack?" Molly asked.

She sat across from him. The two men settled into the two remaining chairs. The woman stood close to the table. Looming, playing with the hilt of her belt knife. They all looked hard as kerosene, stank of horses, sweat, and black powder. These three had a shared knack and it didn't take a knack to see what it might be. Their kind always survived when times turned mean.

"So, you're the Apple Man?" the woman said. "Hell, we—"

"—figured you'd be bigger or tougher looking —" One of the men jumped in.

"—or something," the second man finished.

Their voices sounded similar too. Deep. Sharp-cut. The three weren't triplets—that wasn't genetically possible—but family. Two brothers and a sister.

"Jack," Molly said, "Meet the Boones. Dewey, Hugh, and Louise, our traveling companions."

Long past twilight.

More people than Jack had come upon in ten years crowded the common room. A few had to be locals, but the rest must have settled for the Pair-A-Dice because their gambling and whoring money had been spent. Jack didn't need a knack to see that that was so. Folks might be looser these days about what they considered money, but when you didn't have any, all the old rules still held.

Molly and the Boones left hours ago, out the door and somewhere else. Jack hadn't been invited. It didn't matter. He felt far too tired to do much of anything, even to get up and take the long walk to his room. Timothy still manned the bar. A group of men gathered about an upright piano near the bar, singing *Hey Jude*, doing it justice too.

"Mr. Everett, the man playing the piano, thinks they're better than The Beatles," someone said. "Timothy thinks Mr. Everett's full of shit."

Jack turned in his seat. He found himself nose to nose with a little girl swaddled in initial clothes. Rags from L.L. Bean and J. Crew. The yellow-brown of a fading bruise peeked from the torn collar of her striped shirt. She couldn't have been more than ten or eleven. Her mass of white-blond hair so fine it looked like spun sugar, her jet-black eyes so sharp they cut to the very depths of Jack's sorry soul.

"Hello," he said.

"Hello." Her ancient's voice didn't match the rest of her. Jack could see the child had witnessed miseries most folks never faced in their entire lives.

"Molly said Tim had a granddaughter," Jack said.

The little girl shook her head. Her dandelion tuft of hair swayed back and forth. "That's what she tells everyone. I'm not related to Timothy, not any way I can figure. I stay with him sometimes."

"Molly's your mother."

"Uh huh."

Jack should have seen it right away, but he was so damned tired. Molly had wrung him out. He smiled at the little girl. "My name's Jack."

"I know," she said. "My name's Cassie."

"Pleased to meet you, Cassie."

The girl curtseyed. "Pleased to meet you too. I always figured Apple Jack was a fairy tale Molly told, like the three bears or the turtle and Bugs Bunny."

"Bugs Bunny isn't a fairy tale. He was—"

"I know," Cassie said. "It's a joke."

Jack grinned. "I see that now."

"And you see how I know who the Beatles are," Cassie said.

"You've got a knack."

She nodded. "Little magic for a little girl. A knack as handy as the one you got."

"You hear things."

"Uh huh. Everything inside most people's heads. I remember every little bit I hear, too." Cassie tapped against her temple with her knuckles. "It's so full in here."

She leaned close, ready to share a secret. "I call it my hearing aid."

"That's a good joke, too," Jack said.

"Thank you. I knew you'd understand."

As Cassie spoke, she patted the back of his hand, offering sympathy without pity, something only the young ever master. "It's not easy having such a good knack, is it?"

Jack shook his head, silent, waiting, hoping.

"I hear things no one should have to hear, and I'm just a poor child," Cassie said. "At least, that's what Timothy says."

"But he wants you to tell him what people think, anyway." Jack leaned closer, whispering now.

"Uh huh. He doesn't care if it hurts me or not. Some days the listening drives me crazy."

"I know how you feel. You can't make it stop. It was like that for me too, when I was your age."

"Uh huh. And I can hear anyone, anywhere. I just give a little push, some direction. If they're alive, no matter how far away, there I am."

"That's *very* useful," Jack said.

"Thank you. I've been listening to you, for longer than you know, and I've decided I like you."

"I like you too."

Cassie nodded. "I thought you would. Anyway, even though Molly told me I'm not to tell anyone about my magic unless she tells me to, I told you because I want to tell you something."

Cassie mumbled to herself, counting on her fingers. "Told. Tell. Tells. Told. Tell." She looked back to Jack, those dark eyes full of mischief. "That's right."

"What—"

She interrupted, began to chant. "Three things only will I say, though you beg and plead and pray."

She giggled. "I just made that up. It's funny, isn't it?"

"Tell me the three things," Jack said, very close now.

"First, Timothy's—"

"You keep you trap shut, girl!"

Timothy had come upon on them as each focused on the other. He clamped his hand onto Cassie's shoulder and jerked her away from Jack. She squirmed, Jack could see her pain, but she remained silent.

"Sorry, Apple Man," Timothy said. His eyes stayed on Cassie. "Child don't know her place."

"I wasn't offended," Jack said. "We were just having a chat."

"Uh huh," Cassie said. "Just talking."

Her teeth chattered as Timothy rattled her back and forth. Her face pinched with the pain.

"Told you to shut it," Timothy said. "Damned brat."

He pulled her close and raised his free hand, ready to strike her. She flinched but didn't cry out, didn't draw away, ready to accept the blow. It never fell. Jack came to his feet, grabbed Timothy's wrist.

"Let the child go, Tim." No hurry in Jack's voice, but the room fell silent. Everyone watched.

"Ain't your business," Timothy muttered. He tried to wrest his wrist free.

Jack squeezed until he heard wrist bones grate, saw Cassie's pain mirrored in Timothy's eyes.

"Let her go," Jack said.

Timothy eased his grip. Cassie scrambled away, clutching her injured shoulder.

"I'm sorry," she said. "I'm sorry!"

Timothy gritted his teeth against the pain. "Not half as sorry as you're gonna be. Count on it, you -"

Jack stepped in tight, so that he and Timothy breathed each other's air. "Here's *my* promise, Tim. If I ever hear that you've touched this child again, I'll come back, do to you whatever you do to her, do it worse. You understand?"

"Molly—that is, the lady ain't going to like this, when I tell her."

In an instant Jack's free hand clutched Timothy's neck, thumb pressed to that prominent Adam's apple.

"*If* you tell her, you mean."

The two men stood for a time, noses almost touching, neither blinking.

After a time Timothy turned his eyes away. "I won't say nothing."

Jack kept his grip on wrist and neck. "Good. And the girl?"

Timothy's chin came up and he met Jack's gaze again, then he looked away. "I won't touch her."

Jack released his neck hold. "I knew you'd see the right of it." He released Timothy's wrist but didn't look away.

"Now, Cassie," Jack said. "Go run along."

In his dream Jack awoke with a pistol in his hand, alerted by some uncommon noise.

Early-morning sunlight filtered through a frost veneer on the interior walls of his expedition tent, lighting the narrow confines with a diffuse glow.

"Annie?" Jack said.

His words weren't much more than a whisper. He had no wish to notify any inadvertent neighbors that he'd spent the night in their vicinity. Since Collapse, survivors had flooded north. The few cities were over-crowded, violent crimes high. Jack had taken to the woods for what little safety could be found. He had no notion of what he'd do, now that he'd survived, but he knew he no longer wished to frequent crowded places.

No one responded to his whispers. Jack threw back the edge of his sleeping bag, sat up, and slipped his feet into his boots. When he undid the tent flap, the outer layer of fabric crinkled like tin foil. Temperatures had plummeted while Jack slept.

Almost a foot of new snow covered everything. The little thermometer he'd sewn onto the flap showed twenty below zero, but it felt colder, fresh from the warm nest of his dreams. Jack eased his head from the tent, holding his pistol inside, out of sight but ready.

A woman sat upon a stump, across the remains of his fire. She faced away from him. Her white-blond hair lay gathered by a ribbon at her neck. Jack knew that ribbon.

"Annie?"

She nodded. "Hello, Jack. How are you, sweetie?"

"It can't be, it can't." Jack shook his head.

"Of course it can. You're dreaming."

A jump cut and Jack stood just behind her. All around him the snow melted, green grass and foliage returned, as if poured from a bucketful of summer.

"I'm lost without you, Annie. I missed you so."

"I miss you too."

Jack circled her, kicking through the weeds and vines. Even the stump Annie sat upon showed signs of renewing life. She spun about with him, refusing to show her face.

"I don't know what to do, Annie. Most days all I can think about is suicide." Jack settled onto the ground.

"Don't you dare say that word. I'll tell you what you're going to do. Plant trees for me."

"What do—"

"You know what I want. Plant apple trees for me, all over. Go out, be my

Apple Jack again."

"I should have come for you. I'm a coward."

"Shush! Now throw that worthless gun away. What would you do with it? You have too much compassion, you always have."

Jack pitched the rusting pistol off into the weeds.

"Good. Now go see who's knocking on the door."

Jack woke upon his back, hands behind his head, lying in the darkness on the lumpy bed in the room Timothy provided. He made it to the door in two strides, almost before the echo of the knock faded. Cassie stepped inside as soon as she found an opening. Jack could see she had been crying again. Her lower lip quivered but the set of her chin, the direct way she looked at Jack with those jet black eyes, told him she'd reached a decision.

"I came to finish talking," she said.

"No need for that."

Cassie's chin came up a bit, her curls bouncing. "Uh huh, there is. I need to make it up."

She drew a deep breath. "I said I'd tell you three things."

Jack nodded. He stepped to the bed and sat on its edge. She moved toward him, taking that stance he'd seen earlier, holding herself as if older than her years.

"First, I can't listen inside Molly's head, something stops me. What I'm going to tell you I know because I listened to you or because I heard her and Timothy talk."

"I understand."

She stopped just short of his knees.

"Don't blame yourself for things that happened long ago," she said. "All you could have done, going back to Detroit that day, would have been to die, too."

"Annie's dead, then," Jack said.

Cassie reached up and brushed at his cheeks with the tips of two fingers, wiping at the tears that had begun to fall. Jack twitched at her touch, his heart tripping behind his ribs.

"I've tried and I can't hear her," she murmured. "That's the second thing."

"And—" Jack said.

He held his breath. It shamed him to use the child but he had to know. Cassie withdrew her hand, pulled her shoulders back, and placed her fists upon her hips. Her brows hunched low and her nose twitched as if she'd smelled something bad.

"Don't you trust her. Molly, I mean. I don't care if she's my mother. She won't help you, even if it would save the world."

"And—" Jack said.

"She wants you to be confused. There's something she's not telling you. Something –"

Cassie's eyes grew wide. "That's four things, no, five. I said three things only. I have such a big mouth. Timothy thinks that all the time. I can't tell you anymore."

"Tell me what she's hiding. I can't see it!"

"I've said as much as I can, can't say anymore. *Can't.* I'm trying to help you, but she's so strong."

Cassie drew her index finger along her lips as if sealing them. "Duct tape, hot wax, and tiny little nails," she chanted.

She stepped close, stretched upon tiptoes to place a soft, warm kiss upon his forehead. "Thank you for helping me," she murmured. "No one's ever understood."

Then she turned and scurried from the room.

The Fifth Day

The five of them—Jack and Molly, Dewey, Hugh, and Louise—rode out of Christmas just after first light. Dewey and Hugh each led a mule laden with canvas-swaddled gear. Louise drove a wagon packed high with canvas-covered crates.

"You forgot to label that stuff 'machine parts,'" Jack said to Louise.

"Go fuck yourself, old man," she replied.

He turned his horse away. Molly rode up next to him. "What was that about?"

Jack grinned. "She didn't get the joke."

"Don't piss off the Boones, Jack. I need you but there's only so much I can do."

"Uh huh."

It rained all night, a long, soaking downpour that didn't appear ready to go dry just because the day had begun. As they set out, it let up long enough to suck in a second breath, then fell again in heavy, piercing sheets.

If anything, the Boones smelled worse wet than dry, and despite rain gear and tarpaulins, everyone and everything soaked through before they made the first mile.

Upset by his dreams, unsettled by Cassie's words, Jack hadn't managed more than an hour's sleep the night before. Even so he could see that Molly and the Boones hadn't slept at all.

Louise appeared in a foul mood. For no reason Jack could see, he became her target. She plucked out her misery in profane rants, taunted him about the Apple Jack legend. Old man this and old man that. He soon had had his fill of her and the rain. Even so neither stopped by the time Molly called a halt, just before last light.

The five of them slouched around a sputtering fire in the shelter of another of Jack's orchards, sharing watered beans and lukewarm coffee. Jack sagged against one of the apple trees, drawing comfort from its scaly bark. He pushed his food about on his tin plate, too tired to care whether or not he ate.

"You plant these?" Louise asked. She patted a tree.

"Yes," Jack replied. "Years ago."

"Why?"

"I wanted to."

"Smart ass."

Jack ignored her. From the size of the trees, he suspected it was one of the first groves he'd planted. He kept no records though, and after all the years one bunch of apple trees looked much like another. Even so it always felt as if he'd come home. Annie would have loved every single tree.

"Dewey's got extra weapons, old man," Louise said. "Why don't you take a gun?"

"I don't care for guns," Jack said.

"Don't have the stomach for killing, I suppose," Louise said. She dug at her beans. "Fucking useless old man."

Before the others could react, Jack was behind her, using her as a shield, gripping her braid in one hand as he pressed the jagged tip of a rusted piece of metal packing strap tight against her neck. She pushed hard against him.

"It's taken years but I have the stomach for it," he said, breathing the words into her ear. "You don't stop calling me old man, you won't have a chance to join me in my infirmity."

"You two stop it," Molly said. "Or I'll turn you both to frogs."

Jack and Louise ignored her, continued to struggle.

"Goddamn it. I'm serious. Stop it."

Molly's right. Fighting's wasted effort.

Jack leaned back from Louise. "Leave me be, you hear?"

"I hear you, old man," Louise said.

Jack let her braid go, tossed the metal strip into the fire, and moved away.

Dewey and Hugh inched back from the fire, as far away from Molly they dared. Louise didn't move. She fussed with her braid and straightened her vest.

"Don't you ever touch me again," she said, not looking at Jack. "You do, I'll tear you to pieces and fuck the cost."

"Now, now, Louise," Molly said. "To subjugate the enemy without doing battle is the highest of excellence. That's from chapter three of Sun Tzu's *The Art of War.* You ever read it?"

Louise scrawled. "I can't read."

"Why doesn't that surprise me?" Molly said between one mouthful of beans and the next. "Take a gun, Jack. Humor her."

No use arguing.

"All right."

He grabbed a chunky, black-matte Glock nineteen, stuck it into one of his bags, and curled into his blankets. The camp remained silent. No one wanted to upset Molly any further. Jack soon dropped away into his dreams.

Jack shivered from the cold. He crouched within growing shadows upon a snow-dusted rise, dressed in jeans and a tee shirt, bootless, without even his mailbags to ease the chill.

The beanpole child stood next to him, tight against his bony shoulder. Try as he might, he couldn't see her clearly but the scent of her fear remained palpable. Her ragged fingernails clawed at his bare arm.

"Oh, Daddy," the little girl whimpered. "Save them."

"Shhhh!"

Below, Annie stood with her back to Jack and the girl, her long russet-red hair unfettered and flowing in the wind, facing a dozen Scavengers, back-to-back with Seth and Virginia, her parents. Jack ached to step from hiding, to fight beside them, but he couldn't move. They fought well, all three seasoned veterans by now, but the inevitable outcome played out in grisly detail.

Every blow. Every cut. Every scream. Every single hot drop of blood in vivid red against the cold white snow.

"Help them, Daddy!"

"I can't." He hated himself for having to mouth the words. "There's too many Scavengers."

"You could try!" the girl shouted. Her voice climbed in volume, become more and more adult with each word. More and more familiar. "You could have tried, you bastard!"

He came to himself in the Michigan woods, clutching wet and tangled blankets.

The Boones lay nearby wrapped in steaming wool and canvas, heads together, snoring, oblivious to his cries. But Molly sat across the fire bundled in her own thoughts, watching him with those damnable new-charcoal eyes. "Bad dreams, Jack?" she asked.

He ignored her, settled back down into his blankets. The familiar scent of apples all about him was nearly more than he could bear.

The Sixth Day

Once upon a time, it had been K.I. Sawyer Air Force Base. Then it became K.I. Sawyer International Airport and Business Center. Now five thousand acres of no-man's land. Nothing but one big jumble of broken concrete and brick, pocked by craters and deadfalls.

"Unload the gear," Molly ordered.

They stood within a cluster of crumbling buildings near the southeast edge of the compound. The structures were set around a pond fed by a fast-running stream.

Louise muttered something but Molly ignored it. She slid from her horse and stalked toward the center building. Jack followed, picking his way along the edge of the pond. The ground felt like rotten sponge.

Molly stood half hidden in a doorway. Beyond her Jack saw a broad and shadowed wall. Centered upon it, two-feet-high white letters spelled out a single word. *DELPHI.*

"Come over here, Jack," Molly said. "And look in there."

Jack peered into the moldering interior. Molly moved close, leaning into him, one hand hooked around his elbow. She tilted her head so that her lips lay next to his ear.

He could feel the heat of her breath, moving across the fine hairs upon the whorled inner ridges of his ear. It didn't rouse him half as much as the thought of touching a computer keyboard after all these years. Molly laid her hand upon his forearm.

"What I want is behind that wall," she said.

"Damn it, Jack! Can you do it or not?"

Molly sat upon the edge of a folding table littered with cables and computer gear. Her legs swung back and forth, as if she pumped a swing. Nearly six hours had passed since Jack began to set up equipment rebuilt from components of a dozen different brands.

A heavy cable snaked down a corridor to where the portable generator from Hugh's wagon fed juice to the building's defunct electrical grid.

"Well, can you?" Molly asked.

Jack recognized her growing tension. "Not if you keep pestering me," he said. He wouldn't look at her. "I'll get it. It just takes time."

"We ain't got all day, old man," Louise said, from her seat atop a second table. "No telling who might come nosing around, wanting what we're after, too."

Two figures appeared at the entry just as the generator kicked in. Its clatter shook the floor and walls, made further conversation impossible. Louise leaped from the table, gun drawn even before she was on her feet. She relaxed when she recognized her brothers.

"That racket don't help the cause none," Hugh said. "Any more than the damned rain."

"Anybody out there?" Molly asked.

"Nobody wants to be out in this shit," Dewey said.

"Dipwad," Louise said. "Don't mean nobody's out there."

The generator shut down just as she spoke. In the silence Dewey stared at his sister, eyes narrowed. "Who you calling dipwad?"

Louise straightened, brought her gun back to the ready.

The room was silent except for the click of Jack's keyboard and the drum of the rain on the sagging roof. Hugh stepped close to Louise.

"Apologize," he said.

"For what?" Louise said. "He *is* a dipwad. He don't have enough brains —"

Dewey took a step forward, kicking up water from the puddles gathered on the tile floor, swinging his shotgun out from under his canvas duster.

Hugh pinched Louise's earlobe, held it. "Apologize. Now."

Louise froze under her brother's touch. Her eyes shifted from one brother to the other. She lowered her handgun. "I'm sorry, Bro. Didn't mean what I said. Waiting on the old man's making me grouchy."

She didn't sound sorry.

Dewey stared at her, still cradling the shotgun, then he nodded and let the gun swing back under the coat. He glared at Jack. "Okay. I'm itchy too."

The rain thundered on the building roof loud enough to drown the sound of the generator. A broad puddle coated the floor and Dewey kicked at the water as he stood at the door, peering into the deluge.

"Fucking rain," he said.

No one responded. Molly sat cross-legged upon the worktable beside Jack, elbows on knees, chin on fists. Hugh and Louise had settled on the second table. Louise pulled five metal balls from her knapsack.

"C'mon, Hughie," she said. "Wanna juggle?"

Hugh tossed away the old chair rail he'd been whittling on, folded his knife and slid it into a jacket pocket. "All right."

Louise tossed one ball to him and then another. Soon all five were in the air, flying back and forth between them.

"They're juggling hand grenades," Jack said, not looking up from his work. "That backpack is filled with the things."

Molly popped off the table. "Goddamn it," she said. "I told you no explosives. I swear, talking to you three's like telling rain not to fall."

"You ain't the boss," Louise said.

Hugh kept juggling but glanced at Molly. He sighed, a loud grunt of air. "Put the toys away, Lulu."

One at a time Louise caught the grenades and didn't throw them back, returned them to the backpack, instead. Jack could see her from the corner of his eye. She didn't look happy. Molly returned to the tabletop.

"Thank you," Jack said.

She patted the top of his head. "Don't worry, Apple Tree Man. I've got your back."

Jack turned to her, eyes wide, but returned his attention to his work when musical notes sounded from speakers set into the computer monitor. He studied the screen for an instant, then rocked back in his chair, stretching, cracking his knuckles above his head. Molly jumped from the table, wrapped her arms around Jack's neck, and peered over his shoulder.

"You got it!" she said.

Jack reached out to the control mouse and clicked a button. Hidden electric motors hummed. A crack appeared across the center of the logo wall, splitting the letters in half. Dewey spun away from the entry. Hugh jumped from the table.

"Ta da," Jack said.

He stood, scooped up his mailbags. The generator clattered into life. Within a minute the wall was gone, replaced by the dark maw of a freight elevator.

"Dewey, stay here and keep watch," Molly said.

"Should we bring our gear?" Louise asked. Molly waved the words away as she moved toward the opening.

"Leave it," she said. "We won't be long."

The elevator gaped, big as the room Jack had occupied at the Pair-A-Dice. The ride down proved steady and smooth, not dry though. Water oozed from the walls of the shaft beyond the wire cage, dripped from the wire cage, and misted the air.

"Ground's soaked up enough water—" Hugh said.

"—to float a freighter," Louise said.

"Doesn't matter," Molly said. "We're just in and out."

The elevator eased to a stop. Hugh tugged at the gate and the frame slid upward. Blackness lay beyond. Jack heard a click. Light sprang into being just above her left shoulder. She had clipped a camp flashlight there. She stepped off the elevator and reached to the right.

Intense light from overhead fixtures burnt away the darkness. Molly turned off her light. She and Jack, Hugh, and Louise stood at the edge of a high-ceiling room with all manner of test equipment lining the walls. In the center two vehicles took up much of the space.

They had the look of suburban utility vehicles, although sleeker and more substantial than any SUV Jack had ever seen. A film of dust dulled the cherry-red finish of both vehicles. Stylized white lettering along the rear fenders aped the sign on the lobby wall. DELPHI.

"Concept cars," Jack said.

"Uh huh," Molly said. "Not like any automobile ever made." She walked around the first vehicle, pointing out features as if she would receive a commission if it sold.

"Molded Kevlar bodies. Armored glass. Unified bi-wire chassis control. An electric motor on each wheel powered by hydrogen fuel cells with an internal hydrogen conversion plant."

"What the hell does all that mean?" Hugh asked.

"They're test vehicles," Jack said. He walked around one of the prototypes, studying it. "Look at those tires. They're armored, self-inflating, and all-terrain too."

"Uh huh," Molly said.

"So what?" Hugh said.

"They'll go anywhere," Molly said. "Take all sorts of punishment without

191

stopping."

"And they don't run on gasoline," Jack added.

"What are they worth?" Louise asked.

"Before Collapse? Upwards of twenty million each," Molly said. "These days, I know someone at the Soo who'll give us enough for them to satisfy our every want and need."

"How we going to get them there?" Hugh asked.

"We're going to drive," Molly replied. "Me and Jack."

"If he ain't so old he forgot how," Louise said.

"He still remembers," Molly said. "Don't you, Jack?"

Jack ignored the two of them. He stepped to the driver's door of one vehicle, pulled on the latch. The door swung up and out with a sibilant hiss. Bucket seats with gray leather upholstery. Deep-pile gray carpet covered the flat floor. It still smelled like a new car. Lights blinked on the control console.

"It has power," Jack said.

"Internal charger," Molly said. "Been drawing juice since the generator kicked in."

"How do you know so damned much about them?" Hugh asked.

"A geezer almost as old as Jack told me," Molly replied. "Go ahead, Jack. Show us you know how to start it."

Jack pulled his mailbags to his chest and settled into the driver's seat. A hum, like the whine of a mosquito hoping for a snack, nibbled at Jack's ears. The seat cradled him in its leather folds. No steering wheel. Instead, a joystick set at the end of each armrest. Jack slid his hands into place.

"Identify yourself." A computer-generated voice.

It sounded so much like the machine in that old science fiction movie. *Blue Danube*, the Strauss waltz, began to play on interior speakers. Someone long ago had had a bent sense of humor.

"My name is John Chapman."

"Good morning, John."

Jack decided to go along with the joke.

"Good morning, Hal," he said.

"I hope you are well today, John."

"I am. How are you?"

"I am well, thank you. Functioning within all program perimeters. Would you like to take a test drive?"

Jack couldn't resist. "Yes, Hal. Open the pod bay doors."

Through the windshield Jack saw glowing green lines appear upon the floor, leading to the elevator.

"Please push the green button on the left joystick, John. I'll take us upstairs and then turn the controls over to you."

Jack extended his thumb toward the blinking button. Before he could engage it, gunfire chattered from above. The elevator gate clicked shut, the platform began its climb to ground level.

Hugh stomped toward the elevator. "Who the hell's up there?"

"Whoever," Louise replied. "Dewey's up there alone."

Jack could just hear the exchange over the noise from the elevator and the hiss of the climate control equipment inside the vehicle. He slid out of the seat, stood beside Molly.

"We gotta go help him!" Hugh said.

"Wasted effort," Jack said. "He's dead by now."

"Shut your trap, old man." Louise said. Jack thought he had seen her pissed before. He was wrong.

"He's right," Molly said. "You know he is."

Louise shook her head, refusing to listen. She and Hugh stood next to the elevator. He beat upon the wire barricade to no avail. The elevator had reached the ground floor. Louise began to prod the control panel.

"How do you make this damned thing work?" she asked.

Before anyone could answer, the elevator came to life again. Louise jerked her hands away as if the buttons had snapped at her. She scrambled back, shouting as she moved. "Find cover, Hugh."

Hugh back-pedaled, hunkered behind a workbench, automatic rifle at the ready. Louise chose a heavy red-metal tool cart but Molly remained standing in the open, waiting.

"Don't be fools," Louise said. "Take cover."

Molly stepped behind the open vehicle door, pulling Jack with her. He didn't argue. The elevator finished its descent, the garage fell into silence once again.

"Open it, Hugh," Molly said.

"Stay where you are, Hughie," Louise shouted.

He ignored her. He scuttled to the elevator, rifle held at the ready, and peered through the mesh.

"Oh, damn!" he said. "Dewey!"

He jerked the gate up. A body sprawled at the center of the elevator car. "Dewey!"

Molly pulled Jack in front of her as Hugh stepped into the car and grabbed Dewey's shoulder. He pulled. A gout of fire roared from the elevator. The vehicle door slammed into Jack's chest. Hugh's mangled body flew across the workshop and slammed into a concrete support pillar, spraying beaded blood in a red fan from one out-flung hand.

"Hughie!" Louise cried. She glared at Molly. "You could have stopped him. Why didn't you?"

"He wouldn't wait," Molly said, shrugging.

Louise spit onto the floor at Jack's feet. "They have to pay for that. What are you going to do?"

"I'm going to wait right here," Molly said. "But don't let me hold you back. I'll even give you protection." She flicked her hand toward Louise and muttered something unpronounceable.

Louise nodded. "When I get back, one of those is mine." She entered the elevator, slammed the gate. It climbed away.

"You didn't shield her," Jack said.

"More for us," Molly replied. "After Louise wears them down, you and I will go up and finish it. Then it's a nice, easy drive to the Soo."

"If you eliminate me, you could have it all to yourself."

She smiled and shrugged. "I need you as second driver."

"Bullshit," Jack said. "Those things drive themselves."

Molly studied him for a moment, one eyebrow raised. When she spoke, her voice trembled just a bit. "Why would I want to kill you—Daddy?"

Jack blinked and pieces twisted into shape.

"I was eleven when Mama died," Molly said. "She never stopped hoping you'd rescue us. She used to say, 'someday, Molly Marie, someday your daddy will find us.'"

She glanced at the elevator, tilting her head. From above gunfire grew louder. Molly nodded, as if she heard things Jack couldn't. After a time she returned her attention to him.

"What happened, old man? Why didn't you come for us?" She laid her right hand on the juncture of her neck and her shoulder and rubbed. One of Annie's poses. Those dark eyes, blacker than his own but not by much, drilled into him.

Memories and dreams tugged at Jack, almost overwhelmed him. He had to force himself to remember she had lied to him, that it was all performance.

"You didn't have to run this shabby con game," Jack said. "I didn't have to kill those men. The Boones didn't have to die. If you'd come at me straight, told me who you and Cassie were, what you wanted, I'd have come gladly. We could have had fun driving these things back to the Soo."

"It's not a con game."

"The hell it's not. I can't mutter an incantation like you do and see the way of it, but it always comes to me, sooner or later."

She remained silent and the last piece dropped into place.

"But then you knew that," Jack said. "You pushed me so hard and set Louise on me to distract me, to keep me from seeing. You don't have big magic."

"To hell with your silly knack," she said. "It's wrong."

"Not about this."

She turned away from him even as she interrupted, and moved toward the elevator.

"We'll settle this after we get out of here," she said.

Okay.

Jack would play her game until then.

"Whatever you like," he said. "Once we get upstairs."

"Agreed," Molly said. "Louise should have them hacked to manageable pieces by now."

As if she had been heard, there was a monstrous explosion from above. The concrete floor rumbled. The elevator shrieked, high pitched and metallic, and plummeted into view, jamming to a stop four feet from the garage floor, only half the car visible within the shaft opening. It shuddered, as if caught within the jaws of some invisible Brobdingnagian mutt, and then its front edge dropped another six or eight inches.

"The grenades!" Molly said. "Those damned grenades!"

Jack could see the seared corpse of Dewey Boone, tumbled toward the lip. No sign of Louise. The overhead lights flickered and went out, drowning them in darkness.

"Now that's a surprise," Jack said.

"To hell with you, old man!"

Light winked into being. Molly had turned on the flashlight once again.

Water gushed from the shaft. Jack figured the explosion must have opened a channel to the swollen pond. The workspace flooded as if by magic. By the time Molly and Jack reached the wreckage of the elevator, the water wetted the cuff of Jack's jeans. He kept an eye out, mindful of shadows in the water.

"We'll have to climb out of here," he said.

A growing cataract roiled over the broken lip of the lobby opening. The tang of spent explosives saturated the damp air but the rush of the water was the only sound.

195

Jack snaked his way into the tangle and began an ascent, placing hands and feet just so, easing upward. Molly clambered into the wreckage behind him.

"Where are you going?" She had to shout to be heard above the rush of the water.

Jack hung at his own height above the top of the mangled elevator frame, already out of breath, but able to reply. "Out of here. You coming?"

"You think I'd stay if I could make that climb?"

"Use your magic, if you really have it," Jack said. "Fly out or transport yourself upstairs. It's all the same to me."

"I can't do either one, old man!"

"Necessity teaches fast and well, Molly Marie."

The water almost reached to Molly's knees now. She glared up at him. If she could have reached him, she would have ripped him from the wall, no doubt about that.

She swallowed, frowning as if something bitter had gone down. "I can't do magic. All I have is a knack, like you."

The exchange required more effort than Jack had expected. His heart sounded in his ears, a trip hammer. His lungs burned raw from the effort. He almost choked on the wetted air.

Even so he grinned.

"It's in the genes," he said. "I see patterns. Cassie hears what people think. You must be able to persuade people using your words. I always thought Annie had a touch of that."

"If she did, it didn't always work. It took us 'til I was seven to make it across the Bridge. We heard about you, looked for you for four years, but you weren't so famous then."

"I didn't know."

"Right. Scavengers caught the four of us outside Kipling, in December. Mama made me run away!" She was crying now. Jack gave her points for style.

"I wanted to stay and fight with them," Molly said. "She wouldn't let me. They overran the three of them, Mama, grandma, and grandpa, there in the snow, and ripped them to bloody bits. I had to watch it all!"

"My dream—"

Molly rubbed away her tears. "Folks are most suggestible when they're nodding off or when they're tired. Or when they're under stress. Now *get down here, help me up that fucking wall!"*

"All right," he said. "Here I come."

Jack gave up two feet of wall before he could slow himself. Even seeing she'd played him, seeing how she yanked his strings, he still had to fight the urge to work his way down the wall.

Time to make a sacrifice.

He shrugged the mailbags from his shoulders, dropped them onto her. She cursed and the compulsion weakened. Jack focused on the sound and the feel of the water rushing over him. Tried to ignore the sound of Molly scrambling about the wreckage.

Even so her words got through. "Come back here!"

Maybe—

"God-damn you, Jack. Come here!"

Her own panic weakened her. She began to rant but the sound of the falling water hid her words from him. He continued upward. Halfway to the light, a great chunk of concrete fell away below him. Molly screamed. Jack couldn't ignore that. He paused to risk a look back. The concrete had pinned her in place. She lay pressed to the opposite wall, skewered at the shoulder by a rusted twist of re-bar. The surface of the water swirled at her midriff. It ran red.

"Come and help me!" she called.

Perhaps—

Jack didn't heed her call, didn't feel quite such a need to do so. He hung there, watching.

Molly marshaled her strength and tried again. She sounded so much like Annie. "I'm your daughter. I swear I am!"

"I believe you," Jack said. "But I'm not certain I can get out of here myself. I know I can't help you."

"You could try, you bastard! You could try!"

I could—

He turned away but her magic lingered. He couldn't summon effort to resume his climb. Molly's voice settled.

"Don't you go away," she said.

Jack's resolve wavered. He looked again. The water washed against her collarbones. She reached to him, beckoning.

"Give me a hand here, Apple Jack. Can't do this by myself."

Annie's words. Molly had used Cassie to read his memories.

The water showered over him in its chilling headlong rush, washing thirty years of guilt away. The taste of champagne still lay upon his tongue, the appled scent of Escape enveloped him, but this time he clearly felt Molly's handiwork behind it all.

"You've played me for the last time," he said.

"No, I swear, I won't do it again!" She sputtered as water lapped over her chin.

Since seeing it for what it was, Jack had never questioned his small magic. He didn't doubt it now. Molly was his daughter, no doubt of that. He wanted desperately to go to her.

"Daddy, you've got to help me!"

She would continue to use her gift against him. Would end his life, if and when she could. He saw that as if it were an old motion picture.

Jack tasted sour tears. He had lost her for a second time, just as surely as he'd lost her and Annie all those years ago. He'd failed both of them in his indecision then, and he was so very sorry. Molly would never forget, though, never forgive him, never give him a chance to make up that single act of cowardice.

"Daddy, please!"

But Cassie waited in Christmas, alone with Timothy. Jack would be damned if he'd fail his granddaughter, too. His eyes lingered below but his fingers skittered across rough concrete, searching for something to hold on to. Something real and solid. There.

"Daddy!" his prodigal daughter stretched her hand toward him again. "Don't let me die."

Jack felt a mild need to heed her words but he managed to ignore it. He turned to face the concrete wall and climbed away from Molly's screams.

We Who Are Ernest Now Salute You

Darkness lay deep and comfortable upon Key West.

The few who noticed figured it for another power outage. The Florida Keys Electric Cooperative had never been the most dependable of systems, even when a minion of supreme evil wasn't strutting about the city plying his trade.

The minion in question, known to his many sudden acquaintances as Gnash, blinked into being outside Sloppy Joe's Bar at the corner of Duval and Greene Streets. Nothingness to full presence in a nanosecond. He towed a little man in a threadbare hospital gown in his wake.

Their sudden appearance didn't seem to bother passersby, any more than the widespread darkness, but strange occurrences go unnoticed every day in America's Southernmost City.

Gnash stood tall, broad-shouldered, and shaggy blond. A dude dressed for the Florida Keys. Worn flip-flops, tattered jeans, and a faded red tee shirt, announcing in cracked white letters across his chest that the floggings would continue until morale improved.

He pointed into the bar through the building's open west portico. The interior was lit by candlelight but the fellow seated at the short bar was easy to spot. A large man, built with plenty of beef, sporting a thick, white beard.

The fellow pounded back the latest in a long chain of Hammers. Two ounces of Bacardi rum, one ounce of blackberry brandy, one ounce of strawberry liqueur, and one ounce of banana liqueur. A drink that flowed like cough syrup and hit the throat like molten steel.

"You see him, Roger?" Gnash asked.

Professor Roger Cooperman, B.A., M.A. PhD, winner of the 1995 Heineker Prize for Literary Excellence, noted author of *Ernest: A Complicated Man and His Simple Works*, reached behind him to tighten the laces of his gown, trying to cover his scrawny ass.

"Is that Papa?" he asked, almost whispering.

"What do you think?" Gnash replied. "You're the one with the deathbed wish."

Roger sidled into the bar, careful not to lose his cardboard slippers or his gown, and eased up to the bearded man. He pointed to the fellow's almost empty glass and was offered a seat on the adjoining stool. The bartender, duly summoned to do his duty, filled the empty, and settled a new glass full of liquid courage before Roger.

The two men soon stepped away from the world, wandering into conversation about the intricacies of writing simple words and what it meant to be a man. Gnash stepped to a nearby parked car and leaned against the fender. He chuckled. Arranging the meeting had been more fun that taking candy from small tykes and that sat very high on his list of jollies.

"Up to the old tricks, I see."

The newcomer was dressed in pressed khaki slacks and a crisp pale blue oxford shirt. Something about him hinted that he had arrived in much the same manner as Gnash and Roger, although with a more divine assistance.

"Hiya, Gideon," Gnash said. "Too late. You can't have him."

"No. You can't have him, at least not for another thirty-seven years."

"What are you yammering about? The geek's dying of inoperable cancer. I read his charts before I snatched him from that hospital in Seattle."

Gideon joined Gnash against the automobile. He folded his arms across his chest.

"He was praying for a miracle when you arrived," Gideon said. "God has decided, in His infinite wisdom, to allow that miracle."

"The dweeb's healed?"

"Indeed."

"I'll be damned."

"Without question."

Gnash pushed away from the fender and brushed his hands together. "Oh, well, it's not like it's going to be forever, is it?"

"There is the matter of The Accord," Gideon said.

"I didn't lie to him."

"No one said anything about lying."

"Then what do you think I did?"

Gideon opened his right hand, palm up. A thick paperback book appeared from the ether, nestled there, open to a page near the front. Gideon didn't bother to look at the book.

He quoted. "No tempted soul shall be delivered into his or her past or future, or given knowledge of his or her past or future, whatsoever his or her wishes."

The book disappeared with the same suddenness with which it had appeared. Gideon brushed his palms together. "That sort of violation nullifies any agreement you may have struck with him, don't you think?"

Gnash grinned. "You should pay more attention to your timepiece when you go ambulance chasing."

He reached into the air, collected a newspaper, and handed it to Gideon. It smelled a bit mildewed. One corner had turned a mottled blue-green.

"Today's *Key West Citizen*," Gnash said. "Check the date."

Gideon examined the newspaper. "July 20—"

He stopped as he noticed the year. He stepped away from his perch and peered into the darkness, taking a closer look at the automobile. A brand-new Lexus. An HS-250 hybrid.

"You see," Gnash said. "We aren't in Roger's past or his future."

Gideon glanced into the candle-lit interior, toward the two men at the bar. He examined the newspaper again and this time noticed the headline.

"Oh," he said. His voice lost its steam. "Hemingway Days."

"Uh huh."

"Dear God, you've delivered Professor Cooperman to an Ernest Hemingway *pretender!*"

"Uh huh." Gnash peered into the bar, smiling with an almost paternalistic pride. "Damned fine one, too. He could win the competition this year, even if he's so nervous he showed up two days early. In fact, I've guaranteed his victory."

"You managed a twofer out of this deal?"

"Uh huh."

"You *are* evil," Gideon said. "Do you know that? Pure evil."

"Hey," Gnash said, shrugging. "It's a job."

And Bay the Moon

Four months, slipping after-hours into Ravenna Park to take five turns along the narrow path that twisted through the ravine. Four months, and tonight was the first time Borden had encountered another runner.

He listened to the quick footfalls upon the gravel path behind him. Maybe it was a fluke. Maybe he wouldn't have to find another place to run.

A flat, straight stretch afforded a chance to look back. His pulse jumped. It wasn't another person behind him. It was a dog, a huge mutt, and it was gaining. Borden fought away an impulse to pick up his pace. He focused upon his breathing and his heart rate dropped.

"Easy, Jimmy," he said, talking to himself. "You can handle a dog. No big deal."

Borden was a tall man, long-limbed and graceful, with an endurance developed through years of exercise. Running was an integral piece of his regime and he wouldn't allow a mange-riddled mutt to upset the program.

A snootful of oleoresin capsicum would wrap the mutt's tail around his ass and send him whining. Borden's fingers slit the Velcro of the nylon pouch at his waist, settled the aerosol can of pepper spray into his left hand.

"Come catch me, if you can," he said.

The pattern of footfalls changed. Borden risked a glance and his breath quickened. The dog, some sort of flop-eared hound, ran twenty-five yards back. Three other mutts almost as large as the first had joined him, strung out along the back trail but gaining with jointless ease.

The hound's eyes fixed upon Borden's face, would not look away, and as it ran, it lifted its muzzle and howled. The sound raised the hairs on Borden's neck.

He turned away, intent upon a rough patch of trail, and picked up his pace despite his resolve not to do so. When he risked another look back, there were seven of them.

Too many to do battle.

Borden pushed the pepper spray back into the fanny pack. It was just under a mile back to his waiting automobile, time to run, perhaps, for his very life.

And so the night's run became a race. The crunch of gravel under paws grew louder. He could smell them now. A green-grass odor touched by the iron scent of blood. Borden focused on the sound of his own footfalls, the swelling pressure within his chest, and the glow of the lights ahead.

A glimpse of yellow light reflected from his car's windows gave Borden courage to look back. The hound hurried along less than ten paces away. As it saw his face, the dog renewed its baying. Borden shuddered. Clear to see, he wasn't going to reach his automobile. The pack would run him down, rip him to pieces.

As he burst into the clearing, someone stumbled into his path. Borden did a hasty stutter-step, managed to hold his footing, but the other man dropped into a heap of rags and alcoholic curses. The curses became screams as all seven dogs fell upon the ragged man and tore at him with teeth and claws.

Not a single dog followed Borden as he sprinted across the clearing and skidded to a gasping stop beside his car. He had his key out of the fanny pack and ready.

In an instant, he threw himself inside. The growl of the engine drowned the ragged man's screams. Borden caught one final image of the hound's muzzle pointed toward the sky as he skidded from the lot.

Running made sleep come easier. Running away did not.

Nightmare images of the dogs tearing at the ragged man kept Borden at the edge of slumber. Twice he awoke, safe in the bedroom of his condominium on North University Way, to discover himself out of bed, panting, face pressed against cold window glass. Both times he stood for long minutes, staring across the trees to the northeast toward the park.

In the morning Borden felt exhausted, angry with himself for fleeing. At the office he scoured the Internet, the morning newspaper too, but could find no mention of the incident.

He left at noon claiming client meetings after lunch, made a quick stop at home, and spent the rest of the day getting ready to return to the park.

Despite his preparation Borden's heart rate spiked when he slipped onto the graveled path just after midnight. Now he was well into the final lap and he had calmed.

The weight of his pistol, nestled in the holster strapped across his chest, comforted him. As he ran, the musty aroma of sweated leather helped him to remember that payback was a bitch.

A bag lady had been scavenging trashcans when he arrived but she had disappeared when he completed his first loop. Borden hadn't seen another living creature since.

Then the moon broke through the cloud cover and a single dog stood silhouetted against the trees upon a low rise to Borden's left.

The hound.

Borden could hear a note of anticipation as the dog arched its neck and howled. Within seconds all seven mutts were on the trail behind him.

Borden ran with ease, buoyed by anticipation. He knew the pack was just yards behind him but he did not care, did not look back. He hurdled into the clearing near his car, turned in mid-stride, drawing the pistol from its holster as he spun, and slid to a halt against a wooden post.

The weapon was up and aimed as the hound leapt. Borden squeezed the trigger. The bullet knocked the dog from the air and the point-blank shot opened its chest. As the other dogs reached him, Borden shot each one.

His eyes stung from the gun smoke, his hands shook from the pressure of his grip on the pistol, and his ear rang but Borden couldn't remember ever feeling better. He stepped toward the mess of canine bodies, prepared to savor his handiwork.

And the hound began to struggle to its feet.

Borden screamed and fired two more thirty-eight caliber slugs into the animal. All he had left. Even as the hound once more collapsed, the other beasts began to stir. The second and third dogs were up and staggering toward him before Borden stumbled to his car and fish-tailed from the park.

Every crackpot site on the Internet had said Professor Morton Thorn had the last word on strange. And so Borden had expected something leaning toward the arcane. A cramped basement office perhaps, with battered furniture and flickering light fixtures, odd-shaped skulls, and dusty artifacts scattered atop stacks of brittle manuscripts.

Instead Thorn's office at the University of Washington proved full of light and painted in soothing pastels. Books and journals were organized in gleaming, shoulder-high bookcases along the walls and plants hung at two windows. No skulls of any kind were in evidence. Borden didn't see a speck of dust.

"You were expecting Christopher Lee or Peter Cushing, weren't you?" Thorn said. He was compact and fit, maybe thirty-five, with a tidy thatch of blond hair.

"I didn't mean to stare," Borden said. "I haven't had much sleep since Tuesday."

Thorn waved away the apology. "Don't worry about it. Have a seat. You said on the phone that you had questions."

Borden settled into the offered chair. Now that he was here he found he wasn't certain how to couch the questions he wanted to ask.

"I run five nights a week in Ravenna Park," he said.

Thorn propped his elbows on his desk and leaned forward, his eyes bright, expectant. "I know the place," he said.

"For the past two nights while I ran, I've been chased. No, that's not the right word. I've been hunted."

Borden paused, afraid now to say the words. Thorn remained quiet, waiting. Borden thought he saw a certain expectation in the professor's expression. He sighed and plunged ahead.

"I was hunted by some sort of creatures."

"Creatures?"

Borden couldn't sense even a bit of condescension in Thorn's voice.

"They looked like dogs, big dogs," he said. "But they weren't any such thing."

"Did they attack you?"

"No. I got away but I think they killed a homeless man Tuesday night."

"You think?"

"He and I ran into each other and he fell. The creatures jumped him and I escaped, drove away without doing a thing to help him."

Borden watched Thorn, waiting for the professor to reach for the telephone. Instead Thorn sat back in his chair and rocked from side to side.

"What could you have done, Mr. Borden?"

"I don't know." Borden's voice sounded rusty. "Something."

"You said you were chased twice," he said. "Did you go back last night?"

"Yes," Borden said, whispering.

"Why?"

"They were strays. They killed a man in my park for God's sake. I took a gun with me, I planned to shoot them."

"To salve your conscience?"

Borden studied Thorn's face for a time, eyes and mouth held tight. At last he sighed. "I suppose."

"You said you planned to shoot them."

"I did shoot them, all seven of them," Borden said. "They died – and then they came back to life."

Borden knew how that sounded. He waited for Thorn to tell him he was crazy.

Instead Thorn stopped rocking. He sat up straight and slid his chair closer to the desk. Borden pulled back. Thorn didn't look quite so harmless now.

"You're messing with something nasty, Mr. Borden," Thorn said. "You should find someplace else to run."

"Then you believe me!"

"Oh, yes. You're not the first to come to me with the tale. I know for fact that there are several packs of these beasts scattered around the city but the one at Ravenna Park is the largest."

He stood, walked to a bookcase, and began to search titles.

"They're lycanthropes," he said. "A genetic abnormality. Those afflicted with it can transform into any sort of carnivore they want. Dogs. Big cats. Wolves."

He pulled a book from its place and returned to his chair. He laid the book upon the desk between them.

"That is not a work of fiction, Mr. Borden," Thorn said. "Believe what it says. Protect it too. There aren't many copies and writing it cost a man his life."

Borden reached to slide the book toward him.

Thorn laid his hand upon it. "Don't take it unless you intend to see this through."

"Even if it kills me," Borden said. "I have to finish this."

Thorn took away his hand. "That could happen. These creatures are people but they aren't poor souls with a curse. They like what they become and they can change at will. They'll come looking for you now that you've seen what they are."

"Can you tell me how to kill them?"

"If you wish."

"Do I have to use silver bullets?" Borden asked.

Thorn smiled. "No," he said. "They do the job but they're damned expensive. Lead slugs will do fine."

"But I —" Borden said.

Thorn held up his index finger and kept talking. "That little gun of yours just irritated them. You've got to have something big with bullets that shatter on impact."

Thorn drew a breath and ran his hand through his hair. "Look," he said. "Here's better advice. Give me the book back and move away from here, far away."

"I can't do that," Borden said.

Thorn settled back in his chair. "All right. After they're down, shoot them in the head. Destroy the brain and they won't get back up."

Borden nodded. He picked up the book and moved toward the door. Thorn remained seated. Outside clouds drifted over the sun and the office darkened.

"Just in case, Mr. Borden," Thorn said. "You might consider saving a bullet for yourself."

Minutes before midnight.

Ravenna Park felt deserted as Borden climbed from his car, but in the distance he heard a drawn-out howl. He fought back an urge to respond. He trotted to the path and began to run. No waiting tonight. As Borden reached the tree line, all seven mutts materialized upon the path behind him.

As they ran, the others stretched into a line behind him, but the hound wouldn't fall away. Stride by stride the dog closed distance until it ran less than twenty feet behind Borden. Both were gasping for breath when they completed the circuit and broke from beneath the trees.

Borden slid to a stop against the post once more, turned to face his pursuers, and drew his new weapon from its holster. A Desert Eagle. Seventy ounces of nickel-plated steel with an eight-inch barrel topped by a laser sight.

Its magazine held seven steel-jacketed forty-four caliber hollow-point shells and a second loaded magazine rested in Borden's windbreaker pocket.

The hound never slowed; threw itself at him. The red dot of the laser sight glowed on the dog's chest. The muzzle flash of the big pistol almost blinded Borden. The echo of the Desert Eagle rumbled through the trees.

The hound dropped to the path, skidded toward Borden on a ribbon of blood, turned black by sodium security lights. Six more times the red dot touched dog flesh. Six times the gun roared.

Even with the firepower of the Desert Eagle, the first hound was struggling to its feet as the seventh animal dropped.

"Not tonight," Borden said.

He stalked closer, snapped the second magazine into place, and fired another hollow-point slug into its head. Growling, he moved from dog to dog, finishing his wet work.

Thorn had been right. The bodies twitched in transformation and Borden watched as the seven dead canines remolded into human form. It was then, as he listened to the approaching wail of sirens, that he realized the true nature of the feud into which he had fallen.

Before him lay the naked bodies of seven ragged-haired children. Four boys, three girls. The oldest, perhaps thirteen. The youngest, seven.

Borden knew the police wouldn't understand he had killed to save his life and sanity. They'd arrest him for murdering seven waifs, would commit him to a mental institution if he told the truth. He would have to run away again.

As he turned toward his escape, Borden collided with the homeless woman he had seen scavenging the trash bins the night before. She had plumped to the ground and sat, spread kneed, and open-mouthed, her shopping bags a forgotten mound about her. She stared at the seven still forms, tears blurring the dirt smudged on her cheeks.

Borden took three strides past her before the notion struck him. He spun in time to see the giant wolfhound struggle from the pile of rags she had worn in human form.

The sirens' volume climbed as Borden pulled the gun into line one last time. He drew a breath, the red dot dropped onto the dog's breast. The monster hurled herself at his throat as he pulled the trigger one more time.

And heard the dead click of the hammer as it fell upon an empty chamber.

Author's notes

Snapshots I Brought Back from the Black Hole

This one started with that last image, the close-up of Chloe's face. I jotted down the flat-out statement that nothing escapes from a black hole and did a rough sketch of that final frozen image after reading an article in one of the science magazines about black holes. I built the rest of the structure from that and pushed the first scene as far away from that close-up as I could get. The panoramic view of the black hole.

From the start, I intended to tell the story from an omniscient point-of-view that would allow me to present everything that was going on in the story with as much detachment as possible. First draft felt too cold and awkward, though. I decided to warm the story up with a more personal presentation, but couldn't decide which character would be the best choice. None of them felt right. Then the notion of Mikhail, the A.I., as narrator hit me.

Until then, Mikhail had been a peripheral character with no other role than having the speed to juggle communications up and down the black hole's gravity well. But when I did the rewrite, and began using his voice to tell the story, he grew as a character and the whole thing came alive.

I'm interested in the notion of sentient A.I., and got more and more into the character as the story developed. I tried to make him real *and* unreal, to give him attitude, particularly in his view of humans. I think, in the end, he's the most sympathetic character in the story.

The really fun story behind "Snapshots" came after the sale.

When John Joseph Adams, editor of *Lightspeed* magazine, emailed his acceptance of the story, he mentioned that he didn't have a technical education [neither do I] and that when he got a hard SF story like "Snapshots" he like to run it by friends who were experts.

He said: "Mike Brotherton, an astronomer and SF writer who runs the Launch Pad workshop, serves as an informal science advisor on Lightspeed from time to time, as needed. Given that your story is about black holes, I wanted to run it by him to see if he might catch anything that I would have missed science-wise ... I've pasted some of our correspondence about the story."

Mike is an astrophysicist at the University of Wyoming in Laramie. He's also an SF writer and has published two novels, *Spider Star* and *Star Dragon*. He had some nice things to say about the story, so I sent him a thank you email. He responded by suggesting that I apply for the NASA-sponsored Launch Pad workshop he runs every July at the university.

I applied, got accepted, and spent a fantastic week in Laramie at Launchpad in July 2010. The story showed up in Lightspeed in June 2010. Growing up in Ohio, we used to call that 'a twofer'.

In His Prime

Another flash fiction story that appeared at *Every Day Fiction*, October 2008. I cry every time I read this one. The protagonist is one of my favorite sports legends. The story is about standing up for individual rights, about the intricacies of time travel, and about the true champion's drive to win, no matter what he or she faces. All that in less than one thousand words. Who says grand ideas don't come in small packages?

Dial Tone

This story started life as a writing exercise at a two-day SF workshop. What if the last man on Earth heard a telephone ringing? I wrote a drabble [a 250-word short-short] with a caustic punchline [I'm addicted to puns and jokes] and wound up posted it at *A Moving Line*, my blog.

Time passed. A lot of time. Then November 30, 2010, Alex Korovessis, editor of the online magazine *Kasma*, e-mailed me. He had read Dial Tone.

"I'm a big fan of post-apocalyptic stories," he said. "Would you like to rework the story to full flash length [1,000 words) and submit it to *Kasma*?"

No promises of publication. Just an invitation.

Well sure. Did I mention that it was a paying market?

I figured a couple days of work would do it, but I started the rewrite at 11:00 p.m., got gobbled up by the idea, and stayed up until 6:00 a.m. on December 1st to finish it. I sent it along to Alex at 7:30 a.m. (PST) and ran off to a doctor's appointment. When I got home at noon, a reply waited. He liked it, wanted to buy it. Would I sell it to him?

Well sure!

By 2:00 p.m. (PST) that day, "Dial Tone" was posted at *Kasma* and Alex' payment had been posted to PayPal. It was and still is the quickest story submission/purchase/publication turn-around I've ever had.

God, I love electronic publication.

Cretaceous on Ice

Like so many of my stories, this one took root from images.

Discovery Channel aired a dinosaur show in late 2009 or early 2010, one of those CGI-driven programs that juxtaposed animated dinosaurs against real backgrounds. Moving through the forest. Running along a beach. That sort of thing.

Two images in particular grabbed my attention. One showed dinosaurs battling the elements in a winter snowstorm. The other presented a pack of raptor-style hunters covered in feathers. I grew up in Ohio farm country. I've seen and chased my share of chickens, and those raptors looked a lot like bantam roosters to me.

The story of feather-covered raptors, escaped from the Cretaceous through a time gate and free to roam present-day Montana [where else would dinosaurs show up?] just grew from there.

At Both Ends

This one was my second pro-rates sale. It went to Jake Frevald at *Flash Fiction Online* and appeared in the June 2009 issue.

I write a lot of flash fiction. It's a demanding style and offers a real sense of accomplishment when you get it right.

I like to think I got this one right.

Jake said, of this story, "I came to love Spiderman through thousands of pages of comic books and hundreds of minutes of movie-watching; K.C. made me feel for her superhero in just a few words."

Stan Lee at Marvel Comics got credit for being the first to give superheroes real-world problems, but anyone who's ever read a comic book has wondered from time to time about how their favorite super guy or gal would deal with the ordinary details of life. That's what "At Both Ends" addresses.

To quote Stan, "'Nuff said."

According to His Substance

I love living in Seattle. We're into our fifth year here and I can't imagine living anywhere else or fathom why I didn't find the city sooner. One of my favorite things about the city [and its a big, long list] is the ferry system. I ride the boats as often as I can, which isn't nearly as often as I would like, and started this story because I wanted to set a tale on the Bainbridge Island run.

It grew from there, became a story about loss and redemption, about how it feels to be transgendered and at odds with the world around you. Most of all, it's a story about how interconnected we all are, even when we feel so.

Tin Man

This one started as a seminar exercise, too. "A body part," the instructor said. I wrote down hand. "An ordinary object found in the kitchen." A can.

"Select a child's story that you loved." My choice was *The Wizard of Oz*. Write a story using all three choices prominently."

The result was "Tin Man." It showed up in *Big Pulp* June 2009.

It's a dark, mean story about a man who has given up on life and is literally being poisoned by his own bitterness and sense of loss. In the end, he discovers he's not ready to give up his life, but the choice he has to make to save himself is horrific.

Even so, this story is one of my personal favorites, of everything I've written, and the first paragraph is perhaps my favorite bit of writing.

To Home, Out Fish Creek Road

After my experience with this story, I put up a sign over my desk that reminds me not to write for themed anthologies.

"To Home, Out Fish Creek Road" was written for a proposed collection of stories about West Virginia folk tales. I love West Virginia, spent time there growing up, although I never lived there. I've rafted the state's rivers, hiked its forest trails, and written more than one story set there. My novel, *Lifting Up Veronica*, is set in the West Virginia panhandle, around Moundsville.

I also knew that West Virginia has had more reported UFO sightings than any other state in the nation, and so when I saw the anthology notice, I figured a UFO sighting in the hills to the south and west of of Moundsville would be perfect.

After a year of waiting, plans for the anthology fell through.

Anyway, I like this story a lot. It's simple and unpretentious but Mina Herron, the protagonist, is just the sort of plucky, deal-with-what-life-hands-out woman this part of the world is famous for. I hope you like this trip out Fish Creek Road.

Flotsam

This one was my third pro-rates sale, to Stan Schmidt at *Analog*. It appeared in the August-September 2010 issue.

Growing up, James Gunn's novel *The Joy Makers* was one of my favorite books. In early 2009, I was looking for a major writers' workshop to attend and discovered Jim's Writing SF workshop at the University of Kansas. We exchanged e-mails, I sent him some of my stories and he invited me to attend the July 2009 program.

I wanted to make an impression, but Jim wrote hard science fiction and most of what I had written up to then was fantasy and borderline science fiction. So, I plotted out a hard SF piece titled "Fat-Bottom Girl" and took it to Kansas.

First round of critique, my story got shredded, but Jim said there was hope. He gave me a list of things the story needed to accomplish and told me to cut 2,000 or 3,000 words out of it. Over the next ten days, I didn't do much else with my free time but write, Queen's *Fat-Bottom Girl* blaring on my headset as I wrote [read the story, You'll see how that works in.]

Our first-round stories got a second reading before we left. When the critique circle got around to Jim, he said, "Someone was listening. I think "Flotsam" [the new title] is ready to send to Analog."

A reviewer called "Flotsam" "a typical Analog story," as if that might be some sort of put-down. If I were writing it today, instead of two years ago, of course I would have done "Flotsam" differently. It's still carrying too much fat and may be more technical than it should be. But damn, I'm proud of this story,

Nosing With the Four-Stroke Kid

This story wasn't anything but fun. It started with a line I jotted down one morning at 2:00 a.m. on the pad I keep beside my bed. *She looked like Uma Thurman on a bad-hair day.* It's a flash piece that wrote itself in no time. I swear I could hear the Rider say the words, as I wrote the last line.

Terry Martin, the editor of *Murky Depths*, the award-winning British fantasy magazine, snatched it up and ran it in Issue Eight in May 2009. It was my first illustrated story, too. Neil Struthers, an Irish illustrator, nailed it cold. I was sorry to hear recently [late October 2011] that *Murky Depths* was closing shop after 18 issues. Genre publishing is a tough racket.

Gossamer Yellow

In the late 1990s, I lived in a grand old house just like Chelsea and Michael's place, down to the oak trim and the crystal chandelier. If there were no ghosts in that house, there certainly should have been. "Gossamer Yellow" ran in the May 2011 issue of *Dark Valentine*, along with a lovely dead-on (no pun intended) illustration by Jane Burson. Alas, it was also the magazine's last issue, another great market gone.

Bringing in the Dead

This is my zombie story. Every SF writer's got one, I suppose. I wrote it while at Clarion West, in late July or early August, 2010. I can't recall exactly when. There is a white heat to the CW experience that grabs your imagination and gets you writing, at all hours and whether you want to or not. Ideas explode out of nowhere and won't let you alone until you've committed them to paper. The program asks each participant to write six stories. Most folks write more. I cranked out nine, along with most of "Snapshots I Brought Back from the Black Hole."

I have no idea where the idea came from but I sold "Bringing in the Dead" the week after I sent it to Pill Hill Press for their *Aftermath: 2013* anthology. And for those folks who wonder how writers select settings for their stories, I grew up in Tuscarawas County, in eastern Ohio, and spent many happy hours on that golf course.

But I never saw a single zombie.

Synchronized with Evelyn

Another story sparked by an image.

If you've never seen the famous Life magazine photograph of Evelyn McHale's suicide, you should go looking for it on the internet. On May 1, 1947, 23-year-old McHale jumped from the 86th floor observation deck of the Empire State Building, the last to do so before the wire barricades were installed.

She cleared all the setbacks and landed face up on the roof of a limousine parked at the curb outside the building's Thirty-Fourth Street entrance. In the photograph, she appeared to be asleep.

It's a haunting image, equally repugnant and fascinating. When I began to play what-if with that thought, the notion came to mind of a time-jump service that allowed a thrill-seeker to ride with Evelyn during her ascent and fall.

Serves Him Right

Another piece of flash fiction. This one appeared in *Every Day Fiction* in March 2011. It's a snark on television cooking shows mixed with infidelity and seasoned with a sprinkling of noir. *Every Day Fiction* allowed immediate reader commentary and the readers bantered back and forth about the ingredients of the dish the three protagonists were cooking. Some felt that detail effected the reading of the story. I disagree with that. Like good cooking, I believed that good writing in about the presentation and the final taste, not what went into its production.

A Bannockburn Night

I'm fascinated by the Great Lakes, particularly Lake Superior, which is not a lake at all, but one of the largest inland seas in the world. The Ojibway, the native Americans who have lived on the Lake's shores for millennia, call it Gitche Gumee. Big, shining water. It is that. Cold and deep, too. It devours sailing craft. It's most famous is the lake freighter *Edmund Fitzgerald*, which went down with all hands during a storm November 10, 1975.

Hundreds of ships have been lost over the years on Lake Superior but no single disappearance has become as famous as the *Bannockburn* in a similar storm on November 21, 1902. After more than one hundred years, Lake sailors still swear they see *Bannockburn* from time to time.

"A Bannockburn Night" is a modern ghost story, presented as a recollection of an old sailor who has sailed the Lakes for decades. Sometimes a story and its characters take almost take on a life of their own. That happened with "A Bannockburn Night." I like the solid, matter-of-fact feel of it and I respect the captain of the *Walter A. Hutchison*, the ship in the story that sails for a time with the *Bannockburn*. The story appeared in the December 2008 issue of *Static Movement*.

A Son of the Night

Another superhero story, this one set on the rooftops of downtown Seattle. The what-if question here, for me, was a what-do question. What do those close to a superhero, who care for her or him and know their loved one is out there fighting criminals, what do they do while they wait for the hero to come home? What do they do to support their hero?

This story appeared in the Fall 2009 issue of *A Thousand Faces*.

To Each His Niche and Task

What is real and what is not? That's what I wanted to explore in "To Each His Niche and Task," another piece of flash fiction that appeared in the July 2009 issue of *Morpheus Tales*, a British horror magazine. The story also touches on the things men and women are prepared to give up for something in which they ardently believe. The protagonist of "To Each His Niche and Task" may be a hero or he may be a madman. And who's to tell?

Coward's Steel

I won third place in the 2009 L. Ron Hubbard Writers of the Future contest with this story. I'm always reminded of Bob Ross, the creator of *The Joy of Painting*, when I think about "Coward's Steel."

Bob's syndicated show appeared on public television channels for years. In each thirty-minute episode, he would paint a landscape in oil, all the while explaining his technique. He liked to talk about what he called happy little accidents. Unexpected occurrences that turned out to be worthwhile.